From: Delphi@oracle.c
To: C_Evans@athena.edu
Re: United States Marine, Jessica Whittaker

Christine,

Now that we've learned Arachne's true identity, we can better protect the women she's sure to target.

Jessica Whittaker will be one of them. She and her friend Nikki Bustillo have more to their genetic makeup than good looks and courage. With all the files Arachne's stolen from the IVF labs, she'll know just what talents they possess. Though I still haven't nailed down how Arachne plans to use the women and their special powers, I aim to offer these Athena alums as much warning as I can.

I'll be contacting Jessica, asking her to be cautious. But I've also got a role for her in Arachne's takedown. More information about our enemy lies under the water, in a three-year-old shipwreck off Puerta Isla. With Jessica's special abilities, she'll find what we're looking for. Even with A. on her tail.

D.

Dear Reader,

I'll be the first to admit that I am a sucker for series. I've worked on continuities before and found it one of the most rewarding writing experiences. So of course I was both thrilled and agog when I was asked to be a part of Athena Force—but not too stunned to say, "Yes!"

The fun was compounded when I found out who my characters were: Jess and Zack. The Marine and the Geek.

Jess is tough. A little broody. Loyal. A woman who will fight for both those she loves and what is right, but who is also oh-so-determined to keep her vulnerabilities to herself. I knew she would be a bit of a challenge and I was right. Jess is not an easy character to know. Things I thought I knew about her were true but there were also many unexpected surprises. And no, I am not telling you what they are or they wouldn't be surprises.

Then there's Zack. People hear *geek* and picture a pasty guy who lives behind a computer. Not true! The "geeks" I know (and I know a surprising number) are driven men. They have to be or they wouldn't be able to do what they do, and that drive spills into their personal lives. Zack is that man. Driven. Wicked-smart. A bit of a risk-taker. If he were here, I'd fight Jess to date him. I'd lose, but I'd try.

Love,

Sharron

Sharron McClellan

BREATHLESS

ATHENA FORCE

Published by Silhouette Books

America's Publisher of Contemporary Romance

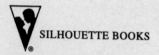

SILHOUETTE BOOKS

ISBN-13: 978-0-373-38978-0
ISBN-10:   0-373-38978-7

BREATHLESS

Copyright © 2008 by Harlequin Books S.A.

Visit Athena Force at www.eHarlequin.com

Printed in U.S.A.

SHARRON McCLELLAN

always wanted to be a writer. There were two things she had always loved: writing and science. In college she thought about being a marine biologist, but there was the whole shark issue (they freak her out). Instead, she discovered the joys of playing in the dirt—a profession more commonly known as archaeology. For years she focused on excavating ancient sites that included projectile points, burn pits and the occasional burial.

But when she took a position during the archaeological off-season and ended up answering phones for a cruise line, she took to reading romance. It wasn't long before she fell in love with the genre and returned to her first love—writing. Five years later she sold her first action-adventure/romance novel to Silhouette Books.

Since that first sale Sharron has traveled both the U.S. and Mexico (ask her about the riots in Oaxaca!) living an adventurous life. Currently, she resides in Annapolis, Maryland, where she races sailboats, dates wicked-smart men and writes every day. She believes in hard work, jumping into life with both feet, and she swears that her Muse spends most of her time in the bar next to the bay drinking gin and tonic with extra lime.

To my best friend and critique partner,
Cathy Pegau, who knows everything about me
(the good, the bad and the Jeez Louise, what were
you thinking!) and loves me anyway.

You know I can't write a book without you.

Chapter 1

U.S. Marine Corp Combatant diver, Jessica Whitaker stepped off the edge of the boat and into the Pacific Ocean, barely making a splash as she entered the water.

With the setting of the sun, the submarine world off Oahu, Hawaii, was dark but also as warm and familiar as her own skin. For a few seconds, the only sound she heard was her breathing inside the full-face mask. Then the rest of her team entered the water, breaking the silence. She counted the splashes. *One. Two. Three.*

A small team, but this was a training exercise, and in the initial stages, she found training to be much more effective if the recruits had personal attention.

Not that they needed or demanded the one-on-one time. They were Marines. They didn't need anything but water, air and the burning desire to do the right thing.

She could train larger groups, but Jess knew one axiom to

be true: there was nothing more detrimental to a mission than a half-assed operative who didn't know what he was doing.

Or worse, *thought* he knew but thought wrong.

"Sound off," she said, adjusting the vocals of her mask's transmitter and receiver.

"Latham." *Newbie One.*

"Taylor." Her first in command and a trusted friend, the older, weathered Marine was an excellent teacher with an innate patience that the recruits responded to.

"Eielson." *Newbie Two.*

The three men gathered around her, their dark, wet-suit-covered forms making them almost invisible in the night water. "As you know, our objective is the enemy ship, *Sushi*," she said. "She's approximately one mile away, and her coordinates were downloaded into your personal GPS systems before you entered the water. Upon arrival, Latham and I will set a charge at the bow of the ship. Taylor and Eielson, you're taking the stern. Latham—" she addressed her partner for the exercise "—tell me our objective."

"Disable and distract. Once she's crippled, the surface team will board her and retrieve the hostages."

"Good," she responded. "Questions?"

Nothing but silence. Not even the sound of burbling SCUBA tanks since they wore rebreathers to give themselves an unlimited amount of time underwater.

Not that we have unlimited time, Jess thought. Nor did they need it. Marines did not screw around.

"Move out," she said. In unison, they swam to the diver propulsion vehicles, DVPs, that drifted in the water next to the boat that had transported them to the drop spot. Taylor and Eielson left first. Sinking below the waves, they'd parallel her and Latham as they made their way to the ship.

She gave a short wave to the boat captain, who stood on the deck watching them depart, then powered up her DPV. Using the GPS coordinates for guidance instead of the running lights, she and Latham headed toward the *Sushi*.

She almost chuckled at the name but kept quiet. Each new training group gave the ship a different name. Some serious. Some funny. Some as imaginative as blank paper.

In this case, the name was given when the entire squad of nine went to a Japanese restaurant a few weeks ago. They'd eaten questionable sushi and sucked down sake.

They'd spent the next day hungover and sick with food poisoning.

She'd used the opportunity to take them on a five-mile run. Cruel, she mused. However, they'd all finished, proving their tenacity and strength of spirit not just to her but to themselves.

"How you doing, Latham?" Jess asked when they were a few hundred feet closer to their objective.

"Good, ma'am," he replied.

"It's just us for the next few minutes," she said. "If you have any questions, now would be the time."

"None, ma'am."

She didn't think he'd have any. One of her best recruits, Chuck Latham was a husky young man from the Atlanta inner city. He'd been given a choice when he was sixteen and standing in front of a judge for theft—join ROTC and get his life in line or go to juvenile hall.

Despite the ridicule of his peers, he chose ROTC. After graduation, he'd put himself through college. He was one of those rare recruits that had brains, instinct and heart. One day, he'd make captain or better. She was sure of it.

"You understand how the charges work?" she asked.

"Yes, ma'am."

She sighed, hating the formal term. She was only a few years older than Latham, and whenever he ma'amed her, it felt like a decade of difference in age.

She was not ready to feel that old. Not yet. "Latham, quit ma'aming me. It's Whitaker."

"Yes, ma'am. Whitaker, ma'am."

Newbies, she thought, rolling her eyes.

The DPV sputtered, almost coming to a halt. Jess let up on the power, smacked the console, and it lurched forward. Damned machines.

The combination of night and their depth in the water column left them blind as they motored along, but Jess knew the water around them teemed with life. Lobsters. Snappers. An occasional white-tipped reef shark. Moray eels hunting for food.

And her favorite animal, mantas. Gentle giants that fed on plankton, their ten-foot-plus wingspans created pressure waves that she sensed, even through the skintight wet suit. Occasionally, one passed close enough that its wake rocked the DPV, making her trainee tighten his grip.

"They won't hurt you, Latham," she said, a chuckle tinting her voice.

"I know, ma'am. Whitaker," he corrected himself. "They just startle me sometimes, and you have to admit those horns are a little creepy."

"They're not horns. They're cephalic lobes that help them funnel plankton into their mouths," she said. "Stop thinking of them as horns, and they won't make you jump when they catch you off guard."

"I'll try, ma'am," he replied, his deep voice taking on a drawl that he managed to hide except when he was nervous.

"You do that," she said, not bothering to tell him to stop

ma'aming her. "There's nothing that'll get you killed faster in the ocean than lack of knowledge and being unprepared."

Ten minutes later, they arrived at the ship, and Jess checked her watch. Right on time.

Opening the case attached to the front of the DPV, she pulled out the explosive device. Flicking on a small, pencil-sized light attached to her helmet, she checked the mine. It wasn't much. This was a training exercise, and they didn't want to actually blow a hole in the ship.

Or a recruit.

She handed the device to Latham. "Tell me what you know."

Flipping on his light, he turned the cylinder over in his hands. "Limpet mine. Magnetic. Capable of a range of charges and producing a range of responses from barely no-ticeable to *what the fuck, there's a hole in my ship.*"

She chuckled at his description but nodded in approval. "Time to get away before it blows?"

Latham examined the timer. "Anywhere from three sec-onds to three hours, depending on the required settings."

"Give me fifteen minutes," she said, even though the ex-plosion would be little more than the equivalent of a child's cap gun and fifteen seconds was plenty. In a real-life situa-tion, they'd need those fifteen minutes, and she preferred to treat this as real even though it was a teaching situation.

Latham set the charge, and in the small line of light from his mask, she saw him freeze. "What's wrong?"

He shook his head. "I'm not sure. I entered the correct num-bers, I swear, but the countdown is starting at sixty seconds."

"Hand it over."

He handed her the mine, and she punched in an abort code. Nothing happened. *Fifty seconds.*

She punched it in again. Still nothing.

She'd have to speak to someone about this equipment. Whoever was supposed to maintain it was doing a lousy job. Irritated, she took the all-in-one tool kit from her belt and flipped out the Phillips screwdriver.

The screws turned. And turned. But otherwise, didn't move outward. They were stripped. She brought the explosive device closer to her mask and noticed scratches around the outside of the case with the majority being around the screws.

Underneath her tight black wet suit, the hairs on the back of her neck strained to rise, as she realized the problem with the timer was not accidental. Quite the opposite.

Sabotage.

Then true horror washed over her. If someone had taken the time to change the timer and strip the screws then it was a sure bet there was a reason.

Like blowing a huge hole in the ship.

Which meant a larger charge.

"Oh my God," she whispered.

The console blinked the countdown. *Twenty-five seconds.* She dropped the mine, pushing it toward the bottom of the ocean and away from the ship, herself and her trainee. "Latham, get to the DVP and get moving. Now!"

He swam over to the idling machine and set it in motion. The engine sputtered, stopped. He pushed the start button. Still, nothing happened.

Her heartbeat pounding in her ears, Jess pushed him aside and pounded on the console. "Start, you bitch." The machine refused to engage.

Perhaps this was a bad joke, she told herself. Taylor, hoping to make her late for the rendezvous so he could win their on-going bet of who bought the beer.

The bitter taste of fear in her mouth told her different. "Taylor, you there?"

There was no reply, but neither did she expect one. Mission protocol, after all. Damn. "If you can hear me, get out of here. We have a problem," she shouted into the microphone.

She prayed Taylor and Eielson were where they were supposed to be. *Sushi* was a big ship. They would be fine unless the charge was so big it disintegrated the entire ship.

However, she and Latham were much too close. "Swim," Jess said to Latham. "Fast."

Latham followed her into the dark water away from the ship, the miniscule beams emanating from their flashlights a thin, bright path into the dark void. "Ma'am, what's wrong?" he asked, his drawl more pronounced than she'd ever heard and his breathing hurried and harsh in her earpiece.

Fifteen seconds. They weren't going to make it. "I'm not sure," she lied. "Just swim."

She pumped her legs and within seconds was ahead. No one was better in the water. She'd never lost a race in school or since she joined the Marines.

If left to herself, she might even outrace the explosion.

But that would mean leaving Latham. A trainee. A young man who trusted her to be a commander and do the right thing.

The right thing did not mean leaving a man behind to die.

She slowed, grabbed his arm and pumped her legs again, pulling him along beside her. He was heavy, slowing her. She refused to let go. He was not going to die. Not here. Not like this.

Neither was she.

"Ma'am, we're not going to make it," Latham said, his voice laced with fear.

"Yes, we are, and Latham, stop ma'aming me," Jess snapped.

Behind her, the limpet mine exploded.

Definitely bigger than a cap gun.

Next to her, Latham's eyes widened in fear. Her gaze shifted, adjusted, and she saw her reflection in his mask. Her dark eyes were wide. Panicked.

Then the percussion wave rolled over them, tumbling them in its wake. Someone screamed, and for a brief, agonizing second she thought her head would explode. Blackness claimed her, and she sank into the dark.

The darkness surrounding Jess was absolute. Almost tangible with its thickness. She swam through it like water. But somehow, she knew it was different. Something evil. Slick. Oily.

Still, she swam. She'd lost something. Something important. No, she realized. Not something. *Someone.*

"Latham!" She screamed for her recruit. Out of the blackness, she spotted him next to her, sinking facedown into the ocean's depths. She grabbed his arm and tried to pull him to the surface, but the darkness dragged her down.

Kicking harder made no difference. Pulling at the dark with her hands didn't help.

Still, she fought. She had to save him.

Then the pull of the abyss flipped Latham over, and she froze in horror. His mask was shattered. His eyes wide and sightless. His mouth gaping in horror.

She tried to let go of the corpse that was once a man—a boy—under her guidance but found herself unable to release her grip. Instead, he acted like a stone, dragging her into oblivion. The farther she sank, the faster she went. Soon, she sped past animals that were the stuff of legends. Giant squid. Eels as long as a barge. Fish with lights for eyes.

Something came from below and grabbed her feet. Shook her like a doll. She lashed out, fighting with every ounce of her being.

She refused to die. Nature would not beat her.

"Jess."

A voice called to her, pushing past the fear and the panic. "Jess." She recognized the insistent, familiar baritone. Taylor.

She opened her eyes, blinking at the lights around her. There was no ocean. No depths pulling her down. No darkness that went all the way to hell.

There were white walls. Stainless steel fixtures. Air. A bouquet of daisies on a small table. She was in a hospital.

Disoriented, she untangled her feet from the sheets and yanked the oxygen tube from beneath her nose. Taylor tried to take her hand. She flinched.

He took a step back, waiting. Patient, as always.

Jess blinked again then scrubbed her face with her palms trying to make sense of the world. How had she gotten to the hospital? Why was she here?

"You back with us?" Taylor asked.

Back with them? She didn't understand. "What?" she asked, her voice croaky. Her throat felt as dry as the desert.

Taylor handed her a glass of water.

She gulped down the tepid liquid then handed the empty glass back to her friend.

"Better?" he asked.

"Yeah. Thanks," she said, feeling more grounded with each passing second. "What am I doing here?"

"You don't remember?"

She shook her head. Trying to make sense out of her jumbled memory.

Taylor took her hand, and this time, she didn't pull away.

"We were on a training mission. There was an accident. An explosion."

"An explosion?" The incident came back to Jess in broken, disjointed frames. The stripped screws. The wrong count-down. The disabled DPV. The fear in Latham's eyes as the explosion ripped him from her grasp.

Latham.

"Latham. Where is he?"

Taylor's gray eyes softened, and he ran a hand over his military short, salt-and-pepper hair. "ICU."

She opened her mouth to ask if he was okay then stopped herself. If he was in ICU she had her answer. She clenched the sheet in her fist, wishing she didn't have to go to the next obvious question. "Will he live?" she whispered.

"No idea. If he does, there might be brain damage." He sighed. "He went quite a while without oxygen."

"His mask broke," Jess said, remembering the nightmare. An image of Latham, his face twisted in death, flashed across her thoughts. *Just a dream, Jess.* She reminded herself. *Just a dream.*

"Yeah," Taylor confirmed. "You were holding on to him when we located you. His mask was cracked. Flooded. It took us almost a minute to convince you to let go of him."

"I was awake?"

"Kind of."

She shook her head as both her nightmare and reality converged until she didn't know which was true. Latham had been unconscious, unable to save himself. She'd tried to take him to the surface. She thought.

Whatever the truth, she told herself, *he's alive, and where there's life, there's hope.* "Take me to him."

Taylor shook his head. "No can do. You're confined to bed."

"No, I'm not." Not even Taylor could force her to stay in bed. Not when one of her men was hurt.

She pushed back the covers and swung her legs over the edge of the cot, wavering as the world tilted around her. Taylor moved to help her, and she waved him off. "I'm fine. Just give me a minute."

He sighed again, obviously annoyed by, and resigned to, her decision.

Making sure the pea-green hospital gown was tied in the back, she rose on unsteady legs. He didn't offer to help again. "Show me," she said.

He led her down the hall, through a set of doors and into a small pale green room. Machines whirred and beeped. The smell of rubbing alcohol, sweat and death permeated Jess's nose. She covered it with her palm before she retched at the scent.

But beyond the sounds and the hospital smell was Charles Latham in a bed next to the window, being kept alive by tubes and a ventilator.

The room swayed, but she took a deep breath and shuffled over to her trainee's bed.

Careful not to jostle any of his tubes, she stroked a palm over his cocoa-colored, shaved head. When he'd come to her for training, his dark, curly hair was just over an inch long and stylish for a Marine. He'd shaved it off. Keeping it simple, he'd said when teased about the transformation.

And now, he lay here. His face puffy. His skin ashen. His body limp.

A shadow of the man she knew.

"I am so sorry, Chuck," she said.

"Chuck?" Taylor asked.

"He hates Charles," she replied, unable to think of the boy in front of her as *Latham*. Under the circumstances, his last name sounded cold. Aloof. Impersonal. The boy in the bed was none of those things. Not to her.

He was a person. Her student. Her responsibility.

She put her hands in her lap and squeezed her eyes shut, refusing to believe that such an energetic, strong young man would not pull through. "You're going to make it," she whispered, praying that this room, and the comatose man in the bed, was nothing more than a continuation of her nightmare.

When she opened her eyes, Chuck still lay in bed. Dead except for the machines breathing life into him. "This is my fault," she said.

"Things happen," Taylor said from behind her.

"Not things," she corrected, anger tinting her voice and wiping away any attempt at professionalism. "Sabotage."

"What?" Taylor asked, surprise in his voice.

Jess shifted to face him. "When we were going to the ship, the DPV gave me trouble. I should have stopped. Aborted the mission. Instead I kept going."

"Those things foul up. We both know that."

"Yeah, but if I'd stopped…" She glanced at Latham then continued her story. "We set the limpet. The timer didn't work. Wouldn't abort. I looked closer, and the screws were stripped. When we tried to bug out, the DPV failed."

She met Taylor's widening eyes. "You and I both know that explosion was bigger than anything either of us would use for training. Did you hear me call out? Tell you to run?"

He nodded. "Still, sabotage? You've got to be kidding me," Taylor said, the words not doubting her but uttered in surprise.

"I wish I were." She shook her head, a part of her unable to believe it could happen on her watch. On any watch. Who would have done such a thing? "We were set up, John, and Chuck is paying the price."

"You came close," Taylor said. "We almost lost you, as well."

Jess stiffened. "What do you mean? You said I was awake when you found us."

"I said *kind of*. Your mask was filled with water. You were babbling." He squeezed her shoulder. "We must have reached you seconds after it flooded. Otherwise, you'd be in ICU, too."

Jess bit her lip. Taylor was one of her best friends, but not even he knew that luck had nothing to do with her survival. Her mask could have been filled for hours, and she would be fine. She was special. Different.

When she was a child, her parents discovered that her body chemistry was different. She processed gases, like oxygen and nitrogen, with an unnatural efficiency that gave her an advantage when it came to holding her breath. When tested, she discovered that she could remain submerged for ten minutes, and if she remained unmoving, twenty. But it wasn't her efficiency that saved her when she was unconscious in the water.

It was the set of internal gills that rested just below the upper lobes of her lungs.

It was her freakish nature that saved her.

"You were lucky, Jess. Very, very lucky," Taylor said, squeezing her shoulder again.

"Yeah, lucky," she muttered. She took Latham's hand in hers, squeezing his long fingers. He didn't respond. She squeezed harder. He remained inert.

In the background, a monitor beeped. Grew louder and changed into an insistent shrill. The words, "Code Blue," echoed over the intercom. Seconds later, doctors and nurses ran into the room and shoved her out of the way.

Standing against the wall, with Taylor's arm around her shoulder for support, Jess watched them work on Chuck until there was nothing left to do but pull the sheet over his head.

"Yeah, lucky," she whispered.

Chapter 2

Jess shut the door to her apartment and leaned against the solid wood. There wasn't much to personalize the small living space. The few decorations that graced the room were a reflection of her Apache heritage. A woven basket in the corner. A book on Native American art on the carved oak coffee table.

There was little else, since she normally lived aboard ship with the rest of her team, ready to effect search and rescue or infiltration at a moment's notice.

She touched the written order she'd shoved into her pocket. She'd been leaving the hospital when the communication from Command was handed to her. She didn't open it. She knew what it said.

Fuming inside, she crumpled the official embossed paper in her fist.

Pushing away from the door, she strode across the living

room to her computer, tossing the paper into a wastepaper basket along the way.

She hesitated, part of her wanting to fish it out and get the waiting over with—like ripping off a Band-Aid or taking the first step into unfamiliar waters—but her hands shook at the thought, and she stuffed them into her jeans' pockets. The letter could wait. It wasn't as if her reading it an hour from now would make a difference anyway.

Marching to her desk, she sat in her black, high-back garage-sale office chair and turned on her computer. Her attention flickered back to the small wastepaper basket.

Wait, she told herself and looked away.

The computer hummed, coming to life, but before she could open up her e-mail, a knock sounded on her door. She punched the button on the monitor. The knocking continued, like a woodpecker's persistent rapping. The screen darkened, and she went to find out who was stretching her last nerve.

Taylor leaned against the sill, his knock turning into a wave of *hello* when she opened the door. "You didn't open it, did you?" he asked.

"The letter?" Turning on her heel, she walked into her living room, finding it annoying that he knew her so well. "I was getting to it."

Taylor stood in the doorway a moment longer then strode past her, stopping to pick up the crumpled envelope before he took a seat in one of her mismatched chairs. He ripped open the end of the envelope and pulled out a piece of folded white parchment with an embossed seal on the top.

"Well?" she asked, watching as he read it.

"Standard. You can't return to active duty until the investigation is complete."

Jess buried her head in her hands, gripping her long black

hair between her fingers. It was two days since Latham's funeral, but she already itched to engage both her body and mind with something more than working out and running mental scenarios about what might have been. "But I have to do something," she groaned.

"A trainee died under your command. You knew this was coming."

She did. It was also why she had wanted to ignore the letter. She met his gray-eyed gaze. He glanced away, but not before she read him. She knew that expression. That guilty look meant he was withholding information. "Spill it," she said. Sitting in her oversize reading chair, Jess kicked off her sandals, tucked her legs beneath her and pulled her hair over her shoulder so she didn't lean against it.

He sighed and leaned back. "They're looking at human error."

"Of course." Not that it would help, since this was far from a mistake on anyone's part. However, once they got past the mundane they'd have to listen to her. Have to check out her claim of sabotage.

"I don't think you understand," Taylor insisted. "*Your* error. You and you alone."

Her error? Fury bloomed beneath Jess's skin, but she refused to let it show. She managed a tight shrug. "Fine."

"That doesn't bother you?" Taylor asked. His brows arched in surprise.

"It's what I'd do," Jess replied, sounding as unconcerned as possible despite the fact that her insides were twisted into a tight knot. "It's standard procedure. Besides, it's not like they'll find anything."

She would know. She'd gone over that evening in her mind countless times. The preparation. The maneuver. She'd done everything by the book.

She continued. "The only thing I'm concerned about is what happens after they discover it wasn't a mistake. I want to make sure they find out what *really* happened." She rose, pacing as she spoke, her bare feet quiet against the wooden floor.

"Someone did this on purpose, John. We were set up. *I* was set up. I want them to find the perpetrator. Not just a name to expedite closing the file." She reached the far wall and leaned against it, her forehead pressed against the wood paneling. "I want this person found and brought to justice. I want them to pay for what they did."

"I know, but there isn't much to go on."

"How about the limpet?" She returned to pacing, her frazzled nerves demanding movement. "Do you have good news? Any at all?"

Taylor rubbed the back of his neck. "They're analyzing the little shrapnel that was left, but so far it doesn't appear promising. No prints or anything."

"Damn." This just kept getting worse. "Tell them to check for the stripped screws."

"I'll tell them."

Once again, she recognized Taylor's expression of guilt. Her spirit sank. "What is it?" she asked. She didn't want to know what else could go wrong, but not knowing was worse. "What else are you not telling me? And don't bother to lie since you suck at it."

He cleared his throat. "They have found *some* evidence."

"That's *good* news," she said, breathing a sigh of relief. "Geez, John. Quit freaking me out."

"It's not good news, Jess." He stared at his feet. "The log where you signed for the mine shows that you didn't check out a training mine. You checked out a live limpet with enough power to blow a hole in the *Sushi*.

"What?" Jess stopped midstep. An unnatural chill rolled through her.

Taylor continued, "It's your signature, Jess. They had a handwriting analyst check it."

She stared at her first-in-command in disbelief as she searched her memory. But she only found what she knew to be true—she'd checked out a training tool, not an actual, full-scale mine. "You know I would never be that careless."

He didn't contradict her, but his attention remained focused on his shoes. She knew what he was thinking. She saw the uncertainty in the way his shoulders slumped and the way he refused to meet her eyes.

He thought it was her fault.

She sat down in her chair, resting her head in her hands. "I know what I signed for. I checked it. This is all wrong."

"Maybe you were in a hurry," he offered.

"No," she shot back. She did not need anyone to make excuses for her. Especially one of her best friends. "I was not in a hurry. I know what I signed for, and that wasn't it."

"I know. We all do." Taylor sighed again, a man at a loss and caught between the differing sides of the stories. "Hang in there, cookie."

She smiled despite the frustration and shock. He hadn't called her "cookie" since her days as a new recruit when she was a newbie and he was her trainer. "Thanks," she said, squeezing his hand. He was still her best friend. And if there was one thing she knew, he might have doubts—hell, she had to admit she would if their places were reversed—but he would stand by her no matter what happened.

That's what people like Taylor did. They were rocks in a stormy sea. "You better go," she said.

"Yeah, if they spot me here they'll be asking questions."

"With you so close to retirement, we can't have that," she said. "Catherine would never forgive me." Jess loved Taylor's wife but cheerfully admitted she was in awe of the petite red-head since anyone who could keep Taylor in line was a little scary.

Taylor paused in the doorway. "I'll see what else I can find out. Don't count me out yet."

She met his steady gaze. "Never."

When the door closed, Jess leaned over, hands on her knees, as she absorbed the reality of her predicament. If convicted of sheer idiocy, she'd receive a dishonorable discharge at best.

At worst—Leavenworth.

It wouldn't come to that, she told herself. She'd make sure of it.

She straightened and returned to the computer. Once again, she tossed the letter in the wastebasket.

This time, it could remain there.

She turned the monitor back on and opened her e-mail program. There was the usual. Her parents. Something about buying land in Costa Rica. A notice requesting an alumni up-date at aa.gov—the Athena Academy Web site.

Athena Academy. Her high school alma mater and where she'd spent her teen years. Normally, the teenage time frame from twelve to eighteen was reserved for angst, indecision and drama. Instead, the Academy, and its intense curriculum and supportive teachers, had made it challenging, empowering.

It helped that while the school was an all-girls, private in-stitution, entrance was based on merit. Not money. And there was no application for enrollment.

They sought out the best and the brightest and offered them a full scholarship. So all the girls who attended were smart. Inventive. Talented and unique.

She trailed her fingers down the screen, wondering what they would think of her if they knew her situation. Would they be disappointed? Worried?

Pissed and eager to help?

Damn, she missed them. Her friends. Her teachers. Even her much-loathed language classes.

She missed it all.

But above all, she missed the atmosphere. People believed in her. If Principal Evans was on the Inquiry Board—there would be no question as to the truth.

"Principal Evans isn't here," she said to herself. "It's just you."

She glanced down through the rest of her e-mail messages, coming to one from Nikki Bustillo, her best friend from the Academy and the one person she'd kept in touch with on a consistent basis.

I heard what happened. Call as soon as you get home and let me know you're okay.

Jess wasn't surprised that Nikki had gotten wind of the accident. A lieutenant in the Coast Guard, she always heard about ocean-related *incidents*.

And what had happened to Jess was definitely in that category.

Jess pulled out her cell phone.

There weren't that many people Jess was close to. Her ability to breathe underwater made her wary of letting others in. But Nikki was an enhanced human, as well—though her gift was different. She smelled emotions.

Jess smiled. As best friends and schoolmates, Nikki's gift was both a blessing and curse. When Jess had developed a

schoolgirl crush on Johnny Depp, Nikki had figured it out by
the scent. Said it smelled like socks after a soccer match.

And she'd teased Jess. A little.

However, Nikki had also known when Jess was homesick.
Sad. Angry.

Known and been there.

Jess sighed. She could use Nikki's counsel right now.
Her support.

Before she hit the speed dial, another e-mail popped in with
a familiar beep. Jess snapped the phone closed. No subject
line, but the unique sound told her it was from Delphi—her
contact at Oracle, the secret agency with a computer network
that matched intel from all the U.S. agencies and assigned
projects to people like her when needed.

The e-mail was dated prior to her accident.

Jess, a word of warning. We have reason to believe that
you are being targeted by Arachne, an enemy of Athena
Academy. We're not sure what Arachne is planning but
be watchful.

The chill she'd felt when Taylor told her about the limpet
mine grew stronger with the solid confirmation that she'd
been framed. Clicking the e-mail closed, Jess leaned back,
gazing up at the ceiling and letting the reality sink in that if
she had bothered to check her e-mail, the whole situation
might have been prevented.

Charles might be alive.

She'd been in a hurry the day of the accident, and her
computer had locked up. Instead of rebooting and checking
messages, she'd turned it off and left.

Probably nothing but spam, she'd told herself.

"Not spam. A boy's life." She pressed her palms against her eyes, forcing herself not to cry. If she'd looked…if she'd taken the time… Her hands slid down to her mouth as she tried to come to grips with the news, her head telling her that it wasn't her fault.

Her heart feeling otherwise.

The phone rang, jarring her. "Damn it." Now wasn't the time. She wiped her eyes, blew her breath out through tight lips and picked up the receiver.

"Good afternoon, Jess." The voice was garbled, computer enhanced and changed. She couldn't tell the gender of the caller but she knew who it was.

Delphi.

"Good afternoon," she replied.

"Condolences on your loss," Delphi said, the altered voice surprisingly warm.

"Thank you," she replied. She always wondered what Delphi was. Male? Female? But it was comments like that, the moment of spoken compassion, that made her think Delphi was a woman.

"You read the previous e-mail?"

"Just now."

Silence, but Jess waited.

"According to Oracle, you will be on leave for quite a while. Arachne is working to manipulate the outcome of the investigation."

Always to the point. Jess swallowed, wondering how much more bad news she would have to endure. "Will I be court-martialed?"

"We will do what is needed to prevent your conviction."

A typical quasi-evasive answer but still, Jess's muscles relaxed a micron. If anyone could bring the saboteur, Chuck's killer, to light, it was Delphi's network of agents. Delphi continued, "In the meantime, we have an assignment for you."

Jess perked up, grabbed a pad of paper and a pencil, relieved to focus on something besides images of Leavenworth. "I'm listening."

"We have booked you a flight to Puerto Isla, an island located two hundred miles off the coast of Belize. Once there, we want you to rendezvous with Zach Holiday. He runs a salvage operation. A cocaine ship named *Paradise Lost* sank off the coast three years ago during the Puerto Isla Revolution, and we want you to locate it."

Jess scribbled the information in her personal shorthand then stopped. "Three years?" She knew how the ocean worked, and three years was a long time. Objects moved. Or were buried by sand.

"We've collated the available data and have come up with a search grid," Delphi said.

"Of course," Jess said, knowing Delphi *would* think of everything. "How much does Zach know?"

"Minimal. That we're looking for a specific ship but not why."

"Didn't he ask questions?" Jess asked.

"Yes, but I chose Zach and his crew because they have worked with the government before, and Zach is aware that he cannot be privy to all details."

"What type of projects has he done?"

"Recovery of drug planes and cargo. Some data encryption. Even a recovery mission for the Marine Corps."

Jess perked up at the information.

Delphi continued, "Still, I would prefer our information remain on a need-to-know basis. I'll trust your judgment in that regard."

"Thank you," Jess replied.

Delphi continued. "We believe the ship contains equipment, a laptop that belonged to Arachne and data that might lead to her whereabouts."

The hairs on Jess's neck rose in response to the name. "The one who set me up? The one who killed Chuck?"

"Yes."

She could have sworn she heard a smile in that singular, positive response. "Good." Whoever this Arachne was, Jess wanted her dead.

"Jess, do not underestimate her," Delphi warned. "Arachne's vendetta against Athena Academy and her students goes back twenty-four years."

"Twenty-four years?" The thought that a criminal had been around that long and had not been caught boggled Jess's mind.

"Yes," Delphi confirmed. "All the way back to Marion Gracelyn's death."

"She killed her?"

"Coordinated it, at least. Since that time, she's threatened the Academy, tried to destroy it and now she's showing an unusual interest in the *special* attendees."

"Special? Like me?" Jess asked. She'd always wondered if there were others, girls with gifts. She and Nikki had discussed it before and had found they had something in common—they were both conceived using in vitro fertilization, IVF. Since that time, she'd met more than one IVF at the Academy and had watched her, looking for anything that made her different. She'd seen nothing but that didn't stop her from watching and wondering.

"Yes, girls like you," Delphi confirmed.

Interesting. Jess filed the information away for future reference then returned to the topic at hand. "Do you know why she wants us?" Jess asked.

"No. Perhaps breeding—"

Jess shuddered in disgust.

"—study, or just to hurt the Academy as much as possible. It's hard to say. But she knows about your ability to breathe underwater and has obtained information on other women and girls conceived using IVF at one specific clinic in Zuni, New Mexico."

Nikki.

"Don't worry about your friends," Delphi said, answering her unspoken worry.

Jess stared at the phone in surprise, unsettled that Delphi knew her so well.

Delphi continued, "We'll make sure everyone else is safe. The best way for you to help is to obtain the laptop and anything else you deem useful," Delphi said. "Delivery will be to Allison Gracelyn."

Curiosity made Jess want to ask why Allison, but she held back her question. Allison Gracelyn was a member of the Athena Academy Board, and one did not question that kind of influence or importance. "When do I leave?"

"This afternoon. Check your e-mail. I have sent you directions for meeting with Zach, the search coordinates and an airline ticket."

"Thank you," Jess said. "I appreciate the opportunity."

"Jess," Delphi said, a cautionary tone evident despite the voice distortion. "Be careful. Do not let vengeance cloud your judgment and do not underestimate Arachne."

"I won't," Jess replied. "I know the order of importance. If this brings us closer to catching Arachne, revenge is icing on the cake."

"Understood."

The line went dead, and Jess set the phone back in its cradle. Arachne'd had twenty-four years to plot revenge on

Athena Academy and its students. Chuck never stood a chance. Neither had she. But now that she knew the enemy, maybe she could help bring her to justice.

"Arachne will pay for what she did, Chuck," Jess whispered. "I promise."

"An e-mail? You sent me an e-mail and expected that to be enough?" Nikki said as soon as Jess answered the call.

"Hello, to you, too," Jess replied, a small smile curling the corners of her mouth as she held the receiver away from her ear. After her conversation with Delphi, she'd e-mailed Nikki the basic information about what she was doing. She wanted to call but e-mail was easier. Impersonal. And right now she needed the distance.

She should have known it wouldn't work.

"Yeah. Well. Hi," Nikki returned.

Nikki still sounded irritated. "I was going to call as soon as I packed," Jess explained. "I'm just on a tight schedule right now."

"Packed?" Nikki asked. "Where are you heading?"

"To the beach," Jess said, cradling the cordless phone between her neck and ear. As much as she loathed hauling her personal dive gear—she didn't need much other than a wet suit for protection against coral and fins for additional speed—it would look strange for her to use rental when she was a professional.

Besides, the thought of putting her mouth around a used snorkel and regulator was repulsive. "Since I have time on my hands, I thought I'd work on my tan."

"They're letting you leave? What about the accident?"

"It's under investigation." She tucked her fins in the bottom of her dive bag.

"You mean, *you're* under investigation," Nikki said, her voice terse.

"*The situation* is under investigation," Jess corrected as she folded her full-body black wet suit and tucked it on top of the fins.

Through the receiver, she heard Nikki inhale. "I bet if I was there right now, I'd smell honey, wouldn't I?" Nikki pressed, her voice terse.

Jess sighed. That was Nikki's undercover way of calling her a liar. Trust her friend not to let her get away with anything. Even a fib. "Yes," Jess admitted. To Nikki's olfactory-based psi sense, spoken lies had always smelled a little too sweet. "But I don't want to talk about it."

"Okay," Nikki said, her tone finally softening. "Anything I can do to help?"

Find Arachne? Bring Chuck back to life? Jess wished she could tell Nikki what was happening and hated the fact that she couldn't. If she did, then Nikki would want to know how Jess got her information, and getting into a discussion about being an Oracle agent—especially a discussion on an unsecured line—was as dumb as one got and would put them both at risk.

As much as she hated it, she'd have to trust that Nikki could take care of herself and that Delphi would stand by her word to keep Nikki safe.

"Not really," Jess finally replied. "Unless you know of a way to speed up a Marine Tribunal."

"Not likely." Nikki chuckled.

"So don't worry. Everything will be fine." Jess tossed her dive knife and mask into the bag.

Outside, a car honked, and Jess peeked between the curtains to see her taxi. *Nice timing.*

"I gotta go," she said, jamming the rest of her gear in. "Taxi's here."

"Have fun, and don't worry about the investigation. You'll be proven innocent."

"Thanks," she said. Nikki's forceful assurance caused a true smile to broaden her mouth. "I'll send you a postcard."

She hesitated. "Nikki?"

"Yeah?"

"Thanks, and be careful."

"What?"

She heard the confusion in Nikki's voice, but she'd already said too much. "Nothing. Just be careful."

"I will."

It wasn't much of a warning but it would have to be enough. Jess hung up, grabbed a small backpack that contained her clothes and hoisted her heavier, much larger dive bag over her shoulder. At the taxi, the driver popped the trunk from the driver's seat. Jess tossed her bags in then took the passenger side, sliding the seat belt over her lap.

She never sat in the back.

She glanced at the driver. Tall. Thin but muscular. Dark. Dreadlocked hair.

And *off,* somehow. She cast another quick look in his direction, trying not to stare, but couldn't quite figure out what it was that bothered her. "I'm Israel," he said with a heavy Caribbean accent as he pulled away from the curb.

Jess didn't offer her name, not caring if it seemed rude. Something was making the hairs on her neck rise, and it wasn't just that he was a caricature of a Jamaican.

"Where you heading?" her driver persisted, intent on chatting. "Vacation?"

"Something like that," Jess said, watching the road as they entered the freeway.

"You a diver?"

Maybe he was just nosy, she told herself. And her nerves were overtense. Whose wouldn't be, considering she'd been told that a criminal mastermind was gunning for her? "If you don't mind," she said, trying to relax and to stop seeing danger in every shadow, "I've had a long day and would like a bit of quiet."

"Of course, *mon*," Israel said, "Of course."

She breathed a sigh of relief and watched the pavement slide by—right up until Israel drove past the exit to the airport. Jess stiffened. "You passed the exit."

"I know a shortcut," Israel said. "Miss all the traffic and get you there faster." He turned off at the next exit, then down a side road that led through a warehouse district.

Shortcut her fanny.

The car slowed.

"Where are we going?" she asked. "This isn't a shortcut."

Israel looked at her, all semblance of friendliness replaced by something dark and purposeful. Automatically, her hand went to a gun that wasn't there—the one she'd had FedEx pick up a while ago.

"No, Miss Whitaker, it isn't," he said, reaching into his jacket.

That's what was off, she realized in the split second his hand moved. The bulge in his jacket. It wasn't a wallet. It was a shoulder holster.

Her driver was armed.

Even as her mind processed the information, her combat-trained body was in motion. Unbuckling her seat belt with one hand, she swiveled sideways, bringing her legs up and slamming them into Israel, pushing him against the door as his gun cleared the holster but before he could point it at her.

The car jerked sideways, and the gun fell to the floorboard with a dull thud. Jess grabbed the wheel, yanking it toward her and sending the vehicle skidding in the opposite direction. Israel pounded her hands with his fist, trying to make her let go.

He hit her again. It was like having her fingers smashed in a door, but Jess gritted her teeth and refused to loosen her grip. He was bigger. Stronger. And the moment she gave an inch, he would use it against her.

Changing tactics, he bent over, groping for the fallen gun. *Like hell,* Jess thought. Releasing one hand from the wheel, she undid his seat belt. Reaching across him, she popped open his door.

"Bitch!" Israel screamed, as he realized what she was doing. Forsaking the gun, he grabbed her hair.

Sharp pain reached through her scalp as he yanked her upward. Twisting in his grasp, she bit him until she tasted blood in her mouth.

Screaming, he let go, and she scrambled backward toward the passenger door. With her door at her back for leverage, Jess kicked out with both feet and all her strength.

Israel shot out the open door but at the last minute, managed to grab his flopping seat belt with one hand. Sliding into the driver's seat, Jess punched the gas with one foot, not caring that she dragged her kidnapper wannabe along the asphalt. She reached for the door handle and yanked it inward, slamming her assailant between the driver's door and the car frame until he let go and rolled away.

In the rearview mirror, she watched him come to a stop on the side of the road then stumble to his feet. He didn't run after her, and she didn't stop to make sure he'd live. Her heart pumping adrenaline through her system, she gunned the vehicle. The tension didn't recede until Israel disappeared from sight, and she was back on the main road.

Jess took a deep breath, willing her pulse to slow. Delphi

hadn't been kidding. Arachne was ruthless. Determined. And apparently, she could strike anywhere.

Not that it mattered. Arachne might be determined but so was Jess. Plus, she had a purpose.

Retribution.

Chapter 3

One For The Money. The name made Jess smile. It was appropriate for a salvage boat that hunted sunken treasure. The eighty-foot Swiftship had definitely seen its share of years, but it appeared well maintained. The twenty-foot span of open deck in the back was clean, with gear stowed. There were no oil stains or suspicious spots that hinted at larger problems.

Unfortunately, it also looked deserted.

Jess carried a FedEx box containing her gun in one hand, her duffel tossed over her shoulder and her dive bag in her other hand. Setting box and bags on the pier, she adjusted her black-and-white Hawaiian-print tank top and walked toward the stern hoping to find someone on board. Anyone.

But the deck remained empty. Silent. She frowned, loathed going aboard without permission. Perhaps some people wouldn't think twice about it, but she equated walking onto a ship with walking through the front door of someone's house.

You didn't turn the knob and barge in.

"Hello!" she shouted, cupping her hands around her mouth. She waited for a reply, but the only answer was the slight rocking of the boat. "Hello! Zach, are you there?" Arms crossed, her frown deepened. "Anyone?"

"Can I help you?" a voice inquired. She turned to see the questioner on the opposite side of the pier watching her from the upper story of a double-decker luxury yacht.

Despite her sunglasses, she still shielded her eyes against the tropical sun. "Thanks, but I'm looking for Zach Holiday."

His blond hair sticking up, the man on deck looked younger than her and ready for a beach party. The drink in his hand completed the effect. "Zach? You don't want him. That boat's a piece of crap." He lowered his sunglasses and gave Jess a once-over. "Come on up here, and I'll show you what traveling in luxury is like," he finished, his words slurred.

Rolling her eyes in exasperation, Jess turned away. She didn't have time to deal with a drunk.

"Come on, honey, I got enough for two," he wheedled.

"Jeez." Trust-fund baby.

Trust Fund started whistling at her, and she eyed Zach's boat. The whistling turned into hooting and catcalls. "Time to barge in," she muttered. Hoisting her gear onto the deck, Jess stepped over the railing. Ignoring the drunk's continuing comments, she made her way toward the open door that led below. "Hello? Anyone there?" she shouted down the stairway.

Again, no answer, but from the opposite end of the ship came the distinct sounds of swearing and the clinking of metal.

Walking down the stairs, she made her way to the stern, following the loud clanging noise. Reaching the engine room, she found the origin of the swearing.

Whoever he was, he was on his back, his upper body hidden by the engine. Tools lay scattered at his feet.

"Hello," Jess said.

He jerked upward at the sudden sound of her voice, banging his head with a resounding clunk.

"That'll leave a mark," she said, wincing.

"You think?" the male voice replied. Sliding out, he stared up at her from the ground.

Wearing grimy khaki shorts, a once-green Sex Wax T-shirt, his hands coated with who-knew-what and a greasy red mark on his forehead, he looked like the boat's mechanic.

She knew better.

Zach Holiday. She'd looked him up on Google before she left her apartment, and he'd come up on a number of pages. An independent computer programmer, he solved problems that others couldn't. His skill and business savvy had left him wealthier than most self-employed geeks.

Even more interesting was that he wasn't just a cerebral know-it-all that lived in front of a computer 24/7. He did a lot of physical activities, including extreme sports. Mostly, he used his monies to take time off with his father and hunt for gold in the warm waters off the coast of the Americas.

He presented an intriguing duality of intellectual and adrenaline junkie.

Along with the articles were pictures, which were what gave him away now, despite the grime.

Dark brown hair. Tall, strong body.

And emerald eyes that were so green it was impossible to look away. She stared into them, mesmerized.

He met her steady gaze and raised a brow. "Can I help you, or do you prefer to stare?"

Heat rose in her cheeks, but she blinked, regaining her

composure as fast as she'd lost it. "You must be Zach." She held out her hand. "Sorry, I didn't expect to see you working on the engine."

"You're Jessica?"

"Jess."

He took her hand, using her as leverage to rise. Once on his feet, he shook her hand. His grip was firm. Warm. He nodded toward the engine. "I like to work with my hands, and it's not that different from computers," he said. "Logic and patience will get you what you need."

She gave a brief nod. Interesting man. "Sorry I just walked on board," she explained. "I called out but the only person who answered was some drunk across the way."

"Blond? Invited you on board?"

She nodded. "I guess that's his modus operandi?"

Zach grinned, his teeth bright against his tanned skin. She couldn't help but smile back. "That's Eric. His family has more money than God, but he's harmless."

That was her impression, as well. "What's going on here?" she asked, now that the niceties were complete. She looked past him to the engine.

"Broken belt," Zach said. "One of those parts that are neither expensive nor difficult to install, but essential if we plan to use the ship. So, since we're waiting for Liz to return with parts, how about we get a cup of coffee and talk about this project of yours."

It was a standard request—nothing out of the ordinary—but the shield Jess worked so hard to cultivate rose. Delphi said she'd provided Zach with minimal information. Was he going to try and pump more out of her?

Probably. It was what she'd do under the same circumstances. She remembered Delphi's words: *Need to know.* That was *her* modus operandi.

But Zach didn't need to know that. She smiled at him. "Sure, I'll tell you everything I know."

Her gun loaded and on the bunk, Jess unpacked her bags. Her cabin, eight feet in length and ten feet wide, was small compared to her bedroom at home, but she knew it was probably one of the bigger ones on board.

She glanced around, wondering where to put her clothes, and noticed there were drawers beneath the bed. Bending down, she tucked her few items below.

The door squeaked open. Jess rose and grabbed her gun in one fluid motion. By the time she was upright, she was in ready position and staring at the startled face of a blond girl in a one-piece, red Speedo and a pair of cargo shorts.

"Hi. I'm Liz." The blonde glanced at the gun's barrel and gave a weak smile.

Liz? That was the girl Zach mentioned. Jess set her gun on the pillow—within her reach but not Liz's. "Sorry about that, but you startled me. Ever hear of knocking?"

"I didn't think you were here. I was just dropping off some clean sheets."

Jess noticed the folded cotton in her arms. "Oh." She took them, setting them on the bed and feeling like a fool, even if her actions were justified. "Thanks."

"Anyway," Liz said, leaning against the doorway and giving Jess a curious glance. "What are you doing for dinner? A bunch of us were heading out in a few minutes. Want to go?"

Jess shook her head. "I'm beat."

"You might want to rethink that," Liz said in a singsong voice. "It's kind of a tradition that we take the P.I. out for drinks before we leave."

"P.I.? Private Investigator?" Jess asked.

"*Primary* Investigator," Liz said with a flip of her waist-length, ponytail. "The crew is waiting, if you want to go. It's just dinner. At the bar."

Delivering sheets? Jess didn't believe it. The invitation was the reason Liz was here. They wanted her to go drinking. In other words, *initiation*.

She raised a brow as she considered the request. She'd gone through initiation rites in boot camp when she first entered the Marines then later when she trained to become a combatant diver.

As a Marine, it had included testing her endurance and pain threshold.

She couldn't imagine that initiation to this team was similar, but Liz did make a good point. She should consider going. Part of working with any team was bonding, and it was best to get in good with the crew as opposed to remaining an outsider.

Hell, she might be with these people a few days or a few weeks, there was no way to tell. "I take it this is some kind of tradition?" Jess asked.

Liz smiled, and her face lit up. "Yes." She nodded at the bunk. "But you might want to leave the gun."

Jess glanced at the Sig. She'd feel better if it was with her, but under the circumstances, it seemed a bit like overkill. "I'll see if Zach has a safe."

"He does. Meet us on deck in ten," Liz said with a wicked grin as she shut the door behind her.

When Jess emerged onto the deck, sans weapon, Liz was waiting, a sandal-clad foot tapping on the deck. "Hi." She almost skipped over, took Jess's arm. "We never have another woman on board," she whispered as they walked. "You have no idea how much I'm going to enjoy this. That's Nate," she pointed to an older man. Short and stocky, his head was shaved but his goatee was as blond as Liz's sun-washed hair.

"And that's Diego," Nate said, gesturing at a young Caucasian man with short dreadlocks who walked toward them with Zach.

"Ready for dinner?" Zach asked.

Jess didn't miss his sly grin or the way each member of the crew caught his eye, and she bit her lip in an effort not to laugh at them. They actually thought they had the upper hand. They believed she didn't know what they were doing.

She returned his smile. This was going to be fun. For her. "Born ready," she said.

The bar wasn't what she expected. No tacky swordfish or old nets with the occasional ornamental starfish graced the dark paneled walls.

Instead, it was small. Dimly lit. And crowded with what she thought were locals since there wasn't anyone dancing on the table or doing body shots. Heads turned as they walked past the tables and shouts of recognition followed before everyone returned to their drinks.

She'd called it right—this was a local hangout.

Zach herded the crew toward a long table at the back of the room, and in seconds, two pitchers of beer and a round of shots filled with something dark were in front of them. Jess raised a brow.

"What's wrong?" Zach asked. "You don't drink?"

She looked him up and down. She might have believed his wide-eyed innocence if his grin didn't scream *troublemaker*.

If she had to guess, she'd peg him as the instigator. "I'm a Marine. I can drink you under the table," Jess snapped back. "But we're leaving in the morning. Aren't shots a little excessive?"

"Excessive would be if we made you do all the shots," Liz said. She held the tiny glass in the air. "To the ship!"

They all raised their drinks then paused, watching Jess. She knew that if she refused, she'd always be the one who backed down.

The Marine who backed down.

She raised her shot glass high and toasted the group. In one smooth movement, she downed the drink. *Rum.* The strong liquid burned her throat, but she swallowed the urge to cough. "Smooth," she croaked.

The crew shouted and whistled, as she set her glass upside down on the table in front of her, then all downed theirs in unison.

She glanced at Zach, silently asking him if they were going to push her to get drunk. She hoped not. She'd hate to waste good rum by pouring it on the floor under the table.

Zach handed her a beer, winking at her when the others weren't watching.

She relaxed, confident he wouldn't let her initiation go too far. He was an islander in many ways, but she sensed that his "island attitude" didn't go all the way to the bone. In fact, watching him and how he held himself, she'd bet her weapon that beneath the carefree attitude was steel.

There had to be. Zach was a successful computer genius that worked with the government. Successful men knew when to play. Knew when to work. And knew the line between good fun and excessive stupidity.

It would serve her well to remember the steel beneath the surface, she realized as she caught herself smiling back, and once again, staring into his emerald-green eyes. She turned her attention to her drink.

"They're like emeralds," Liz whispered in her ear.

Jess found herself flushing. "What is?" she asked, play-ing dumb.

"His eyes." She giggled.

Jess flushed deeper and was grateful for the dim lighting of the bar. She realized there was something else she could learn while she was here—how these people related on a more personal level. "Um, are you and Zach…"

Liz's nose wrinkled. "What?"

"You know?" She nodded toward Zach and wiggled her eyebrows. "You? Him? Involved?"

"Oh," Liz said with a start, realizing what Jess was getting at. "Oh, God no. That's just icky."

Icky wasn't how Jess would describe sleeping with a man like Zach. Not at all. Sensuous. Fun. Erotic.

But not icky.

Liz nodded toward Nate. "I'm married."

"To Nate?" He was probably twenty years the girl's senior. At least. She glanced at Liz's bare left hand.

"I kept losing it," Liz said, following Jess's line of sight. "It was simply getting too expensive." She leaned in. "I know. He's older. But he knows *things,* if you know what I mean."

"I get it," Jess said with a knowing nod, praying the young woman didn't elaborate.

"Besides," Liz said, "He's as smart as Zach, and I love smart men, don't you? You seem like you'd need a challenge. Like Zach."

"Um, yeah," Jess replied, not sure she wanted to go where this conversation was heading.

Nate's muscled arm pulled Liz away, saving Jess. "No more girl talk. It's time!"

At the announcement, a cheer rumbled through the bar and the chant of, "Jess. Jess. Jess!"

Heat flamed Jess's cheeks as she realized that getting her drunk wasn't the objective. There was more, much more, and it seemed to involve not just the crew but *everyone*.

"Sorry!" Liz called out over the chanting. Reaching into her pocket, she pulled out a rolled-up piece of paper. "Here." She handed it to Jess.

"What's this?" Jess asked, opening it. The original paper was stained but covered with something shiny and smooth. Jess ran her hand over it. Laminated.

She brought it closer to the light. There was a poem printed on it. A badly written poem, both in content and penmanship. "What am I suppose to do with this?" Jess asked, waving the paper, fairly sure she was going to hate the answer.

Zach leaned in so she could hear him. "It's a song. We want you to sing it."

Jess's smile faded. "Sing this?" She'd rather do rum shots.

"Yes. It goes to the tune of 'Row Row Row Your Boat.'"

For a moment, Jess stared at the crowd, her mouth open. "Of course it does," she finally managed to say.

Zach grinned at her, daring her to back down.

Oh, hell no. She was not going to give him the satisfaction. She gave a curt nod, and he motioned for the bar to be quiet. The chanting died back. She glared at him. He was a dead man. Later. Taking a deep breath, she sang, "Sail, sail—"

"Wait," Liz cut her off.

Jess stopped. "What? Was it that bad? I never said I could sing."

"It's not that," Liz said, looking to Zach.

Zach took Jess's hand. "You have to stand up on the seat. The bar needs to hear it."

Horrified, Jess shook her head. "No. I draw the line at standing on chairs."

The bar started clapping and Zach shrugged. "Okay. It's a bench. Not a chair. And you'll disappoint everyone."

She shook her head. "I'm not doing it," she said through clenched teeth.

"It's *tradition*," Zach countered, his hand tightening around hers.

Tradition. The one phrase he knew she'd give in to. She glared at him. He'd better have steel beneath all that charm, because after this, she was going to beat the hell out of him, given half a chance.

"You're a dead man, Holiday."

The threat only made him smile wider.

She pulled her hand away. "I can get up by myself."

Liz shoved another shot in her hand. "This helps."

Jess downed it and wiped her mouth with the back of her hand. Wobbly with the second shot, she managed to stand on the rickety bench. She waved to the room, and they grew silent.

"I'll get food," Liz said. "When you're finished, we'll eat." She scooted out but not before kissing her husband.

Nate held up a globe candle, spotlighting her. "So you can see," he explained.

"If that's your story." She turned her attention back to the sheet of laminated paper. There were six stanzas. It was signed Diego.

She glanced down at him. The quiet ones. They were the worst.

Diego grinned and gave her a thumbs-up.

"Sing!" an unknown voice called out.

God, she hated this. *"Sail, Sail, Sail a boat, above the briny deep. Watch out for land, watch out for crabs, and never fall asleep."*

She stopped. "Crabs? This is stupid. I mean, really, really, stupid."

"Louder!" someone shouted.

"Fine." She rolled her eyes. *"Catch, catch, catch a fish from the ocean green. Make it fresh, make it large, with scales like aquamarine."*

God help her, Diego couldn't write to save his life.

She began the next stanza, and the crowd joined in, their loud, enthusiastic voices overriding her. Despite the fact that her face still burned from embarrassment, Jess smiled.

The room was hers, and she loved it. And apparently, they were pleased with her, as well.

On the fifth stanza, with the crowd still drowning her out, a sudden movement at the bar caught Jess's attention.

Liz. Her movements were jerky. Wrong. Jess's voice died and the crowd kept singing. Had Arachne followed her here? Jess stood on her toes to watch for trouble.

Liz was trying to make it back through the crowd, and then someone grabbed her arm. Jess stiffened then realized it wasn't an assassin. It looked like Trust Fund. And the idiot was trying to kiss Liz—his friends egging him on.

Another movement caught her eye.

Nate, pushing his way through the crowd to his wife.

She hadn't seen him leave, but from her vantage point, he looked pissed.

Jess shoved Zach's thigh with her foot, catching his attention. "Problem," she mouthed, nodding toward the bar.

Zach jumped up, pushing his way through the sea of people with Diego in his wake. With the crowd still singing, Jess jumped down and followed, arriving just in time to see Nate draw back his arm, and then his fist connected with Trust Fund's jaw. In seconds, Nate was lost in a pile of flailing bodies, and Liz jumped on top to save her husband.

"Get her," Zach said, turning to Jess as he entered the fray.

In his expression, she saw the steel she'd wondered about, and more. Grabbing Liz, she pulled her off the men. Behind her, she heard the distinct sound of fist hitting flesh. "Stay here," she said, turning back.

When she turned around, the brawl was in full force, and she spotted Zach and his men at the opposite end of the bar.

"I swear," she muttered. Why did initiations always seem to end with bruises and blood?

Calmly, she worked her way through the mob, taking time to dodge an uppercut, grab the fist to use its momentum and pull the owner to the ground. She kicked him in the ribs to make sure he stayed down.

Jumping over the moaning man, she reached Nate first. He was standing now, his face dark red as he punched Trust Fund. A few more blows, and Nate would put him in the hospital. "Enough," she said, grabbing his arm.

Nate hesitated, then let go of the man's shirt. He fell to the floor in a heap. "Get Liz out of here before she gets hurt," she shouted, knowing if there was anything that would get Nate's attention, that was it. Nate nodded and went to find his wife.

Around them, the brawl escalated. She spotted Zach as a fist came out of nowhere, clocking him in the jaw.

Jess winced.

Zach shook his head, stunned, and by the time he moved to retaliate, the man was gone.

"You okay?" Jess asked, keeping her head down.

"Get Diego," Zach shouted.

She grabbed the dreadlocked boy and was pulling him to safety when an air horn sounded, cutting through the din like a bell at a prizefight. People stopped, fists midair and then dropped them to their sides. A beefy man stood at the bar.

"That's enough!" he shouted. "You people," he pointed to the group that caused the ruckus, "get out before I call the cops."

They had the sense not to protest.

"You," he pointed to Jess.

"Me?"

"Sing."

Zach thrust the laminated paper back into her hands with a shrug. "You heard the man." Around her the bar chanted, "Sing! Sing! Sing!"

Zach grinned. "And you thought this was over?"

She looked into his dark green eyes. "Bar fight. Rum. Singing. This is some initiation."

With a low chuckle, he wrapped his broad hands around her waist and sat her on the bar.

She leaned forward. "Payback's hell," she whispered in his ear.

She'd make sure of it.

Chapter 4

Seconds after her alarm clock sounded, Jess sat straight up in her bunk and slapped the off button with the flat of her hand.

It took another few seconds to orient herself to her strange location.

One For The Money. Salvage ship. Puerto Isla.

She yawned and stretched. Her mouth tasted horrible. This was why she didn't drink. It seemed to take her forever to get it together in the morning, and she felt fuzzy.

Though last night had been fun, she had to admit. The drinking. The singing. The eating. Even the bar fight had been a good time. Plus, it had given her an opportunity to see the crew in action.

They were a tight-knit bunch. Even Diego—one of the most silent men she'd met who was not a Marine—was in the thick of the brawl.

As for Zach, he was one surprise after another. Charming

as hell, but the way he stood when attacked, held his hands and never hesitated, told her that it was not his first bar fight.

The faint smell of coffee and the steady thump of feet on the deck above caught her attention. The rest of the crew was up and moving and it was time for her to do the same. She grabbed her toothbrush, paste and towel and flung open the door to her private bathroom.

Standing in front of the shower was a seminaked Zach.

Okay, not so private, she thought as she stopped in her tracks.

With nothing but a towel wrapped around his waist and his skin damp from the shower, Zach did not look like a computer geek. Not like a mechanic. Not like an easygoing charmer.

He looked iconic.

His abs were washboard. His shoulders corded with muscle. There was enough hair on his chest to make sure a woman knew he was a man.

Her gaze swept upward, and she met his eyes staring back in surprise. Heat flooded her face. "Um, I…" She held up her toothbrush.

"We share a shower," he said, his voice trailing off at the end as his attention was diverted by her baby-pink, boy-shorts underwear and the thin, white cotton tank top that served as her pajamas.

Jess felt naked despite the clothes and started backing out. "I should have knocked."

He took a step and the towel started to slip and he grabbed it, his eyes widening. "I thought Liz told you. I'm sorry—"

But she was already in her room and shutting the door. "Could that have been more awkward?" she muttered, patting her cheeks to dissipate the heat.

She inhaled, slow and deep. Obviously, it had been much too long since she'd seen a naked man that wasn't wearing military-issue underwear, covered in grease paint and getting ready for maneuvers.

She was a professional. A Marine. She'd seen plenty of naked men.

There was no need to act embarrassed. Straightening, she opened the door a crack. "Let me know when you're done?" she called.

"Give me thirty seconds," Zach replied.

Sounds of hurried shuffling emanated from the bathroom, and she peered inside, catching a glimpse of Zach in the mirror.

His back was to her, and the towel from his waist was now tossed over his shoulder, giving her a perfect view of his perfect backside.

There was a dimple on each cheek.

I could bite that like an apple. She yanked the door shut, realizing where her thoughts were wandering.

Oh, yeah, much too long since she'd seen a naked civilian.

"How are you feeling?" Liz asked when Jess stepped onto the deck wearing her standard boat gear of bikini top, shorts and deck shoes. "Not hungover, are you?"

"Takes more than a few shots and a bar fight," Jess said, glancing to make sure that Zach wasn't around. Taking Liz by the arm, she drew her aside. "Why didn't you tell me that Zach and I were sharing a bathroom?"

Liz shrugged. "Didn't occur to me." She broke into a slow, wide grin. "Oh, don't tell me that you walked in on him."

"He was wearing a towel."

Liz giggled, and Jess found it impossible to be angry at the girl. She wanted to. Really wanted to. But being angry with Liz was like being angry at a puppy.

"Hey, babe." Nate walked past and patted Liz's butt then smiled at Jess. "Slugger."

"Back at you," Jess said.

He pointed to Diego, adjusting lines and prepping the boat. "You ladies going to chitchat, or are you going to help get us out of here?"

Liz gave her husband a peck on the mouth then followed him.

In less than an hour, they cast off and *One For The Money* moved past the moored boats on her way out to sea. Jess realized she had yet to see Zach since their quasi-naked encounter and a part of her—the embarrassed part—didn't want to.

But there was no way she could avoid him forever. Especially when she needed to give him the coordinates for their search.

"Be a grown-up," she told herself. "He's just a man, for pity's sake."

But a finely chiseled man, her libido whispered.

She told her libido to shut up, rolled her eyes at her over-active hormonal response and hurried to the control room before she had a chance to change her mind.

When she entered, Zach had his back to her. He wore black board shorts, a loose T-shirt and deck shoes. Next to him was a man of about the same height and in almost the exact same outfit.

"Gentlemen," she said, stepping inside, curious and cautious as to the identity of the other man. Both turned and in seconds, she knew.

It was Alfred Holiday—Zach's father. A twenty-something-years older version of his son, his hair was more gray than brown. The body a little thinner but just as muscular. He also had the same green eyes. "Pleased to meet you, Alfred," Jess said.

"Please, call me Al. You must be Jess," Al said, coming

forward. "Sorry I wasn't there last night, but I had a previous engagement."

From the way he said it, and from the way he grinned, she had no doubt the previous engagement was of the female variety.

"I hear that you're getting my son into trouble."

She blushed, and glared at Zach. Was nothing sacred? "I know I should have knocked this morning, but I didn't know he was there."

Al's brows arched in surprise. "I was talking about the bar fight." He glanced back at Zach. "Something you need to tell me, son?"

"No. Nothing," Zach said, his mortified gaze begging Jess to shut the hell up.

"Uh, I have coordinates," Jess said, desperate to change the topic. Pulling the worn piece of paper from her pocket, she handed it to Al.

Silently, he read it, stroking his chin as he took in the information. "That's a little far out," he finally said. "Can I ask how you came by these coordinates?"

"You can, but then I'd have to kill you," she replied, falling back on the well-known quote.

"Fair enough," Al said.

Jess smiled. Few people gave in that easily, but Delphi said he'd worked with the government before so it wasn't a total surprise that Al asked pertinent questions but didn't press when she wasn't forthcoming.

Setting the paper aside, Al took the wheel, and Jess realized they'd cleared the small port and were entering open ocean. Al pushed the throttle forward. She heard the slight whine as the engine increased in rpms and the vibration beneath her feet increased.

The engine hiccuped then resumed.

The men glanced at each other at the same time, and Zach started toward the door. "I'll go check it out, Dad. Why don't you come with me?" he asked Jess as he walked past.

Crap. She knew what this was going to be. A talk. An apology. Something that would make her uncomfortable.

Might as well get it over with, she decided and fell in behind him.

"I wanted to apologize for last night," Zach said, once they were in the hallway.

She almost stopped walking. "Last night?"

"I should have warned you about the whole trial-by-singing thing."

"Oh. Yeah. It was a little embarrassing but I've been through worse."

"Marine?"

She did stop. "I never said…"

He kept walking. "You have that look."

She hurried to catch up. "What look?"

"Jarhead."

"Thanks," she said, frowning. It was a common term, but she hated it. She thought it made Marines sound dumb, and the men she knew were anything but stupid. Arrogant? Yes. Pain in her ass? Definitely.

But not stupid.

Not if they wanted to stay alive.

"I didn't mean it that way," he explained, eyes widened as he saw her reaction to the term. "I know most people hear *jarhead* and think that means someone who takes orders without thinking. Dumb. Whatever." He thrust strong fingers through his hair in frustration as he tried to explain himself. "I didn't think that. I don't think that."

"Then what do you think?" Jess asked, as they continued to

the engine room, not eager to let him get away without explaining himself. She'd been uncomfortable. Now, it was his turn.

"I've worked with Marines before. A few rescue teams to be specific."

Just as Delphi said.

Zach continued, "They pay attention. To everything. And they will do anything for each other." He glanced back at her, smiling. "You're like that. My men were in trouble, and even though we embarrassed the hell out of you, you were right there."

"You're my crew," she said, uncomfortable with the praise.

They reached the engine room, and the twin engines ran loud but steady as Al held them on course. No smoke. No fire. All seemed normal.

Until she looked up at Zach.

Head cocked, his eyes were narrowed.

"What?" Jess asked. "What's wrong?"

He held up a finger, indicating that she should be quiet. Walking over to the right engine, he kneeled down, peered between the moving parts and stiffened. "Jess?"

She hurried over, kneeled beside him, and he pointed at something. "Any idea what that could be?"

Her eyes widened. Metal casing. Wires. Timer. She knew what it was, and the thought made her gut twist. "Yes. It's a bomb."

Jess slid out from under the engine and sat up. Whoever had set the device was good. Very good.

Luckily, she was better.

"Well?" Zach asked. At his feet were the tools she'd requested.

"They used an rpm sensor on one of the propeller shafts to trigger the timer."

He appeared confused, but she suspected it wasn't that he couldn't figure out what an rpm sensor did but it was residual shock from finding a bomb on his ship.

"It's a cheap part," she explained. "But clever. It reads the revolutions per minutes of the shaft, and as we speed up it converts them to miles per hour based on the circumference of the shaft."

Zach looked up and to the right, his expression blank as he sorted what she was saying. When he looked back at her, she knew she was seeing the geek. The man that made millions with a single, complex thought.

In this case, not so complex, but so far out of his realm that it seem fictional. "So when we reached speed, it triggered the bomb."

"Yes."

"Will it detonate if we stop?"

She shook her head. "No. But it's not going to stop the timer, either." She braced herself, waiting for the panic that was sure to follow that statement.

He nodded, taking in the information. "This means they knew the circumference of the shaft. They know boats. Timing."

Jess cocked her head, surprised at his calm demeanor. She'd expected fear, but instead he'd accepted the situation with unnatural calm.

Maybe his previous government missions were more dangerous than Delphi let on, and he was more accustomed to danger than she knew. Or perhaps it was simply denial. Either way, it worked for her and there was no time to analyze his psyche.

"Possibly," she said, continuing Zach's train of thought and adding her own. "Or they had plenty of time to figure it out while we were at the bar last night," she said. An alternative thought crossed her mind—that one of his crew set the bomb—but she didn't voice her suspicion.

Zach had kept cool regarding the bomb but she suspected that accusing one of his crew of espionage would send him over the edge.

"What does all this mean to us?" Zach asked. "Do we have time to go back to port? Get the crew off and then deal with this?"

"I'd rather not," Jess said. "We need to stay out at sea. If I screw up, I'd rather do it in the middle of nowhere."

"Good point," Zach said. "But what about my people?"

His people. She prayed that none were involved in setting the device. "Of course," she said. "We can stop the boat and put them in the life raft." She nodded toward the rigged engine. "If this goes south, I don't want their deaths on my hands."

"How long do we have?"

She took a deep breath, held it and focused. "The timer is set for an hour, and we have about fifty minutes left. I want you all in the raft in five minutes."

"There's a bomb on the boat?" Liz's voice squeaked. She was the last to arrive when Zach called for "all hands on deck." The rest of the crew still stared at Zach, stunned.

All of them.

Not involved, Jess thought with relief. She'd seen enough, knew enough, to know a lie when she heard one, and the entire crew looked as if they'd been knocked upside their heads with a mallet.

"That's what I said," Zach said. "Now, everyone in the raft. Jess and I are taking her out as far as we can then she'll dismantle the bomb."

"Jess?"

"Apparently, it's what she does for fun," Zach said, looking at her.

She shrugged.

"Son…"

"Dad, do it." Zach said. "I need you to take care of them."

Still, they didn't move, shocked by the revelation.

Jess walked to Zach's side. This had gone on long enough. Stunned or no, she needed them gone. The longer they took the less time she had. "Everyone in. I need you to leave. Now."

Everybody boarded the Zodiac but Zach. Pointedly, she looked at him. Then the raft.

He shook his head. "You need me to drive."

Dammit, she didn't have time to fight him. "I can pilot a boat, and I don't need heroes," she said under her breath to Zach as the others bobbed on the waves, waiting.

"I'm not a hero," he replied. "Have you ever driven a twin engine?"

"Yes."

"One that has separate throttle and gear levers?"

Hell. "Yes."

"Liar."

She sighed. The others were waiting. "Just go."

He shook his head again. "No. I'm not leaving you here, and the longer you argue the less time we have." Leaning over the edge, he tossed his father a radio.

"We'll be at the dock," Al said.

Jess didn't miss the ashen skin beneath his tan, and she couldn't blame him. Bad enough to lose the boat.

But Zach was his only son.

Zach nodded. "See you there."

Al nodded then revved up the Zodiac engine and sped toward port.

"Get to work," Zach said, walking to the helm. "I'm taking us away from traffic."

Just in case you screw up and we die.

He didn't need to say the words. She felt it. "Give me fifteen minutes of top speed, enough to get us clear of anything, then stop," she said. "I'll need the engines off to do this."

He nodded, and she headed down the stairs while he went to the helm.

Stopping by her room, Jess grabbed her MP3 player then headed to the engine room. Lying on her back, she studied the device. Tried to get into the mind of the person who set it.

Whoever it was, they wanted the boat gone, her gone and anyone who worked with her.

But Delphi said that Arachne wanted her alive. Was Delphi wrong? Did Arachne mean to kill her?

She rolled onto her back, the deck vibrating beneath her. Maybe it was all a test. Or to scare her.

A message that no one was safe with her?

Who knew what these people were trying to accomplish, but she knew she could not let them win. It wasn't in her to toss her hands in the air and cry uncle.

The engines slowed and stopped.

Jess sat up. "Time to work." Turning on the MP3 player, she listened to a compilation of Cake, Fatboy Slim and the occasional top-forty hit.

Zach walked through the door. "Anything I can do?"

"You could have left," she said, her voice tinged with sarcasm.

"Not a chance," he said. "Marines aren't the only ones who refuse to leave a team member behind."

She nodded, admiring him and wanting to smack him at the same time.

Cranking up the music, she wormed her way into the

works of the engine, being careful not to burn herself on the now-hot parts.

Luckily, she didn't have to go far. Using a screwdriver, she removed the bomb casing and breathed a sigh of relief. Whoever set this did not expect her to find the device. It looked simple.

A warning went off in her head as soon as the thought crossed her mind.

Nothing was ever that easy.

Especially disarming a bomb. "The Distance" stopped and Christina Aguilera's, "Fighter," began to play. One of her favorite songs.

She traced the wires. *Good. Good.*

Her hand stilled at a white one. *Not so good.*

There was a false wire in the mix. Meant to mislead her.

And if there was one there might be more.

She glanced at the timer. She had less than thirty minutes.

All the time in the world.

Sweat stung her eyes as she traced the other wires. They looked real. Active.

It was time to make the hard decisions.

She took a deep breath and removed her earphones.

"You okay?" Zach asked.

"Good."

"What next?"

"Now, we see who's smarter," she said. "Me or the person who made the bomb."

She pulled out the set of wire nippers from the front of her bathing suit. "Red wire. Blue wire." She murmured her lucky chant, staring at the green and yellow wires.

Holding her breath, she snipped the yellow.

She exhaled. "Still alive."

"Jess!" She tensed at Zach's shout. "The timer."

She glanced at it. It was counting down now at twice the speed of normal.

She'd screwed up. And bad. She took a deep breath. Now was not the time to panic. "Zach, get out of here!"

He yanked on her foot, trying to pull her out. She kicked him away. "You can do this," she whispered. "You can do this." There were two minutes left.

All the time in the world.

Red wire. Blue wire. Red wire. Blue Wire.

She scooted around the still-hot engine, burning her arm against the metal and no longer caring. She'd missed something.

She followed the wire to the C-4. There. Another wire. Whoever did this was good, she realized. Better than good.

Red wire. Her heart pounded in her ears.

"Jess!"

Seconds now.

All the time in the world.

She snipped the blue wire.

Chapter 5

They were still alive. Jess exhaled.

People who played with bombs were notorious for having short life spans, but she was good at her job.

She knew she was because she still breathed.

Zach grabbed her ankles and yanked her out, sliding her across the floor. "We're alive?"

"Looks that way," she said, pressing her hand to her chest. Her heart pounded beneath it, a steady affirmation of life.

He grabbed her hands and yanked her to her feet, pulling her against him. "Are you okay? You're wet."

"Sweaty," she said.

He wiped sweat from her forehead, pushing stray strands of hair away. "That was too close."

"It was." He licked his lower lip, catching her attention, thoughts of the bomb fading as he spoke. He licked it again.

And her body responded. She wanted his mouth. Wanted

to nibble at the edges. Wanted to taste him and have him taste her.

"Jess? Are you all right?"

Her insides stirred. Flipped. In the back of her mind she knew it was the adrenaline. The sheer joy of being alive that made her respond.

Knew and didn't care.

Her breath sped up. Grew heavy and deep. She put her hand against his chest. "Zach."

His breath caught and his eyes met hers. She saw the same pull in his gaze. Time ground to a halt as they stared at each other. Wondering. Waiting. He wound the length of her ponytail around his hand, answering her unspoken desire.

There was no escaping his grip.

Not that she wanted to.

He drew her closer, and she got her wish. His mouth was on hers, his tongue tasting her. Following the curve of her bottom lip and making its way to the sweet spot where her neck and shoulder joined.

All gentleness evaporated as he pushed her against the wall, the length of his body pressed against hers. She wrapped her arms around his neck, pulling herself upward and pressing herself against him.

He was hard against her. Urgent. His grip on her hair tightened, and she hissed at the pleasure and pain that coursed through her.

She wanted him. Wanted Zach. His body. His mouth. His hands on her skin. She couldn't resist rubbing him with the flat of her palm.

He groaned against her mouth, and his hand slid around her ribs and untied the top of her bathing suit.

Seconds later, Jess found herself on her back and Zach's

mouth on her erect nipples, the smell of sweat mixed with oil and grease tickling her nose. She wrapped her legs around his hips and slid her hand between them, searching for the zipper to his shorts and not finding it.

She wanted to scream with frustration.

"Here." Zach slid the shorts down. She wanted to cry in relief but settled for gripping the length of him with her hand and squeezing.

"No," he groaned, and she felt him pulse in her hand.

He was close.

But so was she.

She let go and settled for biting his shoulder. His neck. Not caring if she left marks. "Hurry."

Skillfully and with surprising patience, he undid her shorts, sliding them down her legs. He kissed her hard then lowered himself over her. Poised. As if waiting. For a moment, she thought he might hesitate. Might refuse her.

She tightened her legs, pulling him closer to her. "Please," she whispered. In seconds, he filled her, and she arched upward. Wanting more.

Needing more.

"Jess." He groaned her name against her ear. "Jess."

She kissed him, whispering his name against his mouth as she moved against him. Urging him with her body to respond.

He smiled. "Greedy." Then moved inside her.

Her breath caught in her throat as chills rippled over her body, but she rose to meet him, matching him as the pace increased, both of them too far gone to stop. To hesitate.

To think.

There was only the need to prove they lived.

His muscles twitched beneath her hands, and he grimaced, driving deep. She felt the familiar heat spreading through her. The tightening. The tension. "Don't stop. Don't stop," she chanted.

He drove deep again, and her body roared in response as her climax claimed her, blotting out coherent thought as she thrashed in his arms.

Then in the back of her semicoherent thoughts, she heard his groan and felt his arms tighten, pulling her near. His shout of release filled her ears and then there was nothing but breathing and the pulsing of her well-sated body as she caught her breath.

"Oh, God," Jess murmured when she opened her eyes again. Zach was on top of her. His weight comforting and oddly familiar. He planted little kisses along her neck and in her hair.

She traced a random pattern on his back. "That was amazing."

Propping himself on his elbows, Zach cupped her cheek in his palm, his bright emerald eyes staring into her. "You okay?" he asked. "I didn't hurt you or anything?"

She kissed him. Gentle now. Tender. "Marine. Jarhead. Remember?" she said, smiling.

He nodded then moved, but she tightened her legs. "Stay."

He smiled down at her. "I'm too heavy."

"No, you're not," she said, loving this part and knowing it wouldn't last—especially when he realized the danger they'd just escaped.

He played with her hair, letting the strands fall through his fingers like black silk as he searched her face. "Did you know you have gold in your eyes?" he said, brushing his hand against her cheek. "Dark eyes ringed with gold. So beautiful."

"My mother's eyes," she said.

He nodded and kept touching her. Stroking her. He stopped, frowning. "Damn, I didn't use protection. Will there be complications?"

She shook her head. "I have an IUD. I won't get pregnant, if that's what you mean," she said. "I just had a checkup and haven't slept with anyone for over a year so I'm disease free."

"Same here," he said, smiling. "The not getting pregnant part, I mean."

She gawked at him. "That is a horrible joke," she chided, but a giggle rose in her throat, and she realized she couldn't stop it if she tried.

Still on top of her, Zach shook with laughter, as well, and then rolled off her and onto his back, his guffaws filling the engine room and echoing to the corridor outside.

"And to think we were worried."

Their laughter stopped as both shot upright to see Al and the rest of the crew crowded in the doorway, staring down at them.

Dressed in tan board shorts and a tan-and-white-striped bikini top, Jess sat on her bunk. She was never coming out of the room. *Never.*

She sighed, knowing that *never* was just a fantasy. She'd made a mistake. They both had.

She thought of how he'd touched her, the intensity of his love-making, and she shivered. Granted, it was a memorable mistake, but she reminded herself, not the best idea she'd ever had.

"Jess?"

Her name was followed by a light tapping on the bathroom door. She hesitated, not wanting to face Zach but knowing that the sooner she got this over with the better. "Come in."

He walked in.

"Should we open that?" he asked, glancing at the door that led into the hallway.

"They've seen us naked after having sex on the engine-room floor, I can't see where it matters what they think of us now," Jess said. Scooting back, she leaned against the wall.

"Good point." He sat on the edge of the bed, facing her, his larger frame making the mattress creak.

For an uncomfortable minute, they stared at each other. Jess tried not to fidget. "About what happened…"

"I'm sorry," Zach said.

"Sorry?" She knew what he meant, but it still stung her pride. "Was it that bad?"

"No. You were amazing."

Jess offered him a halfhearted smile. "I feel the same way, but it was a mistake. You know it. I know it."

"Yeah," Zach said, looking uncomfortable. He sighed and scrubbed at his face. "This is awkward, isn't it?"

"Yes, it is," Jess agreed. Why did the mornings after always have to be so uncomfortable? "How about we forget about it and talk about the bomb?"

Zach sighed again, but she suspected it was in relief and even though she knew it was foolish, it bothered her that she was so easily pushed aside.

He nodded, latching on to the change in discussion. "You want to tell me why I had a bomb on my boat?"

Where to start? It was her turn to sigh now. She could only tell him so much without giving away Delphi and where she got her information. Better to let him ask as opposed to tossing out information. "What do you want to know?"

"Who set it?"

"Someone who doesn't want us to find the sunken ship," she replied. She sure wasn't going to tell him about Arachne. The less he knew the better.

"I figured that," he replied, his tone edged with frustration. "Unless it's a personal thing and they're after you."

Bingo. After herself and all who were like her, but she kept herself from reacting to his alternate assessment.

"Whoever did this, have they come after you before? Tried to kill you?" he asked again, pressing her for either confirmation or denial.

"No," she lied, and hated herself for doing it.

She would tell him about Chuck, she promised herself. Just not yet. She wasn't ready to talk about what had happened to her recruit. In fact, she hadn't permitted herself to even think about either the incident or the inquiry since arriving in Puerto Isla. Both were distracting and distractions led to sloppiness.

And sloppiness equated with dead.

She'd lost one man. She wouldn't lose another.

Zach stood up and paced the small room. "We need to find out what these people are after. I can't have my crew in danger." He stopped at the porthole, pulled back the simple, muslin curtain and peered out at the deep blue water. "The bends? Oxygen narcosis? That I can handle. I understand the ocean. Respect what she can do. But a bomb? I'm not sure how to handle that."

"I know," she said. He was out of his league with explosives, but most people were. "It's a little overwhelming, but as long as we don't go back into port, we should be safe."

"Jess, you and I both know that's not true." He let the curtain swing shut and turned back to her.

She raised a brow, realizing she'd underestimated Zach and the many facets of his personality. The logic and methodology that made him a computer genius also applied in real life.

Oh, goody.

He continued, "This could happen again at any time. People are trained to swim at length to place mines on the hulls of ships."

People like her. But she didn't bring that up. "I won't argue the point, but we have sensors to track something like that. We should be safe."

His mouth thinned. "That's not what I mean, and you know it."

She did, but again, she made sure her expression remained impassive.

"The point," Zach said, "is that my people are in danger." He walked over and sat down next to her, his knee touching her thigh and invading her personal space.

She refused to show discomfort by shifting away.

He leaned closer. "Can you guarantee my people will be safe? Even if we don't have another bomb, can you guarantee that this person won't try something else to stop us? Won't place more charges that are harder to find and impossible to disarm?"

His intensity made her nervous. It was as if he could see into her. She found she couldn't lie again. She'd lied so much that it had left a bitterness in her mouth that refused to go away. "I can't."

"Then I can't have you here. I can't continue this project if my crew is in danger."

Anger flared in her gut. "You can't stop the project. We just started. I don't have time to find anyone else."

His green eyes darkened, and she knew she'd hit a nerve. "It's my boat. I can do what I want."

She leaned in closer, until they were almost touching, his mouth inches from hers.

This time, there was nothing erotic about his proximity. "Call me crazy, but I don't see you as the kind of man to give up," she said, hoping to tweak his ego.

"I'm not," he replied. "Not when it's just my life on the

line, but when it comes to my people, there isn't room for pride. You should know that."

"I do." She respected Zach for having a conscience, but that didn't change the situation. "I don't have time to find someone new."

"I'll help. I know people."

She knew it wasn't that easy. Not when she considered all the parameters. "We picked you and your father for a reason. You've done government work before. You know the risks."

"Not like this. Not *once* did I think I'd be blown up."

"What did you think the money was for? A day cruise?"

He stiffened, and she knew she'd hit another nerve, and as much as she hated taking advantage, she went in for the kill. "I know you were paid a lot. More than any normal job. Somewhere in your head you must have known there would be danger. Otherwise, why the crazy money?"

He looked away, and she knew she was right and hated using it against him.

Finally, he turned back to her, his expression angry and dark. "They tried to kill my people. You can have the money back."

"It's not that easy." She wished it were. "The people doing this, they don't know how much information you possess. Even if you gave back the money and walked away, they'd come after you and your crew. They might kill them but not before finding out the depth of their involvement."

Zach paled as he realized what she was insinuating. "You're saying they'd torture them?"

She nodded. "You want to stop these people? Then help me catch them. Don't abandon this job."

Or me.

He looked grim and angry and ready to break something, but

she sensed his animosity wasn't directed at her—but at himself. He'd known what that kind of money meant, and he'd taken it.

She sympathized. People never thought they'd be the one to get hurt. Bad things happened to other people.

At least until you became the other people.

He stood, his body tense. Muscles tight. "I want to talk to the crew about this. If they're risking their lives they deserve to have as much information as possible."

It wasn't what she would do but Jess nodded in agreement.

They found the crew in the kitchen, going over duty schedules. The room fell silent when they appeared in the door, and Jess felt her face grow hot. Of all the bodily reactions she'd kept from her teenaged Academy days, blushing was her least favorite.

After a few tense seconds, Diego started to clap, and the others joined in, hooting at the same time.

Her blush deepened. "Oh, hell no," Jess muttered, turning on her heel to leave.

Zach grabbed her arm. "Don't," he whispered. "Children," he shouted over the whooping. The applause died down. "We appreciate the enthusiasm, but it's not like you've never seen two naked people before so let's forget it happened."

"Was it that bad?" Al teased. The rest of the crew smiled, knowing that any answer would be fodder for taunting.

Jess realized that this tight-knit group was not unlike her military crews. Show fear and they'd eat you for breakfast.

"No, that good," she said with total truth and a big smile. "We were marvelous, but we'd rather not mar the memory by discussing it with a bunch of adolescents."

Despite her put-down, the clapping started again. She rolled her eyes then followed Zach to the coffeepot. By the time they poured two cups and each grabbed a bagel, the applause had stopped.

"People, we need to talk about what happened with the bomb," Zach said.

The snickers died as Zach reminded them of the danger they'd dodged.

He continued, "Or rather I need to talk, and you need to listen."

Jess sipped her coffee, listening to Zach and adding a few comments here and there as he explained what was happening. "It's up to you to decide if you want to stay or leave," he finished.

"Why didn't you tell us?" Nate said to Jess, his hands grasping Liz's. "You put us all in danger."

Jess didn't back down from the accusation. It was deserved. "I know—"

"Nate, that's not fair," Zach interrupted. "I knew when I took the money that this job might be different. I didn't want to admit it, but I knew."

Jess met his eyes. Thank you, she mouthed. Damn, she admired him. Most people would never have confessed that.

Nate frowned. "That doesn't change anything. Drop us off somewhere. I won't take a chance with Liz's life."

Liz jerked her hand away from her husband's. "Excuse me? I don't believe that is your choice to make."

"I'm your husband," Nate growled.

"Yes. Husband. Not master," Liz said. She tucked a strand of long blond hair behind her ear. "I'm not leaving. This is my job, and no one runs me off."

"Don't be stupid—"

"Stupid?" Liz bolted to her feet, staring down at her husband, hands on her hips, eyes blazing like a Viking Valkyrie.

Go Liz. Jess tried not to smile. She had thought Liz sweet.

Easygoing. And much the way she'd misjudged Zach, she'd misjudged the California blonde.

Liz was kind and perky, but also much tougher than she looked.

"I didn't mean stupid," Nate said, backing down. "It just slipped out."

"Okay." Liz took a deep breath and sat back down. She smiled at Jess and Zach, once again the sweet girl Jess knew. "I'll stay. As I said, this is what I do and what I love. No one runs me off."

"I'm in," Diego said. He grinned at Zach. "But I want hazard pay."

Zach chuckled. "You got it."

"How much hazard pay?" Diego pressed.

Something about him caught Jess's attention. With his dreadlocks and light skin, he looked nothing like Charles but he reminded her of the recruit. There was a tenacity about the boy that intrigued her.

"Twenty percent of what I've received for the job," Zach replied.

Jess blinked. Twenty percent? If he gave everyone twenty percent he wasn't going to make any money on this. At all. That was eighty percent gone and once other things were factored in…

She glanced at Al, but he didn't object. In fact, he hadn't said a word. She tried to ignore the voice in her head that told her his silence did not bode well.

Diego whistled in surprise. "That dangerous?"

"There was a bomb," Jess reminded him.

More silence. Diego rose, stretching. "Well, I better get to work. You don't pay me hazard money to sit on my ass."

With that, he and Liz filed out, leaving herself, Zach, Nate and Al.

"Well?" Zach said, turning to Nate.

"We've been friends a long time, Zach, but if something happens to her, I'm holding you responsible. Both of you."

"Fair enough," Jess said as Zach nodded acknowledgment. Nate rose and followed the others out.

"Will he be a problem?" Jess asked, once the older man was out of earshot.

"No. He doesn't hold a grudge, but he wasn't lying. If something happens to Liz, he'll come gunning for us both."

"As in gunning?" Jess asked, wondering what Nate had been in his past jobs. He was fit. And in that bar fight, she saw skill. Training.

"Yes," Al answered. "He's ex Special Forces."

"I was wondering when you'd chime in," Zach said.

"I don't like to argue in front of the crew, you know that," Al said, sitting across from them. He looked Jess up and down. "You've heaped a world of problems on us."

She nodded. There wasn't much to say other than that was an understatement.

Al toyed with his pencil, doodling while he talked. "Is there any way out of this?"

Zach leaned back, looking more relaxed than Jess felt. "No. These people are ruthless. If we just walk away, they'll still come after us just to see what we know."

Al drew a square and began filling it in. Jess prayed he'd agree. If not, there would be problems even if the other crewmen were willing to take the chance. Finally, he set the pencil down and crumpled the piece of paper. "Meet me on the bridge in ten minutes."

"Thank you," Jess said. The elder Holiday left, and she let her head fall to the table, resting her forehead on her hands. "Thank God."

"One more thing, Jess."

She turned her head so her cheek was resting flat.

"If they're hurt, any of them, Nate isn't the only one your people will have to watch out for," Zach said, his voice low. "When you get a chance, tell your bosses that. I can find them. That's what I do. Find things."

His green eyes were hard. Flat.

And looking into them was scarier than looking down the muzzle of an M16. "And not just in the water," Zach said. "No one can hide in the computer world. Not from me."

"I know." A shiver rushed down her spine. She'd just make sure it never came to that.

And warn Delphi if it did.

Chapter 6

Jess stood on the deck, her black, full-body wet suit unzipped and pushed back so the upper half hung around her waist.

She strapped on her dive knife—something that all divers carried since the sea tended to be full of wayward fishing line that could snare the unwary—to her left calf and stared out at the deep blue waters before her.

Almost a hundred feet beneath them was a shipwreck.

Paradise Lost, she hoped.

It was their fifth, and last, day searching the designated grid area that Delphi had given her, and Jess was frustrated with what felt like unending failure.

It didn't help that every time she saw Zach, his presence reminded her of what had happened in the engine room, making her alternate between acting like a giddy schoolgirl or stumbling over her words like a klutz.

Finally, she opted for professional and cool, and while it

seemed like the best way to keep her emotional distance, she missed the camaraderie from the bar.

She missed the unexpected closeness she'd experienced with Zach.

Jess stared into the blue. "Please be the right boat," she whispered. She wanted—needed—to get back to her life, even if it meant dealing with the inquiry. While that would be difficult, she understood the Marines.

And she'd rather face an inquiry than another uncomfortable silence.

Footsteps on deck caught her attention. Recognizing them as Liz's, she didn't turn. "I meant to tell you that I like the black suit," the blonde said, standing next to her. She glanced down at the knife. "And the knife is very James Bond."

"James Bond?" Jess asked, dubious. "Not what I was going for but thanks."

"I think Zach likes it, too," Liz said, grinning.

Jess's head whipped around. "I bought this before I ever met Zach," she said, knowing she sounded defensive and wishing she could snatch the words back.

Liz's smile broadened.

"Besides, it doesn't matter what Zach thinks," Jess finished.

Even lamer, Jess.

"If you say so," Liz replied in a singsong voice then strolled away.

Jess didn't have the heart to glare at the girl. Instead, she leaned against the railing. Almost a week later, and she was still getting teased for having sex with Zach.

More footsteps on deck caught her attention, and this time she turned to see Zach coming toward her. Also wearing an all-black wet suit, his fins in one hand, mask in the other,

buoyancy compression device like a vest over his chest and
a knife strapped to his calf.

She glanced at him from beneath her lashes.

James Bond, she thought with appreciation. His lean, fit
body. His hands—both sensitive and strong. She swallowed
hard, remembering how his shoulders felt beneath her palms.
His weight on top of her.

Stop it, Jess, she admonished herself. *Daydreams like that
will not help, and you wonder why you act like such an idiot
around him? That's why.*

She turned back to the water to clear her head and look at
something besides Zach and his rock-hard body.

"Almost ready?" Zach asked. His hand touched her lower
back to get her attention.

Her breath caught in her throat at the heat that seemed to
radiate into her, but she stopped herself from flinching at his
touch. Both their egos were already bruised and there wasn't
any point in making it worse.

Swallowing hard, she reminded herself to remain neutral
as she turned to face him. "Yes," she said, forcing herself to
smile. "Gear check?" Zipping up her bodysuit, she slipped on
the rest of her equipment.

The check is standard procedure, she told herself as she
faced Zach and their hands glided over each other, checking
BCDs, weight belts, regulators and air. His hands on her were
practiced. Far from being erotic, the familiar routine helped
calm Jess and banish all thoughts of Zach appearing James
Bond-like.

Mostly.

Although she still breathed a sigh of relief when he finished.

"We're diving to one hundred feet," Zach said, all business.
"We'll have twenty minutes."

Twenty minutes was the safe time designated by the navy diving tables, but Jess huffed in frustration.

"What?" Zach said. "You can go longer?"

I can go as long as I want, she thought, her hand pressed to her side as if to hide the gills Zach couldn't see. Much longer.

But there wasn't any way to tell him how. Or why. Not without freaking him out. "Thirty minutes." It wasn't an unheard of number, but something only obtainable by those who had years of experience, zero body fat and excellent lung capacity.

His brows shot up. "You do breathe down there, don't you?"

Like you wouldn't believe, she thought, but the comment didn't faze her. He wasn't the first to wonder at her skills. "I'm an expert. Jarhead, remember?" she said, surprising both herself and Zach with the joke.

He smiled back, but the moment ended in seconds, and once again, the air between them thickened with silent tension.

"How about you?" she asked, desperately wanting to fill the space between them with something besides silence.

"Twenty-five or so."

Her right brow rose. Not better but unexpectedly good.

He shrugged, reading her surprise. "I'm a big guy but I don't suck air."

She shouldn't have been shocked, she realized. When she was checking his gear, she'd noticed that he wore four pounds of weights around his waist. The low weight was the sure sign of a pro since they tended to use breathing, instead of extra pounds, to regulate their depth. Novices, until they learned buoyancy control, wore twenty pounds or more.

"You two good to go?" Diego shouted from the aft of the boat. He had two tanks next to him.

Thank God. They didn't have to try to talk anymore. Walking over, they both stood still while the crewman helped put on their tanks. One more check to make sure they could breathe with their regulators and they both sat down to finish putting on their equipment.

"Jess?"

The seriousness with which Zach said her name caught her attention more than the words. "Yes?" She prayed he wasn't going to say anything about the sex. Or the bomb. Or their weird silences.

"Any thoughts on what we're going to do if this isn't the wreck?"

Or that. "Other than hoping you'd have saved this conversation for later, no," Jess said, strapping on her fins and not wanting to admit the worry that was prevalent in her thoughts when she gave herself permission to think about it.

"I understand," Zach said. "But it's my boat. My people. And my job to worry. To consider contingency plans. You might want to consider the possibility of what comes next."

She had. More than she wanted to admit to. "We can always go back over the search area," Jess suggested.

"There's nothing there."

"But—"

"That's why you hired us," Zach said, cutting her off and rising. "If I say there is nothing there then the place is a desert."

Standing beside him, Jess shifted her balance with the rocking of the boat. "Can we wait to see what we find before we worry about the next step?"

He slid his mask over his eyes and adjusted his snorkel. "I can do that. Let's hope we don't have to."

Holding her mask with one hand and crossing the fingers of the other, Jess took a giant stride off the edge of the ship and the water closed over her head.

* * *

The tension from even that brief conversation with Zach melted away as she floated in the blue. The water always felt like home to her. She watched from beneath the surface as Zach entered the water. Taking a few seconds, they did a self-check and gave each other the "okay" signal.

They followed the anchor line down to the shipwreck, taking time to hold their noses and blow out to equalize their ears and sinuses to the increasing pressure of depth.

With Zach in the lead and unable to see her, Jess held the regular mouthpiece loosely between her teeth, hesitated and then inhaled water.

Even now, there was a part of her brain that screamed she was going to drown. That humans could *not* breathe water!

But she ignored the voice, and the water flowed cold and heavy down her throat.

Internally, she knew what was happening. A cartilage and flesh flap closed to protect her ordinary lungs and another set opened, allowing her gills to intake the water and extract the oxygen.

It took more effort to push water instead of air and she breathed deep, tasting the familiar salt of the ocean on her tongue.

The first time she'd even dared to do this it had taken coaxing from Nikki and a shot of tequila—not a good idea, but she'd been fourteen and scared. And excited to think that she might be able to breathe like a fish. She'd had a few close calls while on the swim team. She'd breathed water and instead of choking, it had felt odd.

Almost normal.

And then when she was tested and told of the gills, she knew she was anything but normal.

* * *

"Do you know CPR?" Jess asked. She and Nikki had come to the pool to test her underwater breathing ability but now that she was in the water, her excitement faded and all she could think about was drowning.

"Read all about it." Nikki flashed her a smug smile.

Nikki and her damned perfect recall. It made it almost impossible to argue with her when it came to facts.

Nikki continued, "Quit stalling!"

"Stalling?" Jess took a moment to stick out her tongue. Then, holding her breath, she dropped below the waterline.

This was it. The moment of truth. She opened her mouth and…couldn't do it. She popped back to the surface.

"What happened?" Nikki asked, dropping to her knees at the edge of the pool, her eyes wide. "Did it work?"

Jess shook her head. "It just seems wrong. Unnatural."

"Unnatural?" Nikki leaned inward. "You have gills," she hissed under her breath. "What's unnatural about it?"

"Just give me a minute," Jess growled, splashing the younger girl.

Nikki pushed herself to her feet and stared down at Jess. "Are we going to do this or not?"

"We?" Jess said. "I don't see you in the water with me."

"You know what I mean." Nikki snorted and turned on her heel. "I guess you're not all that, are you?" she said over her shoulder.

Jess frowned. "What do you mean?"

Nikki stopped and slowly turned back, hands on her hips. "You talk a good game, tough girl. But when it comes to something risky, you can't even take the first step."

Jess held up her middle finger as a response, sank beneath

the water and, before she had time to consider the consequences, she inhaled.

Panic overwhelmed her as her brain screamed that this was wrong, humans did not breathe water, but in the back of her mind, she realized she didn't choke. Didn't die.

Still, she shot up, breaking the surface with a giant splash and exhaling the water she'd taken in.

"You did it!" Nikki whooped, running over.

Jess nodded, wiping the water from her eyes. She had, she realized.

She'd breathed water.

"What did it feel like?" Once again, Nikki dropped to her knees; this time her eyes were bright with excitement.

Jess pressed her hand to her chest. Her heart pounded beneath her palm. "Weird."

"Do it again."

Jess nodded. As pushy as Nikki could be, she was right. She'd do it, but not because it was fun.

She'd do it because she was scared. She'd never let fear rule her, and she wasn't about to start now.

Exhaling and taking a deep breath of air, she sank to the bottom of the pool. Sitting cross-legged, she inhaled, fighting back the panic and ignoring the primal screaming in her head.

She exhaled. Inhaled.

The chlorine burned, but she was breathing.

Zach tapping on his tank caught Jess's attention. They were almost at the bottom and below them rested the ship.

Even at depth, she could see that it was a yacht—approximately thirty feet in length. It could be *Paradise Lost*. The dimensions were about right. Her blood pulsed harder and her breathing quickened. Turning on her flashlight, she let go of the anchor rope.

She glanced at her partner, a check now that they were at depth, and he gave her the "okay" sign with thumb and forefinger. She returned it then swung the light. They were far down, but a school of silver fish swam past and fragments of coral and rocks littered the sandy bottom.

Swimming side by side, they reached the deck of the ship and swam over the top. There was a hole in the side, and Jess gave it a brief glance but wasn't sure what had caused it. Perhaps a collision with another boat. Explosives?

It was hard to tell, considering the evidence was three years old and had been underwater and subject to tides, time and the sea.

Zach touched her arm to gain her attention again, and they opened the hatch that led belowdecks, being wary of any animals that might be living inside the ship.

Even at this depth, there were predators and animals that, due to their size, were dangerous. She did not want to piss one off. Not that she was scared, but she didn't have the time.

With the exception of a few fish, the ship was empty. Swimming down the stairs, she flashed her light along the walls. Words painted on the overhang at the end of the stairs caught her attention.

My Wish. Papeete, Tahiti.

The name of the ship and port of registration.

My Wish?

Jess *wished* it was the right, damned boat. *Fuck.*

She pointed the name out to Zach. He nodded and even through the mask, she saw the deep disappointment in his eyes that mirrored her own feelings.

He wanted to find the boat as much as she did. Albeit for a different reason, but still, it was disappointing.

They ascended, and she breathed deep using her tanks, knowing that when she reached the surface, she was going to have to make some hard decisions.

They stopped fifteen feet below the surface to give their bodies time to adjust to the change in pressure and avoid the bends, not that Jess ever got the bends due to her body's unique structure, but she was used to the routine and liked the alone time.

She floated in the open water, scenarios racing through her head. She'd have to contact Delphi. Tell her or him that the information was wrong. That the ship wasn't here.

Perhaps they could rerun the data.

The familiar sound of a boat engine caught Jess's attention and goose bumps covered her skin despite the warmth of the water and wet suit.

After a week of being on *One For The Money,* she knew the boat's many sounds. This wasn't one of them.

Zach glanced upward, as well, and despite the fact that they had thirty more seconds of decompression, he swam toward *One For The Money*.

She grabbed his right fin and pulled hard, stopping him before he broke the water surface. It might be his ship and people in danger, but if these were pirates, it was best to play it careful. If not, then there was no rush.

He tried to pull away, but she held tight and pointed to the boat that was now twenty feet from his. Perhaps thirty feet in length, it was dwarfed by the larger salvage ship.

That was one thing in their benefit.

She shook her head and tugged him toward the stern of their boat. Zach nodded, and they swam over.

Rising to the surface, they hugged the hull and listened.

There was talking. Arguing. Then a sharp pop.

Gunfire. Jess jumped at the sound.

More popping sounded, but all came from *One For The Money*. Nate, she surmised. As specialized military—even ex-military—he wasn't going to tolerate pirates.

Or anyone that pointed a weapon in Liz's vicinity.

But Jess doubted if the rest of the crew was as well trained, and that was a problem. She had to stop the firefight before someone was hurt or killed. That meant taking down the pirates. She had no idea how many were on the smaller boat, but from their shouts of surprise she'd say not more than a few.

She could handle a few—even without a gun.

She pulled Zach close. "Stay here," she whispered in his ear.

"Not a chance. I'm coming with you."

"You're not trained to do this." This was her expertise. Stealth. Surprise. And the occasional killing, if the situation warranted it.

"I'm not letting you do this alone."

There was a break in the gunfire and some shouting, but no screams. So far, it seemed as if neither side had taken casualties.

"Dammit." She did not need Zach getting in the way. He had the courage of a Marine, not many would have stayed with her while she dismantled a live bomb, but he did not have her expertise or experience.

She also knew he was as stubborn as he was brave. He wasn't going to give in on this, and she didn't have time to argue. "Fine. I'll distract the pirates. When I do, board the ship and start her. We might be able to get away before this turns into a bloodbath."

"How do you plan to distract them?"

"I'm going to board them."

His eyes narrowed. "Bad idea."

"I'm trained." She pulled her dive knife free and flashed the blade at Zach. "And I'm armed."

The gunfire began again. "I'll signal when I'm ready," she said, and dived under the water before he could stop her or argue.

With Zach no longer at her side, Jess resheathed her blade, and swimming with a speed she reserved for just such occasions, was at the other boat in less than thirty seconds.

Focused and ready, she came up on the backside of the pirate ship and listened to the gunshots and occasional chatter in order to surmise their locations. From the pattern, she'd guess there were two men at the front of the boat occupied with the crew of *One For The Money.*

Plus, a set of heavy footsteps pacing the deck.

Number Three. Probably watching for her and Zach.

The footsteps came closer, and she swam beneath the hull of the boat until they passed. Removing her gear, with the exception of her wet suit and knife, she let the equipment sink to the bottom.

When she surfaced, the footsteps had faded. Grabbing a stray line someone had left hanging over the side, she used it to reach the lip of the deck and haul herself on board, trying to remain as silent as possible.

Crouching low, she unsheathed her knife and waited for the third man to make his round. A few seconds later, his footsteps shook the deck. He rounded the corner, and across from them *One For The Money*'s engines started. Zach had done it. She knew she could count on him.

Three looked toward the salvage boat, and his few seconds of distraction were all she needed. She moved in on him, her mind clicking off options. The easiest would be to kill him.

It would send a message to Arachne that mere words couldn't convey.

It would also bring her to the attention of the local police. They could also be connected to Arachne.

By her second step, she'd shelved the killing option and settled for wounding Three.

After all, who could bitch about a little wound?

Her fourth step caught Three's attention and he turned, raising his gun.

But she was already on him. Driving her knife into his shoulder, she twisted the blade. He screamed, and his gun clattered to the deck.

She shoved him into the water, then dived over him. Above her, bullets from the other pirates peppered the surface, creating white lines that petered out before they reached her.

She swam fast and deep, reaching *One For The Money*. Using the anchor line, she pulled herself onto the boat. Zach was at the wheel, and she gave him a thumbs-up.

Behind her, she heard the anchor line clank as the hydraulics pulled it in. They'd be moving in a minute. Until then, she just needed to make sure that no one was killed.

Following the sound of gunfire to the front of the boat, she saw Nate and Al using the oversize, plastic storage bins for cover. Nate had a 350 Sig. Al had an 9 mm HK.

Other than the two men, the deck was empty. That gave her fewer people to worry about. She crawled closer and Nate glanced at her.

Reaching next to him, he slid a gun to her from across the deck. "Thanks," she said, but he had already turned away. Beneath her the boat shuddered as Zach pulled away.

The pirates fired faster, obviously hoping to stop them.

Kneeling down, Jess returned gunshot for gunshot, making sure she hit their hull as close to the waterline as possible.

With a handgun, she wasn't going to do much damage to the thick fiberglass but between that and their wounded man, they might think twice about approaching the Swiftship.

The pirates shrank into the distance. She rolled onto her back. Damn, that was close. And exhilarating. She grinned, watching the clouds roll across the sky.

"Jess, we need to talk."

Zach stood over her, blocking out the sun. She turned over. Al and Nate were gone.

"Everyone's okay, aren't they?"

"Yes. This time," he said, his expression blank.

"Good." She rose, leaning against the railing in relief. If one of them had been hurt, someone like Liz or Diego, she'd never forgive herself. "They did great, but next time, we should make sure that your Dad and Nate join them. It's my job to be the badass. Not theirs."

A hint of a frown turned Zach's mouth downward. "Are you kidding me? There isn't going to be a next time."

Chapter 7

"People could have died," Zach said, pacing the upper deck. "My people."

Jess sat in one of the deck chairs, feeling like a child sent to the principal's office. She still needed to contact Delphi, but that could wait until she had something to report.

Well, something more than that they couldn't find the ship.

She prayed the communication wouldn't include the phrase, "Zach booted me off the boat."

He stopped in front of her, planting his feet wide. Anger burned on his face.

She understood the anger. Anger was easier than fear.

Fear of death. Fear for his friends.

She also knew that one couldn't be ruled by fear. Not that she wasn't scared for the others. She may not have been with the crew as long, but they were her team, and that meant something. The thought of Liz, or any of them, wounded, or worse, made her shudder. "You don't think I know that?"

He remained impassive. "You might have died, as well. Did that occur to you?"

Fear for her? It didn't surprise her. He was that kind of guy. The kind of guy who cared.

It also didn't change the situation. "No." It never did. She did her job, and her job involved dangerous situations.

"Well, it occurred to me," Zach said, his fury unabated.

The way he looked at her, looked *into* her, made her uncomfortable. "What would you have me do about it?" she asked.

"Finish the job as fast as possible."

"I want that, too."

He continued, "But to do that, I'm going to need the information you used to create the search grid. All of it."

She shook her head. "There's nothing to give you. They only gave me the search area. Not the data."

Zach leaned on the railing, watching her. "Do you trust me?"

Jess tilted her head, squinting in the sunlight. "What do you mean?"

"Do you trust me? Does your gut feeling tell you that I'm the kind of guy who'd sell government secrets to the enemy or the kind of guy who would fight to protect them?"

She stared into his eyes. She knew the answer, but it was hard to let go of habit. Of rules. Rules and secrecy were what kept her alive. She blinked. "The latter."

"Good. Then ask for the data. Not just a search area. Convince them to trust me with it."

She hesitated. If some of the information had electronic footprints that led back to Delphi, it wouldn't be as easy as asking and receiving.

Her doubt must have shown on her face because he sat

down at her feet and pushed a strand of her hair from her cheek. "This is what I do, Jess. Solve problems no one else can. Let me solve this before anyone else gets hurt." His touch lingered. "Before you get hurt."

Her breath caught, and it took every ounce of her strength not to lean into him. Not to reciprocate his obvious feelings.

But she was on the job, she reminded herself. And despite their tryst in the engine room, she couldn't afford to get emotionally involved with Zach. Involvement lead to bad decisions and bad decisions led to people being killed.

She took a deep breath, turned her head away from him, and focused her attention on Zach's request.

She couldn't argue that it made sense. She knew his expertise and now, she knew it was their only hope of finding *Paradise Lost.* As much as she hated to admit it, Delphi had missed something.

Delphi would have to trust her and her decision to trust Zach.

Besides, at the rate they were going it would take another month or two to find the boat. She didn't have that kind of time. Not with the escalating attacks and the inquiry waiting for her when she returned home.

If she got home.

"Don't worry," he said, reading her hesitation as second thoughts. He took her hand in his and gave it a brief squeeze. "We can do this."

"I know," she replied, surprised at the simple truth.

Jess stood outside Zach's door, breakfast tray in hand, and knocked for the second time.

And again—no answer.

What was Zach doing in there? she wondered, tapping her foot. Yesterday, immediately after her conversation with him, she'd e-mailed Delphi, explaining the situation and asking for the raw data. Much to her surprise, she'd received the requested information in less than an hour—and with no caveats attached. She'd downloaded it to a flash-drive and handed it to Zach.

She hadn't seen him since.

"This is getting ridiculous," she muttered. "I just want an update," she shouted, "and I brought coffee."

No answer.

"And muffins!"

There was a stirring on the other side of the door, and seconds later, Zach flung it open.

Her jaw dropped. Clean-cut Zach was gone. In his place was a man who hadn't bothered to shower or shave. His hair stuck up in every direction, and while she didn't see bags under his eyes, she guessed he hadn't slept.

His clothes? They were the same ones he'd had on yesterday. She sniffed. There was only one word to describe them.

Rank.

She'd heard the term *absentminded professor,* but this was the term in action.

She regained her composure and held out the tray. "I brought breakfast—"

He took the tray and slammed the door shut.

"You're welcome," she said to the wood that was now mere inches from her nose. She knew it should insult her that he was as rude as hell. Her men would never treat her that way. Nor her friends.

Not even her parents.

Instead, she found it appealing in a weird way. To see a man focus on a project with such intensity that nothing else mattered. She lay a palm against the door and wondered what it would be like to be the object of such scrutiny.

The stray thought was both sexy and disturbing. To have him give her body that kind of undivided attention was a captivating thought.

"Knock it off, Jess," she reminded herself. "It's not all about you."

She dropped her hand away from the door, pushed the disturbing train of thought to the back of her brain and went to the upper deck to enjoy the morning and clear her thoughts.

Leaning against the railing, she closed her eyes and tried to think of other things besides an intense Zach.

Diving. Nikki. The Athena Academy.

Anything.

"I see your head is still attached," Al said.

She turned, unaware the elder Holiday had come up behind her.

He handed her a cup of coffee then took a seat in one of the deck chairs.

"What do you mean?" she asked, sipping the hot, thick brew.

"Zach. I heard him slam the door on you. He can be a little *focused* at times."

She chuckled and took the chair next to him. "Yes, he can be a little abrupt."

"That was diplomatic of you," Al said, patting her hand. "Don't take it personally. He's always like that when he has a big problem to solve. Has been ever since he discovered math and then computers."

"When was that?" Jess turned in her deck char, pushing her sunglasses up.

"When he was three," Al said with a smile. "He doesn't like to brag, and you won't see it listed anywhere, but he was a prodigy. We wanted him to have a normal life so we hired private tutors and homeschooled him."

"When did he graduate?"

"He could have graduated when he was eleven."

Jess's eye widened.

"I know," Al said. "That's my boy."

"But he didn't attend college until he was seventeen," she said, thinking about the articles. That was young, but not unheard of.

"I know. We kept him busy, and then when we found out Jenny was dying…" His voice trailed off.

Zach's mother. She'd read a short blurb that Mrs. Holiday was deceased but nothing more than that.

"I couldn't send him away," Al continued. "College would be there for years but his mother wouldn't. So we traveled. Explored the world." He sighed, and she recognized the look in his eyes. It wasn't unlike Zach's when he was solving a problem.

Except, for Al, this wasn't a problem to be solved. It was a memory. He was watching the past. Playing out memories that only he was privy to.

But there was more than memories in his sigh. There was pain. A longing that would always be present. The thread of *what-if* that those left behind always carried inside.

She thought of Charles and the many *what-ifs* that plagued her when she gave herself time to consider them.

Al took a gulp of juice, returning his attention to Jess. "Then later, there was the grief."

She nodded. Grief she understood, all too well. "I read he graduated college when he was twenty," she commented, changing the subject.

"Bachelor's. He got his Master's by the time he was twenty-two and then started the consulting firm."

"It's impressive," Jess said, leaning back into her chair, glad to be back on more mundane topics.

"I know. He got that from Jenny." Al leaned back, also, re-trieving a pair of sunglasses and slipping them on—but not before Jess caught the shine of tears in his eyes. "He's like her. Her brilliance and her ability to focus so hard that every-thing else is just peripheral noise."

"I noticed." Jess chuckled. She wanted to be insulted but if slamming doors got the job done, who was she to complain?

"He has her smile, too."

"It's a nice smile," Jess said, closing her eyes. She let the morning sun warm her and the motion of the ship lull her.

"He likes you," Al said, startling her from her doze.

She didn't say anything. What was there to say?

"I'm telling you this because I think you're good for him. It's been a long time since a woman challenged him, and he needs that."

Jess turned again, this time, resting her hand on Al's fore-arm. "I'm not staying. You know that."

Al shrugged. "Things change."

She frowned. She did not need Zach's dad playing match-maker. It was already hard to keep Zach out of her thoughts. The additional pressure of someone pushing them together would make it impossible.

She closed her eyes. There was *one* way to make Al think twice about pushing her and Zach together. *The inquiry.*

She'd kept it quiet until now, but she'd have to tell them sometime, and if she told Al, it was sure to make its way to Zach.

A coward's way, she knew. The easy way out.

But sometimes, she grew tired of being brave. "Al, I'm under inquiry right now. I can't entertain the idea of seeing someone, much less act on that idea."

He straightened. "What do you mean, 'under inquiry'?"

She told him the story. About Chuck. And her suspicions.

"And this boat we're searching for has something to do with this?"

"I think so," she replied. "If we can find out the identity of the saboteur, it'll make it a helluva lot easier to clear my name."

"And if you can't? If they find you guilty?"

"Leavenworth," she whispered. Until this moment, she hadn't allowed herself to think of a guilty verdict, had intentionally kept it from her thoughts.

But if she were found guilty, she'd spend the rest of her life in a military prison. She'd prefer the death penalty. To spend the rest of her life away from the ocean was a fate worse than death, and she shuddered at the thought.

"Don't worry," Al said, finishing his juice and setting the empty cup next to the untouched muffin. "Zach will find *Paradise Lost*. I've never seen him fail. Not when he set his mind to something and right now, his focus is on helping you find this ship. He won't let you down."

"I know," she replied, wishing she felt as positive as she sounded. Zach was good but if he failed, if *they* failed, she was screwed.

Al wound his fingers through hers, and she forced herself to think of other things besides a ten-by-ten jail cell.

A shadow settled over her and, shading her eyes, she looked up to see Zach. The sun was higher in the sky, but not quite noon. She realized she must have fallen asleep. "You making time with my dad, now?" he asked, smiling down at her.

Al snored next to her. "Just sleeping with him," she replied with a grin. She sat up and stretched, the underside of her arms and legs striped with the combination of body pressure and the webbing of the lounge chair.

Pushing her legs aside, Zach sat down and leaned in, keeping his voice low.

He'd showered Jess realized. And smelled like soap.

"I have good news and bad news," he said. "Which do you want?"

"Bad," she said, trying not to inhale. He smelled like salt, too. Like the ocean.

"I was right. We are in the wrong area, and I mean hell and gone in the wrong area in terms of searching for a wreck."

"That far off?" she asked, wondering how Delphi could be that wrong.

He nodded. "What they did was technically correct, but there are a lot of other factors they didn't consider. I added them in and voilà, I have the coordinates."

"What did you add in?" she asked, curious as to what Delphi missed.

"There are worldwide events that affect the parameters of the search grid. Especially one that's three years old. I factored in things like earthquakes, currents, weather, even the changes in the ocean floor. Events that occurred when the wreck happened and events that occurred after the wreck and continue to affect it." He pointed to the ladder that led to the lower deck. "I can show you if you want. I have all the data—"

"That's okay." Jess cut him off but smiled at his enthusiasm. "What's the good news?"

He handed her a piece of paper with coordinates written on them. "We can be there by this afternoon."

We're unsure of Arachne's motives in trying to blow up the boat. This is a new tactic for her. But we'll let you know what we discover. Remember—she is capable of anything.

Disappointed, Jess finished reading the e-mail then logged off her secure account. She'd e-mailed Delphi details about what was happening and had hoped for more.

At least Delphi wasn't telling her to scrap the mission. Swiveling in the chair, Jess turned back to watch the sonar, but it remained black. A blipless screen.

"A watched sonar never boils," Liz said, sticking her head in the control room.

"A botched metaphor is always ignored," Jess shot back.

"And you're also missing dinner," Liz reminded her.

"Later." Jess turned back to the annoying screen. She couldn't even think of food until she found *Paradise Lost*.

"Anything?" Zach asked, coming in and relieving his dad at the wheel. The older Holiday gave a wave over his shoulder and followed Liz.

Zach had taken a nap after he'd given Al the new coordinates, and he drank coffee even though it was growing late and the sky was starting to turn pink.

"That smells marvelous," Jess said through a yawn.

Zach handed her his mug. She took a sip and handed it back, wishing she could gulp the entire cup. Any more than that, and she'd never sleep, and when they found *Paradise Lost*, she wanted to be rested and ready to dive. She returned her attention to the screen while Zach piloted the boat.

"My dad told me about the inquiry," Zach said, interrupting the silence.

"I figured," she said.

"You should have told me," Zach said.

"Why?" Jess shot back, embarrassed. Of course Al would tell his son. But still, now that Zach knew, she felt like a screwup.

"I just…" He ran a hand through his hair. "After what we've shared."

Jess felt heat flood her cheeks. "Zach, what happened with us…we got caught up in the moment. The adrenaline. Nothing more."

His back stiffened, and she knew she'd said the wrong thing.

He put the ship on auto. When he turned around, his eyes were dark. "If it meant nothing, then why not tell me? What would it matter?"

The heat deepened, and she hated that he saw her embarrassment. "I don't like talking about it. It makes it more real," she finished, turning away and willing her skin to return to normal.

"Makes what real? The inquiry or sleeping with me?"

Both, but she didn't say a word.

She felt his hand under her chin, and he tilted her head up. His eyes were still dark but his expression had softened. "Sometimes saying things out loud does that, but that wasn't my intent."

She nodded, feeling like a fool. "I know."

Taking her hand, he pulled her to her feet and into his arms. God help her, he felt safe. Warm.

His arms tightened around her. "I just wanted you to know that I will do everything I can to help you," he whispered in her ear, his breath warm against her neck. "To keep you safe."

She shifted until her mouth was less than an inch from his. This was wrong, she told herself. Dumb.

Just take a step back.

But the way he looked at her tossed the more sensible thought aside. She didn't need him to protect her, but the knowledge that he wanted to touched a part of her she didn't know existed. She wanted to hold on to his promise. To keep it close. "I know," she replied.

His mouth brushed hers. A whisper of a kiss so unlike their last encounter.

She traced his lower lip with her tongue. He tasted like coffee.

He groaned and nuzzled her hair. "Jess, we shouldn't do this. Not here."

She swallowed. Much like the engine-room encounter, she knew this was a bad idea, but her mouth opened, and instead of a protest, she whispered, "Where?"

"My bunk."

"But the others."

"Screw the others," he growled. His hands wrapping in her hair, he pulled her head back to expose her throat. "Let them get their own bunk." He kissed the hollow in her throat, working his way up and biting her chin.

She tried not to groan or call attention to what they were doing. But when his hand slid up her thigh and under her shorts, teasing the edge of her panties, she hissed at his touch.

"We should go," she said, starting to throb. "Now."

"In a minute," he whispered, no longer teasing as he slipped his hand under the elastic and between her legs.

Jess leaned back, the edge of the counter against her thighs as he touched her. Caressed her until she was ready to rip his shorts off.

Her breath was loud in her ears. The voices of the others eating dinner carried down the hall, but the thought they might get caught by their friends added to the eroticism. "Zach," she whispered. "Please."

The answer was a beeping. A persistent beeping.

Zach's hand stilled. Her eyes popped open. They looked at each other.

Then the sonar.

The heat between them faded as quickly as it had roared to life.

There was a blip. A discernible shape.

A ship.

And it was directly beneath them.

Chapter 8

Suited up and waiting for Zach, Jess stared into the water. Beneath her, two hundred feet below the surface and at the bottom of Drifter's Abyss was *Paradise Lost.*

She hoped.

Based on his calculations, Zach was confident it was the right boat. She wouldn't be certain until she saw the name written on the stern.

She had to admit her feelings about finding the wreckage were mixed. If the boat below them was *Paradise Lost,* the evidence found might clear her name. She'd be free to go back to work. To doing what she both loved and was trained to do.

And once they had the evidence, they'd capture Arachne and everyone—from the crew of *One For The Money* to the women of Athena Academy—would be safe.

She should welcome the turn of events, and she did. Or would, except that she'd miss this. The camaraderie. Her new friends.

Zach.

Her mind flashed back to yesterday, how he'd touched her. Kissed her. How much she liked it. Wanted it.

Craved him.

She let her head drop to the railing, resting her forehead on her hands. A flicker of wind blew across her back, tossing her ponytail.

Another reason to finish this, Jess, she told herself. Becoming attached to Zach, to any man, was not in her five-year plan. Relationships complicated things, and she already had enough complications in her life.

"You about ready to go?" She straightened at the question and saw Al striding toward her. Nodding, she tilted her face upward, letting the morning sun warm her face. "It's a deep dive," he finished, coming to stand at her side, his legs set to keep his balance even in the gentle waves that rocked the ship. "You are certified, aren't you? I don't want any surprises."

She raised a brow. Two hundred feet was a hard dive, but not unheard of—especially in their professions.

"I'm certified," she replied.

She'd been deeper. Much deeper, in a personal campaign to test her gills. What she'd discovered was that it was harder for her to breathe at depth—not unlike what a normal person felt at high altitudes—since there was less oxygen in the water, but it was possible.

She'd also found out that, for her, the bends were not a problem. Her unique chemistry had a much easier time with the nitrogen formation that came from deep diving.

"How about Zach?"

"He's the best," Al replied. She didn't miss the paternal pride in his voice.

"If you say so," she said, watching him out of the corner of her eye.

"I do." Grinning, he offered her his arm.

He really was a charmer, she thought.

Unable not to return the grin, she shook her head in defeat, linked her elbow through his, and let him escort her to the stern and the rest of the crew. Once out of the wind, a new noise caught Jess's attention.

"It's the crane," Al explained, answering her question before she had time to ask what was going on. "A little extra precaution since this is a deep dive."

They rounded the corner, and Jess slowed, not wanting to get in the way. The dive bell hung over the water with Liz and Nate guiding it by hand while Zach worked the crane. Disengaging herself from Al's arm, she walked over to the water's edge but out of the way to watch the progress.

Shaped like its name, the giant bell hit the water with a splash. Controlled with a steel cable to keep it from dropping, it sank just below the surface.

She had to admit, it was a wise precaution. Weighted to keep upright, it would also provide them with additional air if they, or rather Zach, needed it.

"Ever use a bell?" Liz asked, once the piece of equipment was stable.

"Once," she replied. They were archaic and only for deep dives. Her job tended to keep her in the upper water.

The blonde smiled. "Zach modified this one. It's very cool."

"Modified?" Jess asked.

"You spoiling all my surprises?"

Jess jumped and glanced up to see Zach leaning over her shoulder. "You could warn a person," she said, but without any real annoyance in her voice.

"I thought you heard me. You know, all that Marine training," Zach teased.

Rolling her eyes, she turned back to Liz. "What kind of modifications?"

Liz looked past her at Zach then nodded. "You'll find out."

Jess sighed. Let them have their games and their secrets. "Whatever." She waved as Liz sauntered away.

"Ready?" Zach edged past her, his green eyes bright and all hints of teasing gone.

"Let's do this," she replied, her pulse kicking up a notch. There was something about deep diving that was compelling. Much like scaling a mountain, one did it because one could.

Gearing up, they went through the dive check. Standing at the edge, with her fins hanging over, Jess peeked at Zach out of the corner of her eyes.

He returned the glance, his expression eager. Excited.

And something more. Something intimate.

Her breath caught in her throat. This, she reminded herself as she turned her attention to the water in front of her, is why you don't get involved. It's too distracting.

She took a deep breath.

Please be the right ship. She mouthed the silent prayer. *Because I can't take much more of this.*

Wearing tanks with mixed air that would allow them to dive to depth, Zach entered the water, and she followed, both grabbing on to the cable that kept the dive bell attached to the crane. He gave her the okay sign and she replied with the same.

Dropping through the water, the bell carried them downward, and as always, a sense of peace washed over Jess as she fell through the water column.

Her breathing loud in her ears, she watched Zach. His attention went from her, to the water column, to his gauges and then back to her.

He might be a bit of a tease on the ship but once he was in the water he was the consummate professional.

She smiled, realizing she was following the same pattern, and turned her attention back to the blue and her own gauges.

All was good. Her legs floating behind her, she wondered if it was like this in space. Zach tapped her on the arm, jolting her out of her almost-hypnotic state and making her jerk in surprise. Even with a regulator in, she saw him smile at her reaction to his unexpected touch.

He pointed at the bell, motioning her to swim inside.

She followed him. Once inside, he turned on his flashlight and took his regulator out of his mouth. "Sorry about that," he said with a grin.

"Not a problem," she replied, knowing he was anything but sorry.

"I just wanted to point out a few things while we have time," he explained, his voice echoing in the chamber. "First, you'll see there are a number of places to attach anything from dive bags to a wounded diver."

She tugged one of the c-hooks welded into the wall of the bell. It felt strong. Solid. She nodded at the useful modification.

"There's a two-way speaker that connects us to the boat." He pointed at the grill in the top of the bell.

"Good idea," she replied. Generally, one only saw full-blown communication in bathyspheres or permanent habitats. Not in something as simple as a dive bell.

He pushed the small black button next to the speaker. "Hey, Dad. Everything good? Over."

"All a go. Over," Al replied.

Jess pushed the button. "How much longer to touchdown? Over."

"Not too far." Al chuckled. "About another seventy-five feet. We'll be parking the bell twenty feet above the wreck. Over."

"Thanks, Dad. Over and Out."

There wasn't an answer, and they floated inside the bell as it descended.

Zach sighed, and Jess recognized the sound. It was his *we need to talk about what happened* sigh. Worse, the bell emphasized the sound. "Jess, about yesterday—"

"I don't want to talk about it," she said, cutting him off. Now was not the time.

He frowned. "Neither do I, but I want to apologize. Normally, I have control over my actions, but there is something about you, about us, that makes control almost impossible."

Dammit. What part of not wanting to talk about it didn't he understand? Before she could cut him off again, the bell halted, catching them both off guard.

"We'll finish this conversation later," Zach said, pulling his mask over his eyes.

She shrugged, although as far as she was concerned that was a conversation she never wanted to have. What more could he say? Sorry I felt you up? And her reply? Sorry I let you?

No, some things were best forgotten. Or ignored.

Zach's flashlight pointed downward, illuminating the depths and shadowing his face. "Ready? Or do you want to go over the plan again?" He was all professional. No hint of intimacy.

She shook her head. It was a simple plan. Confirm they had the right ship. Get in. Go for the logs and laptop in the captain's berth. If there was time, go to the control room and retrieve anything else she deemed useful.

"Let's get this over with," Jess replied, eager to find the information and get her life back.

They put their regulators in and entered the water column. It wasn't pitch-black at two hundred feet but it was close. Jess flicked on her flashlight.

It was also cold. Jess shivered, glad she'd worn her full-body wet suit instead of a shorty that left her bare from knees and elbows down.

They scanned the darkness with their flashlights, stopping when they found the ship twenty feet below them.

Right on target.

Swimming through the twilight zone of the ocean, they made their way to the stern. The water pressure and current changed, catching Jess's attention. Something was over them. Something big.

Damn it.

She flipped over, swinging her light upward.

Manta.

Harmless as long as it didn't hit you with its five-hundred-pound body.

Flipping back, she caught up with Zach in two kicks.

They reached the stern, and spanning the width were the words, *Paradise Lost,* Puerto Isla.

Thank God. Jess gave Zach a thumbs-up, smiling around her regulator. With only twenty minutes of bottom time, they swam with strong strokes over the main hatch. Shining a light down the stairs, Jess noticed that the ceiling had collapsed inward, blocking the entry.

She pointed the blockage out to Zach. He nodded then motioned upward, then down. If she understood his sign language, he suggested they go in through the hole the collapse had created.

Backing out of the door, she followed him to the top of the ship. The hole was partially filled with sand.

It would be a tight fit but they should be okay.

Jess shone her light inside. She didn't see anything but that didn't mean there wasn't anything there. In a ship like this, there were plenty of nooks and crannies for animals to occupy.

Careful not to disturb the already unstable ship, she swam inside. Other than a few fish, the ship was empty. Zach followed, his flashlight joining hers and flooding the room with light.

Dishes and cups littered the floor. Stainless steel utensils glittered in the light.

It seemed they were in the galley.

She swung the light. In the corner, disturbed by their movement, was a skeleton floating against the wall. Held together by the dead owner's clothes, it waved a macabre greeting as they disturbed the water.

At least it wasn't gooey, she thought with a chill that had nothing to do with the water temperature. She'd take a skeleton over a fresh body any day.

Zach tapped on her arm and pointed to his watch then the hallway.

She nodded. He was right. They didn't have time to gawk. Two doors later, they found the captain's quarters and what was left of the captain.

Much like the galley occupant, he wore scraps of what was once clothing. Creepy, Jess thought.

Ignoring the remains, Zach was already going though the papers and books floating in the water, searching for the logs.

She turned away and started ransacking the desk for the logs and the laptop. The upper drawers were open but she found nothing except pens, papers and other office supplies that washed out with her movements to litter the floor.

The lower drawer was locked. Her heart pounded in her ears. That had to be it.

She yanked on the handle, but it refused to move. Dammit. She needed something heavy. Rummaging through the flotsam on the floor, she found a bookend made of cut agate.

Bracing herself against the wall, she slammed the lock with the bookend and found that she couldn't get enough force behind her hit.

Too bad she didn't get strength along with the gills. Endurance in the water was all well and fine, but at times like these, extra muscle would be a welcome bonus.

She swam over to Zach, handed him the bookend and pointed at the drawer.

He hit the drawer as hard as he could, the sounds of cracking wood loud in the silence.

He did have his uses, she thought with a smile.

Grabbing the handle, he yanked the drawer from the desk. Jess shone her light in. There were the leather-bound logs. *Bingo.*

She pulled the fragile, wet books out, wrapped them in her dive bags and then put them into Zach's bag.

There was no laptop. Nothing other than the logs to give to Delphi. They'd have to get to the control room and pray the laptop was there. She glanced at her watch. Ten minutes already? She hoped that they didn't run into any more locked drawers or other obstacles.

They swam down the hallway toward the helm. The door was closed. *Of course.*

She turned the knob but the door was jammed tight.

Zach motioned her out of the way.

Show-off, Jess thought, trying not to smile. Ask him to open one drawer and he thought he was the Incredible Hulk.

Taking off his fins, Zach braced himself against either side of the hall and kicked, using the power of both legs and with his feet hitting the door dead center. It flew open, almost off its hinges.

A low rumbling shook the ship. An unmistakable cracking that made Jess's blood pound hard. But before either she or Zach could react, the ceiling came crashing down on Zach.

"Nooo!" Jess shouted, bubbles from her scream filling the water even as she dropped her flashlight and pushed herself backward, pulling herself with both hands along the wall until she could go no farther. Kneeling, she covered her head, waiting for the chaos to end.

Finally, quiet reigned, and she uncurled herself. There was a dim light coming from under the pile of debris in front of her. It wasn't much but it was enough to see that she was alone.

Zach was buried.

Once again, her heart pounded in her ears and her control was slipping away. She forced the panic back. Now was not the time to give in to unreasonable fear. She breathed deep, each inhalation flooding her with calm. Each beat of her heart seemed to say "save Zach."

And she intended to do just that. Swimming through the sandy water and praying that nothing else fell from above, she pried boards from the pile, tossing them behind her.

Be alive, Zach. Be alive.

The chant circled through her head, but she refused to think of the alternative. If she did, if she gave in to the negative, she might make it real.

And that was too horrible to consider.

Be alive. Be alive. Be alive.

Please.

Something grabbed her. Jess shrieked into her regulator and yanked her hand away.

Whatever it was refused to let go.

She realized it was fingers. Five of them.

Zach.

He clutched her wrist. Hard. Bruising her beneath the wet suit.

She didn't care. If he was that strong that meant he was very much alive.

It seemed to take hours to uncover Zach. Jess wanted to yank him free but couldn't take the chance that she might damage his regulator or that she'd bring the rest of the boat crashing down around them.

When she uncovered his head, she made the sign for "okay." He returned it back with his free hand.

Thank God. He was all right.

Carefully, she followed his BCD to his hoses and then to his gauges. She pulled them toward her until they cleared the boards.

He had less than five hundred pounds of pressure left.

A death wish at this depth.

And his pony tank, the spare reserved for emergencies, was still buried. Although she knew he'd fight it, she was going to have to give him a tank. She checked her air.

Almost empty. Dammit. All that exertion. She should have taken the regulator out.

She'd have to give him her spare pony tank. It only held ten minutes' worth of air, but with both his and hers and the bell, he'd stand a chance as long as they were out of here in a few minutes.

Unhooking the smaller tank from her side, she handed it to Zach. He pointed to her gauges, obviously questioning her air supply.

Damned professional. She gave him the "okay" sign. She

could come up with a lie later as to why her own tank was so empty and she was able to survive. Right now, she needed to focus on saving the man in front of her.

Zach helped toss boards away with his free hand and then both hands as he was uncovered. Finally, with his torso free, Jess grabbed his hands and pulled. Seconds later, he was in her arms in an embrace made awkward by their diving gear.

Thank God. If she'd lost him she'd never forgive herself.

He touched her cheek. And even with the chaos and the relief and the chill of water at two hundred feet below, she felt the heat between them. A growing bond.

The connection that she didn't want.

Pushing away, she pointed toward the control room. There wasn't much time left but if she was fast, there was just enough for her to get in and get out.

He shook his head and pointed upward, toward the bell.

Ignoring him, she swam over to the hole that was created when she freed him. Not a huge entrance, but big enough for her.

If she dropped her tanks.

It was a chance that a normal diver would be hesitant to take, but she was a Marine and as long as she was careful and didn't stay gone too long, her secret would be safe.

She motioned to the small hole, signaling that she planned to go in.

Zach shook his head no.

She pointed to the bell and pushed him. *Go.* She unsnapped her BCD and started to shrug it off. It stopped halfway when Zach grabbed it and yanked it upward and back over her shoulders. He shook his head again.

Even through the mask and the dim light, she didn't miss his glare. She wished they knew sign language because she had a few choice words for him.

She slapped his hand but he didn't let go. Instead, he pointed at the bell again.

This was going to take deception, she realized. And speed. Luckily, she could manage both. With a nod of resignation, she swam upward, heading for the bell with Zach at her side.

Halfway there, she flipped around, kicked hard and in seconds, was back at the ship. Hurry, she reminded herself as she entered the quasi-collapsed hallway. But don't be dumb.

Holding the flashlight in her mouth, she unbuckled her vest and set her gear on the floor. Widening the hole to the control room, she pushed through. Halfway through, she felt something grab her feet.

She didn't need to look back to know that a *who,* not a *what,* was grabbing her. Damn, he was fast in the water. Almost as fast as her.

She kicked at him but the contact was weak due to the fins. Flipping onto her back, she used the ceiling to brace herself and push herself farther in.

Still clinging to her fin, Zach's head entered the small hole but his tanks hit the edge, jarring the boat. The ship creaked around her.

She winced and kicked again, this time freeing herself.

Between the ship falling on her head, and the fact she *should* be out of air, she had little time.

Where was the laptop?

She swam over to the main console. Laptop. Laptop. Where was the laptop?

Nothing caught her eye, and in a minute, Zach was going to start wondering why she hadn't drowned. Dammit. She'd have to come back.

She turned to leave, and a Pelican case peeked out from under the debris pile, catching her attention. A Pelican? She remembered that the waterproof, high-end containers were used to keep electronics dry.

Electronics like a laptop.

She yanked it free of the debris.

Right size and right shape.

The ship shuddered around her.

Time to go.

She swam toward the exit. Zach was almost inside the control room. She motioned to him to leave. He backed out. She pushed the Pelican case through first, then followed, grabbing her tank and popping the regulator in her mouth. Zach helped her put the tank on, and they headed for the safety of the bell.

There was going to be hell to pay, she realized. Even his swim kick sounded pissed.

But if this was the laptop, it would be worth it.

"Are you insane?" Zach shouted once they were inside the bell. "You know the first rule. You don't go anywhere without a partner—especially a wreck that's falling apart."

"You're right," she agreed. And he was. If she was an ordinary diver. Which she wasn't.

He was having none of her easy agreement.

"Going into an unknown space without a tank at two hundred feet is insane," Zach continued, "You know it. I know it."

"I said I know!" She shook the case. "I'm fine. Safe. And I got the laptop."

"You could have died."

She exhaled in exasperation. "You'll never have to deal with me again if that makes you feel better." As soon as she said the words, she wished she could take them back.

For an uncomfortable moment, Zach stared at her in silent shock. "That wasn't what I meant."

"I know." She propped her mask on her head and rubbed

her eyes. How did things ever get so complicated? Why did it have to be such an emotional mess? "I got the laptop. Let the rest go." She tied the dive bag that contained the logs to one of the c-hooks. "Besides, we need to get topside."

"Good idea."

She glanced at him. His mouth was tight. His body tense. He wasn't in a forgiving mood.

Zach punched the button to call topside. "Dad?"

There was no answer.

Jess frowned. That was odd. "Maybe they're getting coffee?"

"Not all at once," Zach said, his voice puzzled. He pressed the button again. "*One For The Money?* Anyone there?"

"Hello, Mr. Holiday," an unfamiliar voice replied.

Zach's eyes widened.

The voice continued, "We have your father right here, but he's a bit indisposed."

In the background, the sound of a fist hitting flesh and a groan of pain came through loud and clear over the intercom.

Chapter 9

"Who is this?" Zach asked with apprehensive undertones. "And what the hell is going on?"

Jess stiffened. She knew who they were talking to and what was going on.

The pirates had returned, and this time, they'd managed to board the ship. *How,* was the first question that came to mind. But that question could wait. Right now, there were more pressing problems.

Like saving the crew of *One For The Money.*

"What you need to worry about," the deep voice said, "is not who I am but what I want."

Jess cocked her head toward the speaker. The accent was familiar. Latino. But what region?

Zach pushed the button. Hard. "Then what is it you want?"

"Everything you found on the ship and Jessica Whitaker." Brazilian. That was it. The pirate was Brazilian.

Zach's eyes widened. "Excuse me?"

"Mr. Holiday. Do not play games. I want everything you recovered. And I want the girl."

"Stall," she mouthed to Zach. She needed to think. She could give up the laptop. The logs. She'd hate it but she could always get them back.

That's why she carried a gun.

But if she gave herself up—she could almost guarantee that the crew would be killed. As long as they didn't have her, didn't know if she were dead or alive, there was a chance they'd keep the crew as leverage.

"We didn't find anything," Zach said, shrugging as if unsure where to go with the lie.

She nodded in approval. He might appear unsure but his voice sounded confident.

"Mr. Holiday. There are dive balloons with you, are there not?"

"Yes," Zach said, dragging the word out.

"Send up the laptop, now, or I will hurt the pretty blond girl."

Jess tensed as her thoughts went to Liz, and she imagined what hurting the girl would entail. She squeezed her eyes shut and willed her churning gut to calm. Like hell they were going to hurt Liz. She nodded. Do it, she mouthed.

"On the way," Zach said.

Jess buried her face in her hands. "Dammit," she whispered once Zach let go of the button and they were cut off from the ship. The only sound was the water lapping on the inside of the bell in tandem with their breathing.

"We don't have a choice," Zach said, his voice colder than she thought possible. "We can't let them hurt Liz. But I won't let them hurt you, either."

"I know," she said, pressing into him. His desire to

protect her was sweet. Also unneeded, but he didn't need to know that. It would just make him fight her. She held out the briefcase. "We should make sure this is the laptop. Or all of this is moot."

He nodded and unsnapped the clasp, opened the case then snapped it shut. "We got it."

Both relief and anger rushed through her. So close. So very close. And now she had to give it up to pirates. "Here."

With a balloon in one hand, and the case and logs in the other, Zach ducked below the surface. Holding on to the bell as they continued their ascent, he filled the balloon with air from his regulator, attached the cargo and sent their prizes upward. He called the ship. "On the way."

"Good. Now, it seems that decompression is almost over. You have five minutes, and we'll bring you topside." He coughed. "If you are armed, I suggest you drop your weapons."

Zach moved to respond, but Jess grabbed his arm. "Wait."

"What?"

She hesitated knowing she was going to have a fight on her hands, but also knowing that what she had to do was the only chance they had. "If I go with you, they'll have everything they want. You do that, and the crew will die."

Once again, she saw that familiar *far-off* expression as he processed her statement and considered the ramifications and different scenarios. Finally, he returned his focus to her, but his narrowed eyes told her that he was anything but convinced. "They already said if you don't go, they'll kill them. Besides, where would you go?"

"Out."

He raised a brow.

She continued. "Tell them I died in the wreck. I have air. I can stay under, resurface farther away and take them by surprise."

Zach looked at her as if she were insane. "Did the pressure get to you?" He grabbed her gauges. She smacked his hand.

"Fine." He dropped them instead of trying to wrestle them out of her grasp. "I don't need to see them to know you're almost out of air. There's enough to get you topside but I doubt much more."

She pressed her lips tight, forcing herself to meet his eyes. "I have enough. Trust me. Besides, I can hide in the wave troughs."

He didn't appear any more convinced. "Jess, you're a Marine. That makes you tough. I know that. But it does not make you invincible. Not unless you can breathe underwater." He crossed his arms over his chest, daring her to challenge him.

She swallowed. If there was ever a time to confess, to admit to her gift, it was now.

And still, she couldn't do it. Couldn't say the words. She shook her head. "I can do this."

"No. You can't," he countered, his expression softening. Taking her hand in his, he kissed her knuckles, surprising her. "I won't let them hurt you or anyone else." The chill in his voice contrasted with the warmth of his expression. "We both get up there and wait for the opportune moment. We'll get our shot, and when we do, we take it."

He was a good man. He trusted her. She knew he meant to save her and the others. But the reality was that these pirates, mercenaries, really, were ruthless. They'd killed Charles. They'd set the bomb on *One For The Money*. And they knew who she was.

That meant Arachne had sent them.

Her every instinct told her to stay out of their grasp. If she didn't, if she was captured by Arachne's people, all was lost. Including Zach and his crew.

"Okay," she lied, forcing a small smile to her lips. "I trust you."

He kissed her knuckles again and let her hand go. "We'll get through this. All of us."

The bell started to move upward, and he grabbed the welded-ring on the ceiling. The moment of distraction was all she needed. She tapped his shoulder.

He turned toward her, and in less time than it took him to blink, she punched him in the center of his jaw, driving his mandible back and cutting off his carotid artery for a split second.

That was all it took. His eyes rolled back in his head, and he slumped against the wall of the bell.

It only took a few more seconds to use one of the ropes to strap Zach to the handhold. She pulled on the knot. Hard. It held.

He was going to be pissed when he woke and realized what she'd done. But he'd be alive to hate her and that was good enough. She'd take a healthy resentment over death any day.

As far as explaining how she managed to knock him out then survive without tanks, well, she'd cross that bridge when she came to it.

The bell continued moving upward. Unhooking her BCD, she strapped the vest—including tank and hoses—to the hand-hold, as well. They wouldn't believe Zach when he said she was dead, but they'd believe this.

No one could live without air. No one but her. The Marine. The freak.

The mutant.

Water began filtering in under the bell's rim.

Time to go.

"Be careful." She kissed Zach's unconscious mouth, her

lips sliding down his chin and away as he rose with the bell, and she remained stationary.

She inhaled and the tang of saltwater rushed over her tongue, down her throat and into her gills. Comforting in its familiarity, it still left her cold.

Taking one last look at the man and machine silhouetted above her, she swam downward into the darker water. She'd stay for a while, just long enough so that if the pirates peered over the edge, they wouldn't see her. Later, she'd come up and as Zach had said, she'd wait for the single opportune moment. That sliver of time that separated good from evil, success from failure.

She estimated herself to be at one hundred feet below the surface and stopped. The ship was small above her, a dark blip on the water—not unlike sonar—and next to her was another ship.

The current changed. The manta, maybe the same one she saw earlier, swept past, unafraid of her, as if she belonged in the ocean as opposed to land.

She knew the truth. She straddled both but belonged to neither.

"That can't be right." Jess's mom tapped her foot, staring the doctor down and daring him to disagree with her. Jess ducked her head. She was missing a math test, and as horrible as the test would have been, this was worse.

"I don't know what to tell you, Mrs. Whitaker. They're deformed."

Her mother looked at Jess, and she flinched. Home for the summer, her mother had caught her sitting on the bottom of the pool. Thinking her baby girl drowned, she'd jumped in to save her and now this was the result.

"She's a top swimmer," her mother insisted. "If there was something wrong with her lungs, we would have noticed it earlier. This isn't her first physical."

The young doctor scratched his head. "Did she ever have her lungs x-rayed?"

"No." Her mother frowned. "She doesn't get sick."

"There you go." The doctor waved the file at them and flicked on the X-ray light, shoving the slides under a clip and illuminating them for all to see.

"This—" he pointed to her gills "—these lines. That's not normal."

"Not normal?" Jess's mother's frown deepened. Jess knew that look. She was going to blow.

Jess hated it when her mother lost her temper. It made her nervous. Unsure. As if at any minute, her mother's anger would focus in her direction.

"My daughter is not a freak."

"I didn't say she was—"

"And you would do well to keep this to yourself." Jess's mother cut him off. "Jess is an athlete. A competitive swimmer. I will not have her future jeopardized by some quack."

Grabbing Jess's arm, she yanked her from the office, marching her down the hall. "You will not say a word of this to anyone. Do you understand?"

"Yes," Jess replied, wishing she could pull away but knowing that any attempt would only make her mother dig in her nails.

"You have a future. I will not have that ruined."

Jess nodded but knew the truth. It wasn't her future that was the problem. It was her mother's standing with the family. With society.

It was a tight world. Proper. Perfect.

There was no room for freaks.

* * *

A splashing noise broke her from the memory. Jess blinked in the darkness and checked her watch. Fifteen minutes since the bell emerged with Zach and her tank. They had to believe she was dead.

Another sound caught her attention.

This time, she looked up. There were two divers swimming toward her and the sunken ship.

Probably making sure she wasn't hiding in the wreckage.

As if a normal person could stay under that long at two hundred feet—even with an extra tank.

Slowly, so as not to draw attention, she swam away from the two men and into the darker waters. The divers clicked their lights on, letting her follow their movements from afar. They went into the remains of the boat and emerged a few minutes later, heading to the surface.

Satisfied?

She hoped so. Waiting until they were on the dive platform, she followed, stopping a few meters below the waves and away from the ship. From her vantage point, she watched the deck as best she could but only the edges were visible. An armed man stood at the stern. Judging from the wet suit, he was one of the divers.

His mouth moved in answer to a question she couldn't hear then he walked to the bow.

It was her best chance to get closer.

Diving deep, Jess emerged beneath the dive platform. There wasn't much room between the platform and the water. Made of a tight metal mesh, it was almost impossible to see through but it was better than nothing and allowed her to keep her head above the water and hear the man talking above her.

"Where is she?"

"I already told you," a familiar voice said. *Zach.* "She's dead."

There was the sound of someone being hit. Not with a fist, but something else. She flinched at the dull thud. And the next. And the next.

"What do you want me to say?" Zach shouted. "That she's alive? You saw for yourself. You saw her tank. Her hoses. She died to save me, you bastard, and hitting me doesn't change that."

His voice. The pain. Stay strong, she reminded herself, even as a part of her itched to go to him.

Another dull thud and Zach groaned. Jess flinched again at the sound, even as her hands clenched and unclenched. When this was over, they'd pay and pay hard.

In the meantime, she'd stay put. Wait it out.

Opportune moment, he'd said. Wait for it.

The beating continued. "You're killing him!" Liz shouted.

There was a scuffling sound. The ability to maintain emotional distance was almost gone now with only the knowledge that her arrival would mean certain death, keeping her in check.

"Don't touch her!" someone shouted. Growled, really.

No, not someone. Nate.

A gunshot stopped all sound but the waves breaking against the hull of the ship.

Jess's eyes widened. Screw training and screw the plan. The plan was supposed to keep them all alive. If her crew was dying then it as time to change the plan.

Swimming beneath *One For The Money,* she emerged at the bow, since it provided better cover from both the mercenaries on board and on the other ship. Her nerves were tight. Shaking with the need for action. Taking a deep breath, she reined in her emotions as years of training had taught her.

Now was the time to act.

Not react.

Remaining underwater, she scanned what she could of the forward deck. It appeared empty. She poked her head out again just in time to hear Liz scream.

Jess reminded herself to stay cool. Frosty.

Like ice.

Using her fins, she pushed herself up and out of the water, grabbing the edge of the bow with her fingertips. She hung from the wood, her legs in the water.

Had they heard her?

There was more arguing. Shouting. Someone got slapped.

But no footsteps headed in her direction.

Slowly, she pulled herself up until her head cleared the lip and hand over hand, she edged down toward Zach and the others.

Twenty-five feet away, she saw Zach was kneeling on the deck. His hands bound behind his back. But he appeared to be whole.

The crew was huddled against the railing. Nate's arm was around Liz. Al was hunched over as if in pain. Diego stood silent, his face pale underneath his tan.

But they were alive.

She scanned the rest of the scene, concentrating on the pirates. They all carried guns—one on each hip. One had a shotgun, as well. All wore wet suits. Expensive ones.

But they weren't just pirates. Stance. Attitude. The way they maintained control.

They were professionals. Mercenaries was her guess.

That would make this that much harder. If they were just pirates, she might be able to take them, but mercenaries were a different matter.

They were trained soldiers without compunction.

The one closest to her stood over Zach, his 9mm pressed

into the back of Zach's head and his finger on the trigger. Jess's heart beat in her ears, and her body ached to launch onto the deck and massacre the entire lot.

But she held back. Her capture would not help Zach.

The mercenary cocked the gun. She promised herself that if he killed Zach, she would make sure he died screaming.

And slowly.

Instead of firing, the pirate raised the gun until it was upright. "Are you willing to die to prove the truth?" he asked, his voice clear in the sea air.

Jess cocked her head. He was the one Zach had spoken to earlier. Definitely Brazilian.

"Doesn't matter," Zach said, spitting blood. "The truth is the truth."

"How about them?" He pointed the weapon at Nate. "Are you willing to let him die?"

Dammit.

Zach shook his head. "Fuck you. She's dead, and if you kill us the only thing you'll have is both the Puerto Isla and U.S. government on your ass. Plus, every salvage diver along the coast."

The mercenary laughed, but he took his finger off the trigger. "I believe you."

"Then you'll let us go?" Zach asked.

The merc laughed again and said something in Portuguese. One of his men went back to their boat. Jess lowered herself, hanging from her arms before he spotted her.

Was he going to kill them? She thought through the scenario and came up with a negative. He'd have already done so if that were the plan. Ransom was more probable. Arachne might be running the show but mercenaries were always anxious for that extra bit of cash.

And on the ocean, kidnappings were commonplace.

The ship's twin engine started, and Jess slid back into the water. If they were taking the crew to their hideout, she'd make sure she followed.

She let the ship glide over her, avoiding the props to grab the underside of the dive dock again and letting herself be pulled along with the wake of the engines covering her.

Her breathing alternated between air and water as waves washed over her until she ducked beneath the surface as far as possible to keep from getting beaten up.

Around her, the water chilled. She realized they were heading out to sea.

The rate of the ship. The direction. They were in the middle of nowhere and five miles from land if not more. Damn, where was their base?

The engine stopped, slowed and her heart pounded in opposition. There was only one reason to stop in the middle of the ocean and that was to get rid of something.

Or someone. Had she guessed wrong? Were they going to kill the crew?

The mercenaries' boat slowed and pulled alongside *One For The Money*. There was movement, and the boats rocked, knocking gently into each other. Jess raised her head to watch and listen. She peeked through the mesh to see the crew being put on board the pirates' boat.

"Where are you taking us?" Nate asked.

Nate. Liz. Diego. Al. Zach.

"Ready?" Brazil asked, ignoring Nate's question.

"Good to go." The other mercenary handed him a box.

Jess recognized it. It was a demolition control box. They were going to blow the boat.

He continued, "But we might want to get some distance. It's going to be a big one."

"No!" Zach shouted. As the mercenaries sped away, he broke free and leaped over to the deck of *One For The Money*.

The mercenaries' boat slowed.

"You can't leave him," Liz cried out.

The head pirate shrugged and motioned the crew to continue. In seconds, they were on their way with Zach left on board the doomed ship.

"Zach!" Liz screamed, trying to run back to *One For The Money,* but Nate grabbed her, holding her as the mercenaries' boat revved its engines, and they sped away.

In an instant, Jess swam to the opposite side of the boat, fear for Zach and hard-edged training giving her strength and speed that surprised even her.

She kicked herself out of the water, pulling herself onto the deck but out of sight of the mercenaries' view.

Taking off her fins, she crawled along the deck. There was no sign of Zach. She hurried to the closed door.

Sliding through the small opening, she stood. "Zach," she called.

There was no answer.

Flinging open doors, she ran through the ship and found him in the engine room, kneeling in front of the bomb.

"Zach."

"Jess?" He stared up, his eyes wide. "How did you get here?" He touched her. "You're alive."

She was going to have a lot of explaining to do, but that could wait. "Yeah. I am."

"How?"

"Later."

She dropped to her knees in front of the bomb. C-4. Extra wires. These men knew their explosives, that was not in question.

She turned over the timer.

Two minutes. *Bastards.*

Not enough time to figure it out and disarm it. Hell, it was barely enough to get away. She rose. "Let's go."

"I'm not leaving the ship," Zach said.

"Yes. You are."

"Disarm it.

She shook her head. "I can't."

"You did before."

"I had time before." She grabbed his arm and pulled. His eyes met hers, and she saw pain and denial in them. *One For The Money* was more than a boat. It was home. A symbol. His connection with his father and his mother.

It would also be his grave if he stayed.

And the thought of Zach dead was unbearable.

"Please," she whispered. "Please. It's just a boat."

He held her gaze. "Let's go," he said. He rose and they ran down the hall to the open door.

Flinging out her arm, she stopped him before he went onto the deck. "The pirates," she said. Keeping low, they peeked out. The mercenaries were still visible, but there wasn't time to wait for them to get farther away.

"Let's go." There couldn't be much time left.

Hunched over, they ran to the edge of the deck and around to the far side of the ship. "Dive!" she screamed, and Zach was in the air. He entered the water with almost no splash.

Grabbing her fins, Jess dived in after him. Before he could surface, she grabbed his wet suit, pulling him away from the ship. The fins would help but there wasn't time to put them on.

Faster. Faster.

Zach kicked for the surface and she followed.

Behind them, *One For The Money* blew up, the shock wave rolling over her, tumbling her.

This was Charles all over again, she realized.

Stay awake this time. Stay awake.

The last thing she saw before blackness claimed her was Zach floating facedown.

Chapter 10

Jess peered into the mine shaft. The shaft was dark. And deep. And while it was a little dangerous, she wanted to know what was at the bottom.

She glanced over her shoulder at Nikki, who did not look as enthusiastic. In fact, she looked downright pale. Jess knew she shouldn't tease the girl but also couldn't resist. "Nope. Nothing down there but dark, death and a few spiders. Big. Hairy. Spiders." Jess grinned, hearing Nikki's sharp intake. "So, are you coming or what?"

Carefully, Nikki shuffled over to the edge and peeked over. "No way."

Jess arched a dark brow but didn't reply. She'd never had a younger sister but if she did, she'd have hoped she'd be like Nikki. Smart. Competent. And she didn't put up with Jess giving her a bad time. Well, not for long.

Jess slung her climbing rope around the trunk of a mesquite

tree near the cave while Nikki continued to stare into the abyss. "Come on. It's just a little exploration."

"Yeah, exploration down there."

Jess would give her a few minutes, and then Nikki would go with her—she was sure. Nikki might hesitate, but in the end, Jess knew the girl, and she never backed down.

Not without a good reason. Jess slipped into her climbing rig. Nikki looked paler if that was possible. "What?"

Nikki shrugged. "Spelunking. What kind of name is that, anyway?"

"Because if the rope breaks you go 'splunk' at the bottom." Jess grinned, but Nikki didn't laugh. "We'll call it caving instead. Let's go."

Nikki didn't look convinced.

Talk about putting something off. Jess understood she was scared, but looking into the black didn't conquer fear.

Stepping into the black did.

"I just don't like tight spots," Nikki said.

"That's a relief."

"What d'you mean?"

Jess shook out the climbing rope and pulled out the Athena card. If that didn't motivate Nikki, then nothing would. "I thought you were going to say it's 'dangerous' and I was going to remind you Athenas never back down from a challenge."

The look Nikki cast her way told Jess she was far from convincing. With a sigh of exasperation, Jess lashed the belaying rope to a different tree and tied it off on her harness. "You gonna suit up or not?"

"Yeah, I guess."

Although less than enthusiastic, Jess was impressed as she watched Nikki prep for the climb. She'd paid attention to instructions, and in minutes, she was ready. "How are you going to get back out?" Nikki asked.

Jess shrugged, knowing she should tell Nikki about the vertical ascender in her pack, but it could wait. She wanted to see if Nikki would make the leap. "By my fingernails, I guess. Coming?"

"Hell, no."

"Coward." She tossed the word out as a challenge then stepped over the edge, bracing her feet against the wall to keep from swinging. "Come on in. The water's fine!"

Slowly, she walked a few feet down the wall then waited for Nikki to join her. Pushing herself off the wall with her feet, Jess enjoyed the thrill of being suspended over the abyss. She pushed off again. And again.

Nikki remained absent. Jess wondered if she'd gone too far in taunting her friend. She shrugged. If Nikki wouldn't go, neither would Jess. Caving alone was deadly and dumb.

Disappointed, Jess climbed back up the rocky wall—and saw Nikki crouched on the ground coughing. It looked as if she'd lost her breakfast.

"Nikki!" Crawling over the lip of the abyss, her gear still attached, Jess hurried over to her friend. This was her fault, she knew. She'd pushed too far. Teased too hard. Nikki should have told her to put a sock in it.

She hurried over, admonishing herself. She was the older one. It was her job to keep Nikki safe. To push her, but not so far and so fast that the younger girl couldn't follow.

She reached Nikki's side, and Jess rubbed Nikki's shoulder and back, guilt ripping through her gut. "What's wrong?"

"It's back."

Jess hesitated, not sure what she meant. She helped Nikki to a sitting position. "What's back?"

Nikki shook her head. "Something's wrong. I smell things sometimes. Just never this bad."

Smell things? Jess sniffed. There was nothing other than the mesquite trees and the mine. "You mean, like a blood-hound or something?"

"Sort of."

Pushing Jess aside, Nikki scooted toward the shaft. "Call down," she said to Jess. "Call down there. Someone's there."

Jess frowned, getting the distinct impression that when Nikki said she smelled things, she didn't mean anything as corporeal as the trees. "Helloooo," she called out.

A heartbeat later, a girl's voice answered. Jess's pulse jumped. There was someone down there. Someone she recognized. "Marta?"

"It's me!" echoed back.

"We'll get you out!" Jess shouted back, desperately wanting to ask Nikki how she knew. But that conversation could wait for later.

Nikki blinked. "Marta's the first-year girl evreyone thought ran away."

Jess nodded and restrung her rope. "If she can be moved, I'll bring her out." She wished Nikki could go with her, but now was not the time for an amateur. "I got this one. Better you stay here and belay me."

Nikki gazed at her, and somehow, Jess thought, she knew about Jess. Knew that she was different.

Just like she'd known about Marta.

They were definitely going to have a talk. Later.

"Ready?" she asked, standing at the edge of the abyss.

"I'll keep you safe." Nikki wrapped the belaying rope around her waist with trembling hands.

Jess smiled as she stood poised on the shaft's lip. "Don't worry. You won't drop me on my ass. Not accidentally, anyway."

She caught Nikki's smile just as she slipped back over the edge and into the dark.

"Jess? Wake up? Come on." Someone slapped her cheek.

She blinked, and the sunlight cut into her brain like a knife. "Nikki?" she groaned, squeezing her eyes shut.

"No. Zach."

She blinked. She'd been dreaming about Nikki. When she first realized that Nikki might be like her. Different.

"Jess. Do you know who I am?" A rough hand stroked her wet hair. A few more blinks and she could open her eyes without flinching.

She realized she was floating. With Zach.

"Yeah. Zach," she said, as she processed what happened. She was in the middle of the ocean. With Zach. Around them pieces of broken boards bobbed on gentle swells—the remains of *One For The Money*. And they were in trouble. "Oh, hell."

"There's an understatement." Zach grabbed a board and pushed it to her. "How are you feeling? You were out for a while."

"I'm good," she replied as the throbbing in her head faded. "How about you?"

"Sore, but I'll live."

"Okay," she said, although she was sure he lied. There were dark circles under his eyes giving him a tired appearance, but she knew they were not from the simple lack of sleep. The smudges were the kind of bone-deep weariness that came from being beaten to the point of passing out.

Not that either his weariness or her headache made a difference in the fact that they needed to swim ashore. She scanned the horizon, spotting a dark stretch of land. She gestured toward it with her chin. "We go that way."

"Not much choice, is there?" Zach said. Each gripping a piece of wreckage, they began to kick toward land. Jess wished she'd managed to hold on to her fins, but who knew where they were now.

"Do you want to tell me how you managed to stay underwater without a tank?" Zach asked after a few minutes of silence.

Jess stiffened but kept kicking. Dammit. In the chaos, she'd forgotten about what had happened. What she'd done. "Um. No?" she replied.

Zach didn't respond. She glanced at him out of the corner of her eye. He still kicked for shore but his attention wasn't on the land in the distance. It was elsewhere. His gaze was fixed on the horizon as he worked on the problem.

She returned her attention to her forward momentum. Not that she needed to focus on the effort as she never grew tired in the water—another perk from being a freak. But better to think about what she was doing than what Zach was thinking. Was he putting it together?

Could he?

It wouldn't surprise her. She had put it together when it came to Nikki. And Zach was a helluva lot smarter than her.

He stopped kicking.

Jess drifted to a stop, realizing she was about to find her answer. She wished she could run. Hide. At the mine shaft, she'd wanted Nikki to face her fears.

Now it was time for her to do the same. Although she'd take physical fear over emotional fear any day. "What is it?" she asked.

His head cocked, Zach frowned at her. "You owe me an explanation. You knocked me out. My boat is blown up. My crew taken hostage. I think my dad had a heart attack."

Jess swallowed. That would explain the ashen tone to Al's skin when she saw him board the mercs' boat.

Zach continued. "We almost died. You owe me the truth."

Jess sighed, letting her head fall back, her hair trailing in the water. She did owe him the truth. But not now. Not like this.

"I'm not going any farther until you tell me what's going on," Zach said.

She straightened, calling his bluff. She could put this off. Just a while longer. That would give her time to come up with a plausible explanation.

She might owe him the truth but she wasn't ready to spit it out. "I don't see that you have a choice," she said, keeping her voice steady. "What are you going to do? Stay here?"

Frustrated, he rubbed his eyes with a free hand. "No. Of course not."

"Then let's get moving." She continued swimming for shore, but Zach grabbed her foot and pulled her backward until they were nose to nose.

Tension arced between them like electricity but it was far from sexual. "It's not that easy, Jess," Zach said, his eyes burning with anger.

She swallowed. She'd never seen him like this and wished his angry stare wasn't directed at her.

"If the fact that you owe me an explanation isn't enough, I have information you can use," Zach said. "Information about the pirates and where they are headed with the recovered equipment."

Her eyes widened. "You're blackmailing me?"

He shrugged. "You lie. I blackmail."

"I've never lied."

He leaned in, so close his breath was hot against her cheek. "By omission."

Putting her hands against his chest, she shoved him away. "If you know something, it would behoove us both if you said what it was."

This time, he was the one who started swimming away. She grabbed his foot and yanked him to a stop. "Dammit, Zach. Tell me what they said."

He shook his head. "You first."

Jess ran her hands over her hair, smoothing it back. Zach had her. She knew it. He knew it. As much as she hated to admit it, a part of her was relieved to tell her secret. She was tired of carrying it around. Tired of hiding.

She thought about her mother and her reaction. Her father.

Their disbelief and, when they realized what she was, their fear. Disgust. Their desperate need to put as much distance as possible between themselves and her.

She peered at Zach through her lashes.

Maybe this time it would be different. Maybe he'd be like Nikki. He'd understand.

She hoped so, because he wasn't giving her much of a choice, and she was tired of lying.

"Are you sure you want to know?" she asked. "You might not like the answer."

He nodded.

"You had it right earlier," she said. "Right before I hit you."

His forehead wrinkled. "What?"

"Earlier," she said. "In the bell."

He hesitated, as if trying to recall the conversation. "I said you couldn't survive unless you could breathe underwater."

"Bingo."

Zach stared at her as if she'd grown a second head. Finally, he sighed. "Is that how you want to play this? I tell you that I have information that can help you and you joke?"

Great. She confessed, and he thought she was yanking his chain. "I'm not joking."

"Yeah."

Jess rolled her eyes. Short of x-raying her, the only way to prove something like this was a demonstration.

Yanking off her dive watch, she handed it to Zach. "Time me, but keep swimming. No point in losing distance while I convince you I'm part fish."

She dived down, stopping at five feet. Deep enough for Zach to see her but not so shallow that she'd get in his way.

He peered down at her. She tugged on his foot and pointed in the direction of the land. He swam. She stayed beneath him, letting the water fill her lungs.

She relaxed as they swam, taking a moment to dive down a few extra feet then back up, ticking the soles of Zach's feet with her fingertips.

He kicked her away, and she grinned. This was much better than hanging on to a board. Natural. Easy. As always, it was as if the water gave her strength that could not come from mere air.

Shutting her eyes, she let her kicks carry her. Kick. Glide. Kick. Glide. Kick. Glide.

She realized that she was alone, and a moment of panic washed over her at thinking that she'd lost Zach, but when she looked back, she saw him thirty feet behind her and treading water.

He was safe. Relief was just as strong as the panic.

But when she grew closer, she saw she was mistaken. His kicks were slow, as if there were rocks tied to his feet. She smacked her forehead in disgust at her naivety. The water was life for her, but for him—in his already bruised and beaten state—it was a pain in the ass and possibly fatal. She hurried back to him, breaking the surface a few feet away. "Are you okay?" she asked.

"What are you?" he asked, his green eyes wide. Confused. Horrified.

It took all of her training to keep a straight face as every fear she'd ever had overwhelmed her. "Different?" she replied.

He didn't blink.

She closed her eyes instead. "Please don't look at me like that," she whispered, fighting back the tears. She'd hoped he'd accept her. Wanted it so much.

"Like what?"

"Like I'm a monster." The way he gawked at her, as if she weren't human, cut deeper than she'd thought possible.

"No, Jess." Zach's hand, warm but pruned from being in the water, touched her cheek. "Why didn't you tell me?"

"And say what? That I was part fish?" She opened her eyes. His gaze was softer. Perhaps she was wrong?

He shrugged. "Point taken." Then he pulled her closer, wrapping one arm around her while he held on to the board. He buried his face in the side of her neck. "I knew you were special. I just didn't know how much."

She leaned back so she could see his face. His eyes.

They looked sincere.

"I was surprised. That's all," he explained. "You should have told me. I wouldn't have wasted the money and time giving you mixed air."

For a moment, she stared at him.

A grin broke over his face, and she smacked him on the shoulder. "Now is not the time to tease me!"

"You can joke but I can't?"

Chuckling, he pulled her close again, and she sighed against his chest. "You're okay with this?"

"I will be," he said. "It might take some getting used to—"

He had no idea.

"But…wow."

"There are a few other advantages besides the monetary savings," she said, giddy with the fact that he wasn't running away. Didn't think she was less than human.

"Can you call dolphins for help?"

She laughed and pushed away. "I'm not Aquaman."

He smiled in return.

"But I am tireless in the water," she explained. "Plus there is that whole 'I can't drown' issue. Even if I get tired, I can relax without worry."

He glanced at the expanse of ocean between themselves and the land. "I wish I could say the same."

He was going to die if she didn't get him out of the water soon. They were close to the shore but there was at least another mile of ocean in front of them.

Plus, the sun was setting. She did not want to swim over the reef in the dark. "Sorry," Zach said when she flipped around to go back to him.

She trod water as he rested. "Don't be. You're only human."

He managed a weak smile.

She tugged his arm. "Why don't you relax? Let me pull you ashore. I told you I was tireless."

"You did." He took a deep breath and flinched.

Dammit. "Are your ribs broken?" she asked, her eyes widening.

He shook his head. "Do you think I could swim this far with broken ribs?"

"True." But she was still worried. Beneath the dark tan and the slight sunburn, his skin was a shade paler than it had been earlier. She took his wrist and felt his pulse. Steady. But weak.

"Just tired," he said, pulling away. "Getting beaten to a pulp takes it out of you."

It did. And he was beaten because of her. Guilt churned her insides.

"I know that look and don't." He tugged a strand of her hair. "You did what was necessary. You saved us all."

It was nice of him to say so, but that didn't assuage the guilt. She nodded then gestured at the sinking sun. "We're going to get caught out here in the dark. Let me help you." She took his hand in hers.

He sighed again, this time without flinching. "You say you're tireless, but how long will you last if you're hauling me behind you?"

"Let's find out."

He brought her hand to his mouth and kissed her knuckles. "I have a better suggestion."

Her right brow shot up, asking what it was without words.

"Go on without me—"

"I did not save you to leave you out here!"

"—and bring back help," he finished, ignoring her outburst.

She frowned and shook her head. "Not going to happen."

"Dammit, Jess. For once, stop arguing."

"Then let me help you," she snapped. "Or we can both float out here until the cows come home."

He jerked his hand out of hers and started kicking for shore, his legs moving as if he propelled himself through cement, not saltwater. "You have the worst metaphors," he mumbled.

"No, that would be Liz," she said, pacing herself to his speed and making sure not to outdistance him again.

He covered less and less water until he was almost crawling along. "I'm slowing you down," he said.

"Martyr," she snapped.

"No. Realist."

She bit her lip to keep from saying something rude, then realized his grip on the board was weak, and his eyes were closed.

He'd passed out.

Treading water, Jess surveyed the situation. The safety of the beach wasn't far, but she noticed the waves broke quite a way out before they hit the sand. That meant only one thing—

There was a reef below the surface.

Great.

And somehow she'd have to drag Zach's dead weight over it without getting them both killed.

Carefully, she slipped off her wet suit, leaving herself in a red bikini and dive booties but otherwise, with no protection against the reef and the fire coral.

It might be painful if the waves pushed her into the calcifications, but if he could survive a beating she could take a little scraping and burning.

Holding on to the board for leverage, she flipped Zach onto his back, shoved the board under him to support his head and shoulders then used the legs of her wet suit to tie him to it.

He didn't wake.

Which, she realized, was good. If he woke, he'd argue, and they didn't have time for a fight.

Grabbing the front half of the suit, she tied the sleeves around her left ankle so she could tow Zach.

She glanced at the shore and the water between. There was a spot a few hundred yards to the right where the waves weren't breaking as fast. Possibly a way through the reef.

There was only one way to find out, and even if it wasn't a great opening, she'd take it anyway. She needed to get Zach out of the water.

"Let's make some time," she muttered.

Diving just under the surface, she swam a steady pace, pulling Zach along behind her as she sped through the water. It wasn't as fast as she wanted, but it was faster than they'd been going.

She scanned the water as she swam, watching for any sign of danger. So far, they hadn't seen anything other than a few curious fish. But the closer they got to the reef, the likelier their chance of running into animals that were as large as they were.

Could be a few rays.

Could be tiger sharks.

She prayed it wasn't the latter. If so, she wasn't sure what she could do other than try to scare it away.

With what? she asked herself. Harsh words?

A parrot fish swam past her, its rainbow colors catching her attention. If there was a parrot fish, then she was almost there. She squinted into the blue that was now the color of turquoise.

The waves broke ahead. The water, swirling and shallow, was a great place to get killed by getting scraped across the reef, she thought as she headed closer.

Slowing, she glanced behind her. Zach was still out. She'd wanted him that way, but now she wished he'd wake. It would make things a lot easier.

Another thought made her hesitate. What if he were hurt worse than a beating? What if he had internal injuries? She rose to the surface. "Zach?"

He was unresponsive.

Lifting his T-shirt, she gave him a quick once-over. His skin was mottled with purpling bruises, but the majority were around his shoulders leaving his lower abdomen almost un-marred. At least the bruises weren't enough to make her think there was internal damage.

She shook him again. Nothing.

Once again, she took her place below the water. Parallel-ing the reef, she headed toward the potential opening she'd spotted earlier.

She slowed when she spotted the channel. The water wasn't as deep as she wanted, but it was enough. Jess checked the knots she'd used to tie Zach to her. They were solid.

She breathed deep of the water and pushed forward.

Halfway through the channel, there was a yanking on her ankle. A familiar yanking.

Shark!

Even though she was trained, and the water was her home as much as the land, fear raced through her in an instant, re-leasing a rush of adrenaline.

She flipped, ready to take on whatever was attacking.

There was nothing there.

But Zach. Awake. And pulling on the wet suit.

Bastard! He'd scared the hell out of her. She held up a finger to indicate "just a minute." Stopping in the channel was not a good idea.

They cleared the reef thirty seconds later. Untying the beat-up wet suit from around her ankle, she rose to the sur-face. "Are you trying to give me heart failure?" she shouted.

"Sorry." He didn't look sorry. In fact, he seemed annoyed. But the pale undertone to his skin was gone, and that was a good sign. Let him be annoyed.

He shrugged and worked on untying the knotted wet suit. "You made good time," he said, looking at the shore that was only a few hundred feet away.

"Told you I was tireless," she said, smacking his hands away to work on the knots herself.

He smacked back. "Jess, you've saved my life three times. Let me deal with the damn knots."

Her eyes widened. "Excuse me?"

"You heard me," he said.

She rolled her eyes, realizing what was going on. He was a brilliant computer geek and an expert diver, but he was still a man.

Men hated being saved.

"Where do you get three times?" she asked, watching him work the knots as they drifted, the waves taking them ashore.

"Both bombs and just now."

"The first doesn't count. And why are we even having this conversation? I saved both our lives."

He stopped, shook his head and the first knot came undone. "Fine then. Twice."

"It was my fault you were in danger," she said. "In case you're forgetting that."

Her toes touched sand.

Zach untied the last knot, freeing himself. Rising to his feet, he stood, the surf reaching above his shoulders. He didn't say a word.

She swam ahead until she could stand with her head above water.

"What is your problem?" She stopped Zach with a hand to his chest. "An hour ago, you were fine. You pass out and now you're being a jerk."

His face reddened, and she sensed what the problem was. "Is it because you passed out?" she asked. "Is that the problem?"

The red reached the tip of his ears, and he pushed past her, striding through the waves until he was on land. He fell to his knees, and she walked to sit beside him.

Men could be so dumb.

Silently, they watched the rest of the sun slip below the horizon.

"Thanks for saving me," he said, once darkness covered them.

"I'm better in the water," she said. "That's all. It's not even skill. It's a genetic mutation."

More silence. "It's getting old. You saving me."

She sighed in the dark and lay back in the sand. Above her, the stars sparkled and behind her was nothing but jungle. Not a sign of life. If they were on an inhabited island, it might be Puerto Isla—the reef was in the right location. But that meant they were on the far side.

The uninhabited and untamed side.

Fabulous.

"We got lucky, and I have gills," she finally answered, annoyed at even having the conversation. "You know what, I'd trade all that for normalcy. For not hiding who I am, what I am." She sighed again. "You have no idea."

"I know." He stripped down to his swim trunks then lay beside her, his head touching hers. "Sorry for being an ass."

"Thanks. Hell, I'd be the same way," she admitted. "People like us—"

"We like to save ourselves," he finished.

Silence. "I need to confess something," he said.

Jess sighed. "It's already been a long day. Can it wait?"

"It could, but if you're going to get pissed, I'd rather get it over with as soon as possible."

"Spill it." Jess turned onto her side to face him.

"I lied about knowing where the pirates are headed. I don't know anything other than they were after you and the laptop."

"Crap." She rolled back over.

"Pissed?"

Perhaps it was the fatigue or that she'd lied to him repeatedly or that he'd accepted her—gills and all—for what she was, but Jess took stock of her emotions and found a surprising answer. "No. I'm not."

This time, Zach turned to face her. "You've got to be kidding me."

"Nope."

"Okay," he replied, but didn't sound convinced.

Jess chuckled. "Really. It's good." She reached over and took his hand in hers. "And we have bigger things to worry about."

She reached over and took his hand in hers.

He squeezed her fingers. "Like searching for a way overland in the morning," he said.

"And water," Jess said. "I'm dehydrated, and you can't be much better."

"Definitely," Zach agreed.

Jess snuggled close and counted stars, not wanting to tell him that as long as she was in the ocean, dehydration was not a problem. Never was. Her body extracted oxygen but also took what liquid it needed and expelled the salt.

All that changed on land. Without water, she'd dehydrate and unlike most people, dehydration dried out her gills.

A few hours in the tropical sun, without water, and she'd be dead.

Chapter 11

Jess woke to cool morning air, Zach's arm over her waist and a bathing suit full of sand. Being careful not to wake Zach, she moved his arm off her and sat up, grimacing as bits of silica shifted into various crevices of her body.

Judging by the sky, it was going to be a beautiful day. Tropical. Clear.

And hot and humid.

Humidity was miserable, but it would help stave off dehydration until they could find water. As far as the sand in her suit, it had to go unless she planned on an impromptu exfoliation.

Walking into the surf until it cleared her waist, she swam under the waves, relaxing as her body soaked up water. Finally, she took off the bits of red cloth that designers deemed a bikini and rinsed.

"Morning, Jess!"

She looked up to see Zach coming forward with something

in his hand. She realized she must have been under longer than she thought if he'd had time to wake and forage. He waded in, gave her a brief good-morning kiss that made her toes curl then held out the opened fruit. "Breakfast?"

She took it, eyeing the white flesh. "What is it?"

"Breadfruit. There's a tree just over there."

She poked at it, then nibbled at a sliver. It was sweet and creamy.

Picking out seeds, she ate while Zach disrobed, groaning as he moved. She knew it wasn't because she was nude.

"You going to be able to hike?" she asked.

"Just stiff," he said, stretching. "But I think the sleep helped, even if it was on the beach."

She had to admit he seemed better. Lots better.

"Do you ever hold your breath?" he asked.

Jess hesitated at the out-of-the-blue question then a little trill of pleasure ran through her at his curiosity. "Never thought about it, but, yeah. When I just go under for a minute, I do."

"Why?"

She shrugged. "Habit. I didn't know what I was until I was eleven."

"What do your parents think about it?"

She worked at a slice of fruit. "I think *freaked-out* is the technical term."

He gave a thoughtful nod. "I guess I'm lucky to have my dad. I was a bit different, too." He flashed a wry grin. "Nothing on par with breathing underwater, but still different." He ran a hand through his hair, slicking it back. "Being the mathematical savant wasn't easy when I was young."

She hadn't thought about it, but to be a teenager and smarter than everyone else would be isolating. "I can imagine," she said, dropping what was left of breakfast in the water.

"I love my parents," Jess continued, pulling up her feet and letting the waves lift her. "But it would have been nice to have their support."

"You have mine." Zach grinned, and pulled her to him, his trunks in one hand and the other hand sliding up her back.

She sighed at the skin-against-skin contact and put her feet down. He felt familiar against her. Warm. She kissed his chest then licked a path to the hollow of his throat, tasting the salt on his skin and loving it.

Nuzzling her hair, he lifted her until she wasn't touching the bottom and moved them out into deeper water.

His breath was quicker, deeper and his erection pressed against her abdomen. "Wrap your legs around me," he whispered in her ear. She bit the side of his neck, smiling as he groaned, but did as he asked.

He slid into her as if they'd been lovers for years.

Jess shut her eyes and let the waves move her, exquisite in their slowness. She'd never made love in the water before but it felt so natural. The energy of the water elevating the sensation in her body.

"Look at me," Zach whispered. "I want to see those beautiful brown eyes."

She opened her eyes and met his steady gaze, but being in the water under the tropical sun gave the scene a dreamlike quality and she closed her eyes partway, watching him through her lashes.

In the back of her mind, she heard her breath quicken. Heard the moans from her lips. Realized her nails were digging into his skin and she might be hurting him.

She didn't care.

All she could think about was Zach's steady, hot stare.

His face twisted. He was close to orgasm. She felt it in the way his hands gripped her waist and the way he expanded inside her. "Jess." He hissed her name, and the sound tumbled her over the edge.

She arched back as she climaxed, Zach holding her up with his hands, and her legs tightening around him even as he cried out, his shout echoing across the water.

When her breathing slowed to normal, she realized she was floating on her back with Zach's hand under her for support.

And she had no idea where her bikini was. "Dammit!" She righted herself, splashing, and dived to search the sea bottom.

Zach nudged her with his foot and motioned for her to come up.

"Looking for this?" he asked, holding the bikini in his hand. He already had his trunks back on.

"Yes." She smiled, feeling foolish as she dressed. It wasn't often that she lost herself in a moment, but there was something about Zach that made her lose all sense.

She turned around and let him tie the top on for her. Now that she was satiated, she realized her lack of control was something she'd have to watch. Even in the middle of nowhere, there could be danger from any number of predators, humans or even the terrain.

They swam back ashore and stood for a moment, staring into the jungle in front of them. It was a mass of vines and trees. Almost impenetrable. "This is going to suck," Zach said, his arms crossed over his bared chest.

"Yes," Jess agreed. "We need to find water first. And food."

"We have breadfruit." Zach pointed to the shore. "Unless you can catch fish, because I know I can't, not without a line and pole or a net."

"And what would I use?" Jess asked.

"Your hands."

She raised a brow. "I said I wasn't Aquaman. I have gills and I'm fast, but I am not fish-fast."

He shrugged. "Just a thought."

Jess grabbed her wet suit, rinsed it and slung it over her shoulder. It would be hotter than hell to wear and heavy to carry but she might need it if the jungle proved too thick.

A rustling caught her attention, and she turned to see Zach waiting for her with a breadfruit in each hand to be eaten later, his wet suit tied around his waist and the diving booties on his feet.

She grinned. "Wow, Mr. Holiday. You look really hot. Ooh lala."

He rolled his eyes. "Ready?"

She pointed toward what she hoped was the populated side of Puerto Isla. "Let's get to it."

The jungle was thick and green and lush.

That meant water. Somewhere.

Jess stumbled and fell to her knees. They'd been thrashing their way through the jungle and, despite its lush appearance, had yet to find a stream of any sort. Early on, while the morning was still cool, they'd sucked the water off leaves, but that ended when the sun became too hot and the water evaporated. The fruit was enough to keep Zach going, but it wasn't enough for her.

Now, they were thick in the jungle and there was no breadfruit. Only tamarind, jacarandas and the occasional flame tree. They'd seen a few mango trees, but the fruit was green with the local wildlife having made quick meals of the more edible fruit.

Zach kneeled beside her. "What's wrong?"

"Water," she mumbled through swollen lips. "I need water."

"I know," he said. "I'm feeling it, too."

He didn't understand, but she nodded and let him help her to her feet. The ground swayed beneath her, and she took a deep breath to clear her head.

The world stopped weaving, and she started forward.

She could manage a few more hours as long as she was careful, she told herself. She was a Marine, after all.

Thirty feet later, her knees buckled, and she fell again. She wanted to cry in frustration but knew it would be a waste of tears. Rising to her hands and knees, she fought to catch her breath, but her heart pounded, refusing to slow.

She didn't have hours, no matter what she told herself.

Zach pulled her down to a sitting position. "What's going on?"

She rested her head in her hands. It wasn't throbbing, but it felt as light as a balloon. She held on to it to keep it from floating away. "I should have told you," she muttered.

"Told me what?"

"Have to have water. My gills are drying out, and when they do, I'll die."

"Fuck."

She squinted up at Zach. He glared at her but beneath the initial anger was a concern so deep it surprised her. He wavered in her vision. Like water running down glass.

"Yes, you should have told me." He ran a hand through his hair. "We could have waited until nightfall to walk."

"Need to get to a city," she muttered. "Get hold of Delphi."

"What?"

She shook her head, no longer sure what was real. What she did know was that she needed water. "Need water. Soon."

"Can you walk?" He took her arm to help her up, and she teetered on unsteady feet.

The earth fell away, and she realized he carried her. She tried to struggle but couldn't put up much of a fight. "You're hurt," she said, laying her head against him, grateful for his strength.

"I'll be fine," he replied. "Besides, I think it's my turn to do the saving."

She nodded. Too tired to argue.

When she opened her eyes, she was on the ground. Zach was kneeling next to her and peeking out at something through the brush. "Zach?"

He turned at her throaty, parched whisper. "Glad to see you're awake," he replied, taking a moment to run a thumb along her cheek. "You had me worried."

It took effort to breathe. The air was hot. Thick. Her head throbbed as she tried to stay awake. "Where are we?"

"Not sure," he said, glancing back out between the leaves. "There's an airstrip here and a building but no other sign of civilization. My guess is drug runners. There's a field on the far side. I can't see what's being grown, but I doubt it's corn."

Jess crawled over and squinted at the field. The plants were tall, green, with a familiar five-frond cluster. Marijuana. "Not unless you can smoke corn."

"There's no plane and so far, no activity," Zach said, letting the leaves fall back into place.

His voice sounded strong, but Jess didn't miss the pinched look to his skin and the fact that he wasn't sweating. He had to be as parched as she was.

"You wait here," he said. "I'm going to get to the building and see if I can find some water. If they're growing pot then they must be watering the plants somehow."

"Let's get going." Jess tried to struggle to her feet and failed. She clenched her fists in frustration.

"There is no *we* here. You can barely move." Zach put his

hand on her fists. "Let me do this. It'll go faster if I don't have to carry you."

She nodded, understanding how he felt when he woke up and found she'd carried him through the water. There was nothing worse than feeling helpless.

She tried to take a deep breath but her body refused to co-operate. "Go. Watch for booby traps."

Taking one more look to make sure the area was deserted, Zach sprinted for the shed. She watched as he hesitated at the door. Moving to one side and crouching, he turned the knob. It swung open, but since it faced to the side, she couldn't see in.

He gave her a thumbs-up and entered the shed, emerging a minute later with what she thought were two canteens. He ran to her, crashing through the brush.

"Here." He handed them both to her. She opened one and sniffed. It smelled okay. Upending it, she drank, her body absorbing the liquid almost as fast as it slid down her throat.

When she finished, she wiped her mouth with a sigh. "Thanks"

"Better?"

"Much. But I need more."

He handed her the other canteen. She pushed it back. "You need some, too."

He dropped it in her lap. "I already had some. Finish it, and I'll get us more. There's a spigot on the far side of the shed."

As much as she hated to admit it, she wanted the second container of water. Needed it. She chugged it down, making sure she didn't miss a drop, then handed the empty container to Zach.

Already her energy was returning, and her breathing was easier.

"Be right back," Zach said. "Wait here."

He hurried back to the shed and round to the far side.

Thirty seconds later, he ran back with one of the containers in his hand. She heard noises coming from behind him.

Voices. Shouts. Gunfire.

Behind him, three men ran out of the marijuana field.

A surge of adrenaline shot through her as Zach crashed through the bush, grabbed her arms and yanked her to her feet before she had time to rise on her own. "Run."

She wasn't up to par, energywise, but the adrenaline helped. She managed to keep up with Zach as they raced through the jungle, shoving plants aside. Dammit, she should have served as a lookout rather than sitting on her ass, waiting to be saved.

Behind them, the jungle echoed with shouts as their pursuers followed their hard-to-hide trail.

"We're never going to get away," Jess huffed, trying to catch her breath, "if we stay in the jungle."

"I know," Zach said. "And if they catch us in an open space, they'll shoot us like ducks."

They had to stop the pursuers, Jess knew. Catch them unawares. But she wasn't up to full strength and knew she couldn't fight three armed men. Not even with Zach's help.

Maybe she couldn't take the pursuers head-on, she figured, but if she and Zach took them by surprise, they might stand a chance. They had to do something. Already she was slowing down. Despite the two containers, she'd need more water. "Can you climb?" she asked, her voice cracking.

"What do you have in mind?" Zach asked.

"Get above me. Above them. Let them run past. Get them between us. Then take them out."

"You can't run," he argued. "Listen to yourself."

"I can," she insisted. "Please. Only chance."

She didn't miss the initial *hell no* that flickered across his face, but then he nodded. "That'll work," he huffed.

They stopped at a place where the trees were tall and thick. She grabbed him, pulling him to her, and kissed him hard. "Be careful."

"You, too."

Grabbing a tree limb, he climbed up a jacaranda, the dense foliage and purple flowers providing cover. She ran onward, making as much noise as possible.

When she got out of this, she was going to have a chat with Delphi about her assignments. She wanted her next one in someplace civilized.

Delphi. She almost stopped midstep. Had she mentioned her contact to Zach? She pushed giant fronds out of the way. She seemed to remember saying something, or was that her delirium?

She couldn't be sure.

Behind her, the shouts sounded closer.

She concentrated on running. Their pursuers must have cleared Zach's hiding spot by now, she realized. He had to be behind them. Stopping, she took off her bikini, tossed the top to the right and the bottom to the left.

They might expect an attack. But an attack by a naked woman? That would throw them off, she thought with a grin.

Trying not to disturb the plants, she crawled to the side, and ten feet back, along the trail she'd created and crouched low. Wrapping her fingers around the largest rock she could find, she waited.

Thirty seconds later, a set of footsteps pounded past her. They stopped then walked back. "She is here somewhere," the man said in Spanish, standing less than five feet away from her hiding space, her top dangling from his hand.

There was agreement.

She prayed Zach was in position.

Leaping forward, she grabbed the closest man by the ankle and pulled.

He hit the ground with a thud, his gun firing into the air.

Then she was on him, straddling his waist, and hitting his forehead with the rock. His eyes rolled back in his head and he passed out. Or died. She wasn't sure and she didn't care.

Jess looked up at the others. Their eyes were wide. One man's attention slid to between her thighs. "*Hola, amigos,*" she said with a smile.

The words sent them back into action and the one on the left raised his gun—

But only a few inches before Zach was on him. Jess leaped to her feet, and ran at the other, tackling him and knocking him to the ground.

This one was ready for the rock. As she raised her hand, he gripped her wrist, his eyes narrowed. "*Puta,*" he sneered.

No one called her a whore. She punched him with the other hand, and he returned the blow. For a second, blackness wavered in her vision.

Then she was flipped on her back, her skin scraping along the ground as her attacker gained the advantage. She kicked with her legs but even adrenaline wasn't enough. He laughed at her.

Zach came into view over the man's shoulder, a stick in hand.

Jess smiled. "*Pelotudo.*" Perhaps she couldn't ask for directions in Spanish, but she knew how to insult.

He raised his hand, palm open, to slap her, and Zach hit him with the stick. Hand still outstretched, he pitched forward onto Jess.

He smelled like sweat and oil and pot. Jess grimaced, pushed him off and smiled up at Zach. "Nice timing."

He held out a hand and helped her to her feet. "You're naked."

"Yes." She shrugged, picking up her bikini top from the forest floor. "I wanted to catch them off guard."

He glanced at the body of the man she'd pummeled. "I'm guessing you did."

She didn't miss the way his gaze turned back to her. There was something different in his eyes. Not fear. *Realization.* As if he just now understood what she was capable of.

She turned away, knowing there was no way she could take back her actions, and even if she could, she wouldn't.

She was fighting for her life. For his.

All was fair.

Jess searched the jungle floor until she found her bottoms and put them back on.

"We should tie them up," she said, returning to the carnage.

"With what?" Zach asked.

Though he still looked at her with both surprise and a little trepidation, his gaze seemed to be tempered with what she hoped was understanding.

She glanced at the unconscious men. They wore worn cargo shorts and plain green T-shirts, and while it was tempting to take their clothes for herself, they looked as though they hadn't been washed in weeks.

Plus, if they tore up the clothes for rope it would give her and Zach two advantages—it would take the men a while to untie themselves, and when they were free it would leave them naked.

While she didn't mind nudity, especially when it gave her a tactical advantage, most people were not comfortable being naked.

Especially men.

Too many dangling body parts.

She grinned. "Let's tear up their clothes and use them."

Zach grinned, too, as he followed her train of thought. "Get the guns, and I'll get started."

She nodded. "Good idea." As much as she hated to admit it, she was still weak. She gathered weapons, and the ripping of cloth sounded through the jungle.

As soon as they finished here, they'd have to go back to the pot plantation for water. Then they could find their way back to civilization and, with luck, their crew.

Chapter 12

It took less than thirty minutes to fill canteens then hike through the marijuana field to find the small, beat-up four-wheel drive SUV the drug runners used to reach the growing site.

The car looked like crap. Jess wondered if it would be safer to walk than to drive the sketchy vehicle, but when they successfully navigated a rocky hill that was almost vertical, Jess had to admit the little vehicle was sturdy. She patted the dash. *Good girl.*

The sun was already below the horizon when they reached Playa de Palmas, the airport town of Puerto Isla. Still on rutted, dirt roads, they passed shanties that ranged from card-board to tin shacks, and it wasn't until they reached the first of a few five-story, semicolonial buildings that the road became paved.

Zach stopped at a small market that was still open.

He emerged a few minutes later with a plate of homemade

tamales, a jug of Gatorade and a pair of girls' denim shorts that she estimated were one size too small. Handing everything to Jess, he started the car. "Police?" he asked as he pulled onto the pitted asphalt that constituted a road.

"Seems like the thing to do," Jess replied, unbuckling her seat belt long enough to pull the shorts on. The police might know more about the mercs or what happened to the crew. When that was done, she could e-mail Delphi to give her handler an update and see if there was any information that might not be available to the local authorities.

She glanced at Zach as he wove through traffic, ate a tamale and honked his horn at a driver who decided to stop in the middle of the road so he could run into a restaurant and pick up dinner.

Zach hadn't asked about Delphi—even on their overland trek when there was nothing to do but keep the SUV from rolling over or talk during long stretches of nothing—and Jess decided it must have been the delirium making her think she had opened her mouth.

It was nice to know that even when she was at her worst, she could keep a secret. She smiled to herself and turned her attention to the city outside the vehicle.

In a few minutes, they were at the police station. A small, cement building painted sky-blue, it had bars on the window and two green-and-white police cars parked out front.

Once inside, Jess realized the small building could barely be called a police station. One giant room with two jail cells at the far end. One held a drunk. The other was empty, with its door swinging open.

A solitary man, dressed in a tan uniform and sitting at the desk, watched the inmate. He looked up when they entered, smiled and rose, hand outstretched.

"Ernesto," Zach said in greeting.

"I take it you already know each other," Jess said as the two men embraced in what Jess would describe as a "manly" hug.

"Zach's been running his salvage operation for years," Ernesto explained with a heavy accent. "Of course I know him. I know all the local divers."

Ernesto held out his hand. "*Buenos dias.*"

Jess took the offering. "Jess and *buenos dias.*"

The cop nodded, and his smile faded as he turned his attention back to Zach. Jess's stomach dropped. She knew that look. Something had happened in their brief absence. Something bad.

"What is it?" Zach asked, his voice hesitant.

Ernesto sighed, his brown eyes sympathetic. "We found your crew in the lifeboat yesterday, the engine disabled. Al is in the hospital." He rested a hand on Zach's shoulder. "It's not good. You'll want to go to him. He's in room 211. I stopped by yesterday."

"Thanks."

"The others?" Jess asked. "They're all right?"

"Tired. Scared. Dehydrated, but alive." He scratched his goatee. "We'll need to talk about that. About a number of items, but it can wait until you see your father."

A number of items? "Like what?" Jess asked.

"I am curious as to why the crew was left alive. And we were told Zach was blown up and you—" he looked at Jess "—drowned."

Jess shrugged, knowing there was nothing he could say or do about her unexpected status as *living* as long as she kept her mouth shut

She had questions in regards to the crew, as well. As much as she tried to think positively, a part of her had never expected to see the crew alive again. After all, why leave witnesses?

She touched Zach's arm. "We should get to the hospital."

Ernesto walked with them to the door. "Just don't leave town without talking to me first."

"Of course," Jess said, getting the distinct impression he was speaking to her. They walked back to the car. "He's right," Zach said. "The others should be dead."

"I know."

"Any thoughts on why not?"

"Not really," she replied, but she had a good idea as to who ordered the others to be spared. *Arachne.*

But why? She got in the SUV, letting Zach drive, as her thoughts hurried through scenarios but came back to one— Arachne knew she'd only faked her death.

Not a surprise since Arachne knew Jess could breathe underwater.

Which meant that Arachne was using the others as bait. Hoping that Jess would contact them and then Arachne could capture, kill or whatever it was that her opponent seemed to desire.

The wild card was Zach. Arachne would not know that he'd survived the blast.

They turned into the hospital parking lot, and Zach turned off the ignition, but before he could open the door, Jess grabbed his arm. "We need to talk."

He hesitated. "What?"

Inwardly, she flinched at hearing the tension in his voice, and hated the fact that she was about to make it worse. "Look, whoever tried to kill us left everyone else alive for a reason. I think its bait. For me. Possibly for you. If we go up there, we're going to give away the only advantage we have."

"Advantage?" Zach's lips thinned as they pressed tight. "I don't care. My dad is up there. Possibly dying."

"I know. I want to go to him, too, but they might be waiting."

"Doubtful. If my father or any of the crew saw those pirates here on land, they'd be caught."

He had a point, but she knew someone as experienced as Arachne didn't give up that easily. "I'll give you that," she agreed, "but I wouldn't put it past them to have paid someone for information on anyone that goes into that room."

"You really are a jarhead, aren't you?"

If the words were a knife, Jess knew she'd be bleeding. The way he said it made it sound like the equivalent of *stupid*. She swallowed hard and told herself it was fear talking. Fear for his father.

Still, that didn't mean she had to take the insult without comment. "That was unfair," she said, her voice tight.

Zach sat in the uncomfortable silence then finally let his head fall back against the headrest. "It was. I apologize."

She stroked his hair, wishing she could change what had happened. Fix his feelings. Take away the tension in his jaw.

Anything to get back the Zach she knew.

"So you'll wait until it's safe?" she asked.

He turned his head to meet her eyes, his own reflecting the apology. "I appreciate your opinion, but I need to get to my father. You can stay here if you want but I'm going." Opening the car door, he left her sitting there.

Jess flung open her door, stormed to the other side and blocked Zach with her body. "Maybe a jarhead is what you need because barging into that hospital without taking precautions is dumb in the extreme."

Zach stared down at her and crossed his arms over his chest. "What do you suggest I do, Ms. Jarhead?"

"Let me call my contacts for information."

"Who? Delphi?"

Jess's stomach dropped. She had said something in her delirium. She knew it. Knew it even when she'd told herself otherwise. "Delphi?"

Zach's eyes narrowed. "Yes, Delphi. I assume that's your boss?"

She took a deep breath and ran through her options, but the only plausible one was denial, and even that wouldn't work. With Zach's computer skills, he'd find out who Delphi was as soon as he was left alone with some time and an Internet connection. Better to tell him enough to assuage his curiosity and anger. Perhaps it would get her what she wanted because nothing else had so far. "Delphi is my handler. Not my boss."

"Handler?"

She didn't give in to the urge to roll her eyes. Apparently, he never watched *Alias* or any other spy shows. "The person who gives me assignments. Debriefs me. I've never seen her—or him—but she's my contact. Tells me what to do. Provides information."

"Like the crappy coordinates to the ship?"

Jess frowned. "They weren't crappy. They were better than most. Just not as good as what you can do."

Zach's frown deepened. "They were crap, and my point is that Delphi is lacking when it comes to information manipulation. I wouldn't trust her with my checkbook, and I sure as hell don't trust her with my life or the lives of those I love." He shook Jess off. "I'm going to go see my dad. If you're concerned, you can watch my back."

He went around her.

Stubborn butthead.

Jess hurried to catch up with him, grabbing the waist of his shorts to drag him to a halt. "Fine. I can't stop you but at least be smart."

"How?" he asked, still moving and forcing her to either let go or be dragged along.

She kept hold of his shorts and followed. "Haven't you ever worn a disguise?"

"I love the beach at night," Jess purred, touching the orderly on the arm and keeping his attention on her while down the hall, Zach pilfered hospital scrubs from a closet.

The orderly took a step closer, his gaze zoomed in on her cleavage. She was fairly sure he only understood about every third word, but that didn't seem to matter.

Pervert.

Glancing over the orderly's shoulder, she saw Zach give the "okay" sign and walk back toward the parking lot.

Thank goodness. She could only giggle so much. Jess glanced at her watchless wrist. "Oops! Gotta go," she said, tapping on her skin. With a smile, she stepped around the man and hurried back to the parking lot.

"Hey! Number?" the man called out.

Jess shook her head and scooted out the door.

Slipping into the scrubs, Jess stuffed her long, dark hair under a surgical cap, and they drove around the two-story building until they found a side door.

The hospital was in the middle of the evening meal so the floors were busy with assistants serving food and nurses doing their rounds. "Perfect," Jess said, making sure her voice carried no farther than Zach. "No one will pay attention to us with all this going on."

They headed to the stairs. Much like the lower floor, the second-floor hallway buzzed with nurses. Heads down, Jess and Zach walked to the room and slipped inside without knocking.

The room was dark.

And as soon as she cleared the threshold, Jess knew they weren't alone.

"Jess, get the lights," Zach whispered.

Amateur. She knew as soon as he said her name that their cover was blown, and no amount of disguise would save her. Movement out of the corner of her eye confirmed it. Without hesitation, her arm went up, blocking the first blow, and she took a step back, lessening the impact.

She followed with a left hook, the blow landing against the intruder's cheek.

The door shut behind her, and her eyes adjusted enough to see Zach taking on the intruder, as well. Dammit. Now she was afraid she'd hurt him. She blinked and made out the two men just as someone got hit and a crack sounded in the room.

Something was broken on *someone*. She prayed the someone wasn't Zach. The man fell to the floor, and a stripe of light from the window illuminated him. It was Zach, and the intruder had him pinned, his hands around Zach's neck.

Oh, I don't think so.

Slipping behind the attacker, Jess wrapped her arm around his neck, cutting off his carotid artery. He struggled, but as soon as Zach realized what was happening, he grabbed the man's arms, holding him.

The man passed out seconds later. Jess let him fall to the floor. Zach flicked on the light, and looked at the unconscious man at his feet. "You're good at that."

Jess barely heard him. Her attention was on Al. In the bed. Unmoving. Pale with dark circles under his eyes, he was a mere shadow of the lively, charming man who'd sat with her on the upper deck and told her about his life.

She knew this scene. Lived it just a few weeks ago. Charles. In her head, the beeping of life support wailed.

Jess shut her eyes and caught her breath, reminding herself that because Charles died didn't mean that Al would die, too. This was not the same situation.

Not at all.

When she opened them again, Zach was already at his father's side. "Dad?"

The older man didn't respond.

Jess kept her distance, willing him to wake. Perhaps it was selfish, but she couldn't face being associated with another death.

"Dad?" Gently, Zach shook him. This time, Al's eyes fluttered.

Relief washed over Jess, and she hurried over to stand by Zach's side. "Hey," she whispered as Al focused on Zach and then her.

"Zach?" He reached for Zach's hand, his eyes confused and disbelieving.

"It's me," Zach smiled, meeting his father halfway and taking his hand.

"I thought I lost you."

Zach squeezed Al's fingers. "You should know I'm not that easy to get rid of." He nodded toward Jess. "She saved me, Dad. Got me out of the boat before it blew."

Al let go of Zach and patted Jess's arm. "Thank you."

"My pleasure." She smiled, feeling heat rise to her cheeks, blushing at the unexpected praise. "But I think the saving was mutual if anyone is keeping track."

Al smiled. "That's my boy. His mother's smarts and my skill at staying alive." His eyes narrowed. "I thought you drowned?" His voice grew stronger with each passing minute.

Zach glanced at her, questioning. She didn't miss the unspoken question of *are you going to tell him?*

She wished she could tell Al what she was. He deserved

to know, but old habits died hard. Instead, she shrugged. "You thought wrong."

Zach nodded, accepting her wish to keep her secret.

Al harrumphed at her. "I'll let that go for now, but later, when I have the strength to fight with you, we'll talk."

Fight with her? More likely try to charm the truth out of her. Jess leaned down, and being careful to avoid the tubes, kissed his cheek. "Looking forward to it," she whispered in his ear.

His eyes closed in the slow blink of someone who was fighting to stay awake. He'd be asleep in a minute as his beaten body demanded rest, but before that happened, she and Zach needed a few answers. "Al, other than the name of the boat, did you find out anything about the pirates?"

"No names. Nothing like that. They were cocky. Confident. But they received a phone call after they blew up *One For The Money*. Afterward, they were scared. I think they screwed up somehow, and that's why they let us go."

"Thanks," she said.

"You should sleep," Zach said, tucking a blanket around the older Holiday's shoulders. "We'll be back later."

"Good." He patted Zach's hand again. "I'm glad you're okay. Both of you." His eyes closed, and his breathing evened out as sleep claimed him.

"Let's go," Zach said.

"To do what?"

"To contact Delphi. We're going to find out who did this and make sure they never do it again."

Leaving the Puerto Isla hospital was much easier than entering—especially when they told a nurse there was an unconscious man on the floor in Al's room and almost the entire staff hurried to see what, and who, the problem was.

Not that she minded leaving the assailant unconscious, but she was worried what he might do to Al when he woke up.

Now, it was midnight at Al's apartment, and she sat glued to a computer, waiting for an answer.

Zach paced across the tiny room that served as living room and kitchen and office. It wasn't much to look at, but Al didn't need much since he spent the majority of his time on the boat.

"How long does this normally take?" Zach asked. He opened a window and the familiar sounds of the marina—halyard lines flapping against the main, the occasional bell signaling location—wafted in on the night breeze and into Al's living room.

"As long as it takes," she replied, her tone clipped and sharp, before she could think to catch herself. She leaned her head in her hands and took a deep breath, reminding herself that Zach was worried and being bitchy wasn't going to help.

Someone had to remain professional. "We may not hear anything until tomorrow. Why don't you go to bed and get some rest."

He came up behind her and gave her stiff shoulders a gentle massage. "Come with me."

She shook her head. "I'm really not in the mood."

He swiveled her around, his green eyes soft. "That's not what I meant. I meant, come to bed. Get some rest."

Sleep in a bed sounded like heaven, but she shook her head again. "Delphi might reply."

"And we'll do what? Go rushing off at midnight to knock down doors?"

She shrugged. "Maybe."

Taking Jess's hand, he pulled her to her feet. "We'll keep the computer on, and the sound turned up. If we get an e-mail, we'll know it."

She was passing the threshold, and the bed was calling her name, when the computer beeped at her. *Delphi*.

Her stomach did a full-on somersault. She'd had to tell her handler everything, which included the fact that she'd opened her big mouth to Zach.

She was no longer sure she wanted to see the reply.

"Nice timing," Zach muttered.

Jess went back to her chair, and before she could hesitate, she opened the e-mail.

I understand the necessity of telling Zach and considering he found *Paradise Lost* where we couldn't, I'd like you to use him again.

Jess sighed in relief and continued reading.

Based on the information you gave me, I have attached a file on the men and their known locations. Have Zach pare it down.

In addition, I am sending a FedEx file with a new passport and identification.

Delphi thought of everything, Jess had to admit.

Jess opened the files. Delphi had attached pictures to go along with the data. "That's them," Zach said, looking over her shoulder. His hand grasped the arm of the chair, and she didn't miss the way his knuckles whitened with his grip. "That's the leader."

Rafael Vargas. She glanced at his history. Associated with the Shining Path in Peru. Colombian paramilitary forces. The list went on and on.

A nasty character who was probably also a sociopath.

The other two men, Jose Diaz and Antonio Soto weren't in the same league as Vargas, but between them had records of assault, burglary, carjacking and a list of petty crime as long as her arm.

Jess opened the attached file. There were a number of places the pirates could go, and of course, all the locations were spread out over not just Puerto Isla but the entire South American continent. It would take weeks to find them if they'd gone to ground separately.

She hoped Zach was as smart as she thought. "Can you help?" she said, scooting over so he could see the file.

"What is it?"

"A list of known hangouts for the pirates. Delphi and I want to know if you can whittle it down to something manageable."

"Of course," Zach said. "Get up."

She sat up and tilted her head back to look at Zach. All the earlier softness was gone from his eyes and was replaced with a hardness she prayed was never directed at her. "What are you going to do?"

"Set up a program to find them."

"What kind of program?"

"I call it a *sniffer,* but it's more complicated than that. If these idiots show up on the Web at all, I'll know it. If we're lucky, they'll e-mail someone or someone will mention them. And then we have them."

With his skill and knowledge, he was as dangerous as a commando. Jess rose, giving him the chair, grateful he was on her side and prayed that never changed.

Chapter 13

"Are you sure you're okay?" Jess asked, keeping her voice low so it carried no farther than Liz and Nate. She and Zach had walked down the dock from Al's Puerto Isla apartment to the marina below and stood on the deck of *Bite This,* a college research vessel. Around them, the crew hustled, getting ready to head out to sea to do god-knew-what for the next two weeks.

The morning warmed, and Zach's computer program was still looking for the pirates. In the meantime, they'd decided to check on the crew. Nate had a black eye and a few scrapes but was otherwise okay. As upset as Liz had been when captured, she appeared to be cool and composed, though Jess didn't miss the tension around the edges of her mouth.

It would disappear with uninterrupted, pirate-free time on the water. Thank goodness she'd been frightened and nothing more. The mercs could have done so much more to hurt her.

"I'll heal," Nate said. "Though I'm not sure Diego will ever come back to the island."

"I heard he took a flight out this morning," Zach said.

"For Antigua. Got a job with a dive outfit."

"He always preferred to be under the water rather than on it." Zach ran a hand through his dark hair. "I wish there was something I could do to help. I know how much Nate *loves* working with grad students."

The corners of Liz's mouth turned upward at Zach's sarcasm, and she stopped coiling her rope. "You want to help? Get a new ship," she said. "We're on a research vessel, for God's sake. Eggheads."

"Hey, I'm an egghead," Zach said, smiling for the first time that morning.

"Yeah, but you're a cool egghead."

There was a beeping from Zach's pocket. He pulled out a Palm Pilot and frowned. "We need to go," he said, waving the tiny machine.

Liz let the rope drop to the deck and came over to wrap her arms around Jess. "Take care of yourself."

"I will." Jess squeezed her hard, knowing she'd miss the girl.

Liz hugged Zach, as well. "Take care of your dad."

"Always. And I'll let you know when we're up and running again."

The men shook hands, and in a few minutes, Jess and Zach were walking down the dock, leaving the couple to their new job.

"What's the news?" she asked, once they were back at the car. "Did your sniffer program find them?"

Zach pulled out the PalmPilot again, reading. "Two of them and they're here. On the island."

"Excellent," Jess said, glad to see something finally going in their favor. "Where?"

"The morgue."

She stared at him. "The morgue?"

"Yes," he said, putting the PalmPilot back in his pocket. "Seems that both committed suicide. One shot and the other hanged. They left notes."

"How convenient." Jess leaned against the hood of the car. Arachne was covering her tracks. This was going to make getting information, much less finding the computer and logs, a helluva lot harder. "Like hell it was suicide. Your dad said they were scared."

"At least they've paid for their crimes," Zach said through pinched lips.

"So it seems." Jess managed a slow nod. Perhaps it was her imagination, but while he didn't appear pleased, he also didn't appear upset at the news that two men were dead.

"How about Rafael?" she asked. If the leader were alive, and on the run, he probably still had the laptop and logs to use as leverage. If she could get to him before Arachne did, she might be able to persuade him to give them up.

"His last movement was to catch a flight to Brazil. He's not dead. Yet."

The accent. She was right. She should have guessed he'd head for familiar ground. "Good. Let's hope he's alive."

"Alive?" Zach asked.

She couldn't deny there was a certain amount of satisfaction in the thought of pummeling the mercenary. He'd hurt her friends and she'd be all too happy to take payment in flesh.

But there was a bigger purpose than revenge. She needed the laptop and the information on Arachne. To locate it, she needed the merc.

She needed everything.

"Yes," Jess said, drawing a circle in the dust that covered

the car. "There are things I need to know, and he's my best chance to get answers. Plus, he has our stolen property."

"When you put it that way, I guess we're going to Brazil."

We? She held her tongue and kept her face impassive. She knew that Zach thought she was going to beat the hell out of Rafael. And he was right. By the time she was done with Rafael, he'd be begging to tell her everything he knew.

But Zach was wrong on one count.

He wasn't going to be there for the event.

Driving back toward Al's apartment, Jess considered the ways she might ditch Zach. Knocking him out. Sex as a weapon. Starting a fight.

None of the options appealed to her.

She glanced at him out of the corner of her eye. She liked the man, dammit. A lot. More than she should. The thought of flat-out lying to him left a bitter taste in her mouth.

This, she chided herself while turning her attention back to the passing scenery, was why it was always a bad idea to get involved with the people you worked with.

She couldn't count the number of times she'd given that little speech to her team members before they graduated and were assigned to teams with members of the opposite sex.

Keep it simple, she'd cautioned them. You date a team member and then break up, you hurt the team.

It was great advice.

Better advice if she'd heeded it.

"If you don't mind, I'm going to drop you off and then go back to the hospital," Zach said, interrupting her thoughts, and taking her hand in his. "I'd like to go and see my dad for a while. By myself."

Her initial reaction was to say no, but without her at his side, he'd probably be safe.

Plus, it was the perfect way to keep Zach busy while she left town. She knew he could always find her, if he wanted, but this would give her a head start. With luck, she'd have all this solved before he caught up to her.

"Jess?" Zach prompted.

"I don't know if that's a good idea." She sighed, knowing that if she agreed with no argument, he'd wonder what the heck she was doing.

"It's not up for discussion," Zach said.

"Okay, just be careful." She hoped her relief at him leaving wasn't as apparent as it felt.

"It'll be fine," he said. "Besides, they know we're alive and on the island, whoever they are. A visit to the hospital doesn't matter now, and I want to make sure he's protected."

That was a good point, and one she should have thought of, she realized with contrition. "I'll send Delphi an e-mail and see what she can do to make sure he's safe."

"Thanks." He squeezed her hand, and she realized they were at the apartment. "Here's the key," he said, taking it off the key ring, pressing it into her palm and closing her fingers around it.

His hand stilled over hers as he drew her close. "Lock the door," he whispered, then slid his mouth from her ear to her lips.

The kiss was soft. Tender. And Jess fell into it, her heart thumping inside her chest and her breath quickening. All thoughts that kissing Zach was a bad idea flew out of her head and down the street.

She groaned against his mouth. "We shouldn't. Someone could walk by." But the protest was weak.

"So," Zach said, his hand sliding between her legs.

She widened her legs.

"Touch me," he whispered.

She slid her hands up the legs of his shorts until he was hard in her hands. She rubbed her thumb over the top of his erection, and he jumped and twitched at her touch.

She smiled, then gasped, as he unzipped her shorts and slid a hand inside her panties, rubbing her wetness. "Zach…"

He kissed the side of her neck and pulled away. "We'll finish this later." He grinned.

"Bastard," she said, smiling at the same time. "You are a dead man."

He shrugged. "Just wanted to give you something to look forward to."

She wished, because after he found out that she'd left for Brazil without him, she doubted that sex with her was going to be on Zach's agenda.

Breathing a sigh of relief at finding the FedEx envelope with her identification on the doorstep, Jess sent an e-mail to Delphi regarding Al and a request to upgrade the security around him, then she checked the Internet for flights to Brazil. It was a little convoluted, but possible, if she made it to the airport in the next half hour.

Remembering what happened last time she took a taxi to the airport, Jess hesitated but then called a local company. If Arachne was foolish enough to try the same thing twice then Jess would handle the situation again.

Waiting for her ride, she ransacked the small closet, settling on two T-shirts and stuffing them into a small duffel bag along with her bathing suit.

It wasn't much, but it was better than nothing. If she needed more, she'd shop when she got to Rio.

She went outside to wait just as the taxi pulled up. *"Aeropuerto,"* she said, getting into the front seat.

The driver waved a hand in acknowledgment. He was small. Skinny. And from the way his thin T-shirt clung to him—unarmed.

He pulled away from the curve before Jess closed the door then barely hesitated at running a red light, and Jess remembered why she hated taking taxis in Central and South America.

The cabbies saw driving as a competitive sport.

She shut her eyes as he passed a car on the right shoulder of the road.

She was going to die. The driver didn't need a gun because the cab was his weapon. She opened her eyes just in time to see that half a block away, a woman wrapped in a ratty blue-and-white blanket and with her long hair loose and unbrushed, crossed the two-lane road, oblivious of the cars whizzing by her.

The cab driver swerved around her, and Jess couldn't help notice that despite her disheveled appearance, she wore a serene, almost Madonna-like smile, on her lips.

"Ella está en las drogas," the driver said.

She's on drugs? Jess looked back in time to see a truck come to a screeching, swerving halt as the woman stepped in front of him. She also realized that the blanket was the only thing the woman wore.

Jess didn't doubt that the driver was right. She was on something.

She also didn't doubt that the woman was going to be dead either by her hand or by accident very soon. She turned back around, shaking her head and wondering how people let that happen to themselves. What part of their brain looked at something like heroin and said, *Yeah, that sounds like fun. Let me put that in my body and see what happens.*

Still, she had to admit that she had her own addictions. Guns. Fighting. The adrenaline rush that came when she was on a mission.

Everyone had an addiction.

And in her case, she might be dead well before that crazy, serene young woman,

And Zach. Let's not forget him, her subconscious whispered. He was an addiction, she realized with a smile as the driver entered the airport. It wasn't just the great sex. She could get great sex when she wanted it. Maybe not mind-blowing-fuck-me-against-the-wall sex, she had to admit, but great sex? Sure. But he was smart. Caring. And his left hook was a thing of beauty.

When this was over, she was going to apologize for leaving him behind. If she could make him understand that she'd left him for his own good, to keep him safe, maybe he'd forgive her, and she'd come back for a while. Take all that unused vacation time and go diving. Play.

If she wasn't in jail for leaving Puerto Isla without telling Ernesto or if the inquiry didn't toss her in and throw away the key and if Arachne didn't catch or kill her.

Her smile fell. In all the craziness she'd forgotten that she might end up in jail or dead or Arachne's lab rat.

The taxi screeched to a halt. Jess caught herself with one hand before she crashed into the dash.

"Cincuenta," the driver said.

Fifty pesos? He was ripping her off but she didn't have time to argue. She handed him a fifty-peso note and didn't offer a tip.

He gunned the engine as she shut the door.

Jess took a deep breath and hurried into the building that passed as a terminal. The single agent at the ticket counter looked bored, as if she'd rather be anywhere else.

"Rio," Jess said.

The ticket agent raised a manicured, overpenciled brow.

"What?" Jess asked as she handed over cash and her passport, not missing the unspoken comment.

"You are the second person to book Rio today and pay with cash."

The hairs on Jess's neck rose. Arachne knew where she was going? Dammit. That didn't take long.

"Really? What did she look like?"

"Excuse me?" The agent gave her a suspicious glance. "I never said it was a woman. We don't give out information on our passengers, ma'am."

A man? Jess tried to look innocent. "I was hoping to meet my friend but she wasn't sure if I could go. Perhaps she changed her mind. I was just wondering if it was her."

The agent continued to stare.

Jess forced a smile. "Well, it was a thought."

The agent gave a curt nod and gave her the documents and identification. "Enjoy."

Jess smiled and held up the bag. "You know it."

"You can wait over there." She pointed to a small waiting area with a few chairs. It was empty.

That meant the other person, probably an assassin, was elsewhere. Hiding in wait for her? She doubted it. The terminal was too public. And why pay for a ticket? Whoever it was either didn't know Jess was going to Brazil, or planned to do the deed in South America or maybe even on the plane.

Jess leaned against the far side of a pillar, trying to act natural and planning her steps. She'd board. Act as if nothing was wrong. And when he made his move, or her move, he was a dead man.

A movement caught her eye. It wasn't an assassin. It was worse.

Shannon Conner. She'd recognize that blond hair anywhere. Once an Athena Academy student, she'd been expelled—although Jess was never sure why. Now she was a television reporter.

Jess started to turn away, to hide her face, but not before Shannon noticed her. Their eyes locked, and she saw recognition.

The man Shannon traveled with said something. Shannon turned away. When she turned back, Jess made sure she was opposite her on the pillar.

Coward, she told herself, pressing hard against the column. But she didn't have time for a reporter, of all things. Although, she would make sure Delphi knew about Shannon. She hoped the reporter wouldn't work for Arachne, but it was a little too coincidental that she was in Puerto Isla.

Jess counted to fifty before she peeked out from her hiding place. Shannon was gone. And a man walked into the waiting area, a cup of coffee in one hand and his ticket in the other.

She knew him, too. It was Zach.

He sat down, his back to her.

The bag slipped from her fingers and landed with a thud on the worn, industrial carpet. "You have got to be kidding me," she muttered. He'd fooled her!

He didn't see her, and for a moment, she wondered if she could get away with knocking him out and leaving him in Puerto Isla.

She wished. She grabbed her carry-on bag, tempted to choke him with it. Instead, she walked up behind him and thumped the back of his head, making his hot coffee slosh onto his lap.

She hoped it hurt.

"Hey! What the—" He stared up at her.

Jess glared at him, waiting for an explanation.

"Hi, Jess," he said, and went back to his coffee.

"You are a dead man," she muttered under her breath.

She didn't miss his smile. Oh, yeah, he was dead. And if Arachne or her flunkies didn't do it, she would.

Jess fell into the seat next to him. "What are you doing here?" she whispered.

"I could ask you the same thing," he said.

"My job," Jess snapped.

"Same here," Zach said, his expression blank.

"You're not going."

He waved his ticket. "This says otherwise."

She tried to rip it from his hand, but he pulled it away. "You can't stop me."

"Sure I can."

"Nope. You need me."

"For what? Like I don't have enough people to take care of? To worry about?"

He smiled. "You worry about me?"

She rolled her eyes in exasperation. "This is serious."

His amusement faded. "I know. That's why I decided to take care of it."

Jess put her head in her hands. This was insane. Zach was insane. And out of his league. She had to make him see that. She took a deep breath and raised her head. "Have you ever killed anyone?"

Zach shook his head.

"Tortured them?"

He shook his head.

"Listened to them scream? Beg? And ignored them. Just did what was needed to get the information?"

He looked into her as he comprehended what she was asking. "I am not letting you do this alone."

She looked away as the truth she'd hidden—even from herself—reared up. "You don't understand. I can't do this with you." If he saw that part of her. Saw what she was capable of...

Hell, the fact she had gills was nothing.

There was a darkness in her. If he saw that he'd run. And she'd just found him. She wasn't ready to lose him. Not yet. Not like that. "I can't let you see what I can do," she whispered. "And I'm sure as hell not letting you do it."

He caressed her hair, turning her to face him. "I'm not letting you do this alone. I can take it. They hurt my family. They want to hurt you." He touched her cheek, and as always, it comforted her. "We're in this together, Jess. Besides, you'll need me once we get there to find Rafael."

"Do you know where he is?"

"Mostly."

"You're not lying again? Using what I want to hear to get your way?" Jess asked.

"No," Zach replied, looking wounded.

Her brows shot up. "Then why didn't you tell me?"

He shrugged. "I was worried you'd do something nuts. Like try to ditch me and take him on yourself."

Unable to help herself, she smiled. A part of her wanted him at her side for as long as possible, and it was that part that was weak. That part that conceded the fight.

She breathed him in. "It might get bloody. It might get bad."

"Not might." He kissed the top of her head. "Will."

Chapter 14

"Are you sure this is the right house?" Jess asked, flipping down the visor to block the rays of the rising sun.

Parked across the street and down from Rafael's home, she and Zach had been hunkered down in the rental car since they'd arrived late last night in Rio.

So far, there was no sign of the merc who blew up *One For The Money*. The only person in the white stucco building was an older woman who Jess assumed was either his mother or a maid.

"Positive," Zach said, yawning. "He's probably still out. It's Rio, after all."

Jess slouched farther into the seat. "I hate stakeouts."

"Sheer boredom not good enough for you?" Zach teased.

She adjusted her skirt. She didn't like skirts, either, but it was better than the tight, denim shorts.

It was also all she could find as they cruised through the

streets packed with partygoers, looking for Rafael's neighborhood. It seemed they'd arrived during a festival for Joaquim Jose da Silva Xavier, the first freedom fighter and martyr in Brazil's struggle for independence from the Portuguese.

"How long can one man drink and dance?" she muttered, wishing Rafael would come the hell home.

"It's Rio."

She rolled her eyes, but Zach was right. The weekends in Rio tended to be crowded, but when one factored in a national holiday, it turned into a two-day festival, and in Rafael's case, it provided the perfect cover for a man desperate to stay alive.

"We can always knock on the door," Zach said. "See if his mother knows where he might be."

"No," Jess replied. "I can't imagine two strangers showing up at daybreak will inspire her to do anything but call the police."

"Just a suggestion," Zach said, shrugging.

Jess's eyelids flickered as she pushed herself to stay awake. It was so much easier to remain alert when she was in the water. She yawned. Sitting in a car for hours was going to put her in a coma.

"You can take a nap if you want," Zach said.

"I'll be fine," Jess sat up straight. "I just—"

Headlights coming around the corner stopped her midsentence. She pulled Zach to her, and when the beams flashed across their window, she kissed him.

He tasted like coffee. "Nice cover," Zach whispered against her mouth. "We should play stakeout more often."

"Men."

The car slowed, and they broke the kiss to see if the driver appeared suspicious. The car, a dark, beat-up Lincoln, slowed further and stopped at the curb in front of Rafael's house.

"What's next?" he asked, keeping his head close to hers.

"We watch."

A block away, Rafael got out of the Lincoln.

"It's him," Jess whispered. Hands in his pockets, the merc went inside the house, not sparing them a second glance—appearing satisfied that they were parked lovers and nothing more. "Let's give him about ten minutes to get comfortable then we go get him."

"With what?" Zach asked, leaning back. "It's not like we're armed."

"No, but he'll be. I can get his gun."

"And the mother?"

She smiled, loving the way he thought of others even when the situation was tense. "That's your job. Keep her out of the way. Keep her safe. I do not want a civilian hurt."

"I'm bigger. Stronger," Zach countered. "And more motivated. I'll take care of Rafael."

Jess frowned at the word *motivated*. She knew Zach wanted payback for his father. Hell, she wanted it for Charles, but going into a volatile situation with high emotion was how people got killed. It took a professional to turn off those emotions.

And she was a professional.

She shook her head. "I'm trained. You're not."

Now Zach frowned. "Look—"

"No, you look," she said, cutting him off. "This is my job. What I do. You either let me do my job or I end this right here."

"How do you propose to do that? Take me out, as well?"

She gave him a purposeful once-over then gave him a slow nod. "It's close quarters and you're bigger, but make no mistake, I am trained. So, if it'll save you from doing something stupid, yes, I'll incapacitate you."

He glared at her, the morning light stronger now and illuminating his eyes, making them a brighter green than normal. "I'd like to see you try."

She opened her mouth to retort, but another car turned the corner. This time, Zach pulled her to him, kissing her hard, bruising her mouth and pushing her against the door. She kissed him back, just as fierce. Just as tough.

Even so, she kept her eyes open and on the vehicle.

Zach twisted his hands in her hair, exposing her neck and kissing the side down to her shoulder.

The new car stopped across from Rafael's house. "Dammit," Jess growled.

"What?" Zach asked.

"Raphael has company."

Zach followed her gaze.

Whoever the new player was, he stormed up Rafael's steps, kicked open the front door and barged inside. Jess didn't miss the gun in his hand. It was longer than normal.

A silencer, was her guess. Which signaled hit man. "This isn't good." Jess opened her door. "We've got to get in there."

"To do what? Didn't you see his gun? I can't see us going against two armed men."

She gave a curt nod. "I can't let him kill Rafael. He's my last connection to the laptop."

"I want Raphael, too, but I'm not risking you. We're not armed."

Leaning over the seat and across Zach, Jess popped the trunk. "I'll get the tire iron."

Zach sighed. "I'm not going to win this, am I?"

"No."

He opened his door. "Let's go."

Using the house next door for cover, they ran to Raphael's, coming up along the side of the building. The creaking of the front door made them both stop midstep. Zach threw out an arm, pressing Jess against the house.

She glared at him. Did she look new at this?

"You try to call for help or try to get away and I'll come back and kill her," an unknown voice said from the front of the house. The hit man, Jess realized. And he was leaving.

"No. Leave her alone."

No, *they* were leaving. Jess's eyes narrowed. When this was over, she was going to feel good about beating the hell out of the hired gun. Hurting Rafael was one thing. He was scum.

But to threaten an old lady?

That was low.

"Do what I say, and it won't be a problem," the man said, his voice a monotone.

The front door slammed closed. The two men walked across the front porch and to the hit man's car. She and Zach crouched down behind a bougainvillea and watched the two men through the leaves.

They headed to the hit man's car with Raphael at gunpoint. That meant one thing, he wanted to interrogate the merc. That was fine with Jess, but she knew that when the interrogation was over, Raphael was a dead man.

She needed him alive.

They got in the car and drove away.

Inside the house, Rafael's mother wailed. It was a mournful, scared sound, but she was alive, and from the sound of footsteps running through the house, not tied up.

The hit man's car turned a corner and disappeared. "Let's go," Jess said.

They ran back to the car. Zach slid behind the wheel and pulled away as Jess buckled her seat belt. "Ever follow anyone?" she asked as Zach turned the corner on the hit man's trail.

"No."

"It's early so there isn't much traffic, which is a problem. Stay behind by a few blocks."

"What if we get caught at a light?"

"Run it if we have to, but try to be discreet."

"Discreet law breaking. Got it."

Jess spotted the Lexus a few blocks up and making a right. "There they are."

"Got him." Zach sped up.

"Not yet," Jess said, "but we will."

Zach pulled up to the curb at the back of a garage and stopped the car. Just five minutes ago, the hit man and Raphael had stopped out front of the giant metal building and gone inside.

She and Zach had circled the block, giving the hit man time to get comfortable, then parked.

He was smart in coming to the warehouse district, Jess realized as Zach killed the engine. It was a good spot for torture since it was Sunday and there would be no one around. "I'll take the side entrance," Jess said, tire iron still in hand. "You divert them by knocking on the door, but make sure you're gone before the hit man arrives."

"That's the plan?" Zach asked.

"Yes." She knew it wasn't much but there was little choice.

Zach looked as though he might argue then he hesitated.

He was up to something. She was sure of it. Before she could question him, he kissed her mouth. "Be careful." Then he was out the door, leaving it ajar, and heading toward the front of the warehouse.

She went the opposite way, keeping low and praying Zach didn't do something dumb. On the far side, she heard voices. Not intelligible through the heavy glass windows, but the tone was clear. Raphael was screaming, but his mouth was either taped shut or there was a rag jammed into it.

He was alive, and that was something.

Zach's sharp rap sounded like a shot in the silence of the morning. All sound on the other side of the wall stopped.

She knew what would happen. The last thing the hit man wanted was to call attention to himself. He'd answer. Act normal. Or not answer, since no one was supposed to be there.

Either reaction bought her a few seconds.

There was the sound of a door opening.

Jess moved to smash the window then realized it was unlocked. She slid it upward and crawled through. In less than a second, she assessed the situation. The tool cabinet and machinery suggested she was in a machine shop. She'd called it right about Raphael. He was tied to a chair with duct tape over his mouth. The bound man looked at her as if he'd seen a ghost.

Feet pounded toward her. In seconds, the hit man ran into the room, his bulk giving him the momentum of a charging bull.

He raised his gun, but Jess was ready with the tire iron. Putting all her weight behind it, she caught him on the arm before he had time to fire. His gun clattered to the floor, but too late, she realized she'd underestimated him. He gave the impression of being slow, but he was a helluva lot more agile than he looked.

Ignoring her blow, he stopped and pivoted, pulling her to the ground. She tried to twist in midair but his size gave him the advantage, and she landed beneath him. The tire iron skidded across the floor.

She was dead, she realized. Dead. Dead. Dead.

Unless she gained some kind of advantage.

The hit man raised his fist. She turned as he hit her, and he caught her in the side of the head rather than in the face. She saw stars. Her vision blurred, but she kept her grip on consciousness.

This was not happening. She was not going to die. The random thought flashed through her brain even as training commanded all her attention. Thrusting the heel of her hand upward, she connected with his nose, but instead of a full-on blow, her hand slid sideways before she could complete the thrust that would jam his bone into his brain. He *oomphed* but kept his advantage.

She thrust upward again, but he caught her hand then hit her again. The world grayed. With his meaty hands around her throat, the stars came back, winking in her lessening field of vision as she fought to breathe.

Then his weight was off her, and she sucked in air, her lungs burning. Through blurry vision and a fit of coughing, she saw Zach. The men fought but she knew the battle wouldn't last long. Zach had rage, but the hit man had skill.

She crawled toward the tire iron, wrapped her fingers around the cold metal and stumbled to her feet. Waiting for an opportune moment, Jess swung the iron like a golf club into the hit man's head. He fell beside Zach, as solid as a bag of sand.

"Is he dead?" Zach asked, sitting up and wiping blood from a split lip.

"I don't think so." Jess lay her head against the hit man's back and listened to his heart. It was steady. "But let's make sure he stays incapacitated." She hunted around until she found the roll of tape he'd used on Raphael. In less than thirty seconds, the unconscious man was bound and gagged.

She breathed a sigh of relief then sat back on her heels to survey the damage while ignoring the pounding in her head.

This was not going as she'd planned. Not at all. Then, nothing about this assignment—from Zach to the boat blowing up to Al being in the hospital—was, so why would this situation be any different?

She glanced at the still-bound and gagged Raphael. At least some things were working to her benefit. Dragging the tire iron, she walked over to him, staring down her nose. There was blood on the floor, and she realized he was missing a fingernail. She shuddered. Fingertips were one of the most sensitive parts of the human body. To remove a nail like that was brutal and animalistic. She shuddered again at the thought.

She set the tire iron down. "I am going to take the tape off. If you scream, I will put it back on. Do you understand?"

He nodded.

She ripped the tape off.

Rafael screeched then glared at Jess. "You're dead."

"Apparently not."

"How did you get away? We searched that boat." His focus turned to Zach. "I blew you up."

"Wrong again," Zach said, coming to stand at Jess's side.

Jess smiled. "As fascinating as your questions are, we'd rather you answer ours."

"What kind of questions?" His eyes narrowed.

He was tough. She had to give him that. She decided to start at the beginning. "Who hired you?"

His eyes darkened with fear. "I can't say. He'll kill me."

He? She thought it was Arachne. Perhaps the criminal mastermind had a partner.

It didn't matter. Whoever hired him had him scared. Not that she cared. "What makes you think he won't anyway? Your friends are dead. You wouldn't be here if you thought you were safe."

"But if I talk, I know I'm dead," Raphael countered.

Jess ran a hand through her hair. She hated interrogations. She might hurt someone in a fight but that was mutual carnage. To inflict pain on someone who was tied up went against her nature.

She took a deep breath and reminded herself that she was a Marine and an Oracle agent and with those positions came responsibilities and with responsibilities came unpleasant tasks. "I'll kill you if you don't," she said. "Or worse."

Rafael looked at her, hesitated, then said, "No, I don't think you will."

Smartass. She wasn't sure she could pull fingernails, but she had methods. She backhanded Raphael across the face.

Zach jumped but didn't say a word. She breathed a silent *thanks*. There was nothing worse than being undermined in front of a prisoner.

Rafael spat blood and glared at her. "If that is all you got, let me go now."

"No, I have more. Lots more." Jess tapped her foot, counting off the seconds and showing her impatience. "One thought is that I might let you go, even if you don't talk, and just put out word that you snitched."

"No one will believe it."

"Sure they will. Or I work a deal with him," she pointed to the still-unconscious hit man, "and let him finish his job. Now, who hired you?"

"Bitch," Raphael spat.

Before she could respond, Zach flashed forward and hit Raphael hard enough to knock him backward. He landed with a crash and a scream as his weight came down on his bound wrists and wounded fingertip. "Never talk to her that way again," Zach said, pulling him back up. "Or I'll take out every tooth in your head. The hard way. Through your ass."

Rafael glared at him, but Jess finally saw what she wanted to see in his dark-eyed gaze.

Fear.

It wouldn't take much to break him now. Just the suggestion of pain might be enough. "Zach, can you get me a pair of pliers?"

"Sure."

Raphael's eyes widened.

So did Zach's, but he grabbed a pair off the workbench, he handed them to Jess.

She cast one more glance at the hit man. He was still out. Damn. This would be so much easier if she could use him as an example.

Jess walked around to the back of Raphael's chair and squatted down. "Tell me, how much did this hurt?" she asked, caressing Rafael's callused hands.

Raphael whimpered and tried to pull away.

Jess grabbed his wrist and held him still. "Zach, I think he'll fight me. Can I get a hand? No pun intended."

Rafael struggled harder, but Zach leaned on his shoulders forcing him still by sheer weight and muscle.

"What are you going to do?" Raphael asked.

"Yank out the other nails," Jess said, her voice strong. But inside, bile rose to the back of her throat. She didn't plan to do any such thing unless it was neccesary. Even looking at his already nailless finger made her want to retch. Grabbing a dirty shoprag, she stuffed it in Rapheal's mouth, then she clamped the tip of the pliers onto the prisoner's pinkie fingernail. "It might take one or two tries," she said. "I've never done this, but I am sure that by the time I do a few, I'll be a pro."

She clamped harder but didn't pull. Didn't need to, she realized, as Rafael screamed and struggled.

The suggestion was enough.

"Hold up," Zach said, letting the man go.

Jess stopped. "Is he ready to talk?"

Zach took out the gag.

"You whore!" Rafael screamed.

"I said to watch your mouth." Zach backhanded the man across the mouth, then taking a deep calm breath, he crammed the rag back in, gagging Rafael. "Guess he's not ready."

Jess shrugged and rested the cold metal against the tip of Raphael's skin.

He screamed again. She stopped, rose and went around to face him. Zach stepped out of the way, and she removed the gag, placing her finger over his lips. "I do not want to do this," she said, "but I will. I think you believe me now."

Rafael nodded, and she saw his cheeks were wet. She removed her finger. "Give me a name."

Rafael took a deep breath. "Will you give me protection?"

Jess sighed. She'd known this was coming. Known he would ask. She glanced at Zach over her shoulder. His face was red. "He tried to kill my father."

She nodded. "I know. And I'm sorry."

She was. He was going to have a hard time forgiving her, but there was a larger issue. She had to catch Arachne, and if it meant making a deal, then she'd do it. She turned back to Rafael. "Yes. I can do that."

"Juan Mercado Tulio."

She knew the name. He was a Colombian warlord. A drug dealer. A killer with money.

But not Arachne.

Chapter 15

"We appreciate your apprehending him, Ms. Whitaker. Mr. Holiday."

"Not a problem, Agent Valdez," Jess replied, thankful that the DEA had a cordial working relationship with the local police that allowed Agent Valdez to fly in from Brasilia and use one of the smaller precinct offices.

It had taken a few hours to convince the local police to cooperate—including helping move the men and call the DEA—but once that was accomplished, they were extremely helpful.

Not every country wanted to assist the American government, but the Rio cops knew scum when they saw it. She leaned against the desk, eyeing the two detainees—Raphael and the hit man. "You should know, I promised him protection."

"From Mercado?"

"Yes." Zach stood next to Jess, legs wide and arms folded over his chest.

Jess nodded in agreement. She'd hated giving that bit of information away—it was hard to break the habit of working on a need-to-know basis—but it was what had convinced the agent to come in the first place.

She sneaked a glance at Zach, but she didn't need to see his eyes to know his emotional state.

Body language told her everything.

Pissed, she surmised. Catching her glance, he glared at her. She turned away. She refused to cajole him or apologize. Sometimes, deals were made. That was reality.

Besides, she suspected that if she tried to convince him to see her point of view, it would only make him angrier.

It was something he had to come to terms with.

"Mercado has hands everywhere," Valdez said. "It will be very difficult to keep him safe."

Sitting inside his jail cell, Raphael grabbed the bars, shaking them. "You said you'd make sure," he said to Jess. "You promised."

She walked over to the cell. Raphael looked scared, and a part of her was pleased by his fear.

"So I did." She ran a hand over her hair. As much as she hated it, she did have a promise to live up to. "I suggest solitary or transport to another facility. Possibly the United States, but that would depend on the Brazilian government. And get his hands looked at."

She returned her attention to Zach and the agent, and realized that Valdez hadn't been listening to her. He was watching Zach, waiting for him to comment.

"Uh, hello?" she said.

Valdez glanced at her then back to Zach.

She rolled her eyes as she realized what was happening.

She might be a Marine, tough, able to kick ass with the best of them—but she was also a woman.

Zach was the man, and the possession of a penis automatically made him the one in charge.

Damned macho countries.

Zach stared past her at Raphael. "Save him from Mercado since that was the arrangement."

Jess flinched at the animosity in the words.

"But otherwise," Zach said. "I want your assurance that he'll feel my pain. He hurt my family."

"Of course," Agent Valdez nodded. "I understand completely."

Jess bit her lip to keep from making a comment about either Raphael's safety or Zach's request. Although not what she had in mind, they weren't mutually exclusive. It would be enough.

"What about him?" The agent nodded toward the man on the floor of the second cell. The hit man was awake now, but no one had taken the tape from his mouth or bothered to untie him.

Not that it mattered. He wasn't trying to talk, and Jess knew he wouldn't. Men like that were paid large sums to keep their mouths shut.

"I have no idea who he is," Jess said before Zach could reply. "Run his prints, and if that doesn't get you anywhere, I'd say charge him with kidnapping and keep him jailed."

Frankly, she didn't care what they charged him with as long as he stayed out of her way.

"You will stay until the arraignment?" Valdez asked, his attention still directed at Zach.

"We can't," Jess said.

"We're going after Mercado," Zach finished.

Jess bit her tongue, again. What was he thinking? That was definitely a need-to-know.

Agent Valdez's eyes widened. "That is not wise."

"No choice," Jess explained. "I want to catch him before he discovers his man was apprehended."

"*We* want to catch him," Zach corrected.

"May I ask why?" Valdez asked.

Zach glanced at Jess and she glared at him, daring him to mention the laptop. If he did, she might have to tape his mouth shut, as well. "We have our reasons," Zach said.

She relaxed an iota.

"We've been trying to catch him for years," Valdez said. "I can tell you this much, his complex is impenetrable unless you plan to go in with an army."

"Taking on Mercado isn't my idea of a good time, but if we lose this window, it'll be a helluva lot harder." Jess prayed Valdez wasn't going to be a stiff-necked, rule-book-quoting pain in her ass.

The agent took in the information then offered her a slow nod. "And you?" he asked Zach.

This time, Jess didn't bother to hide an annoyed sigh, not that either man paid it any attention. Valdez was too involved with talking to the *man,* and for Zach there was nothing but anger and revenge. She missed the other Zach, she realized. The funny man. Loyal. Smart. Kind.

"I want to end this," Zach said. Taking a piece of paper from the desk, he wrote something down. "Here's my e-mail and phone number. If you have any questions, let me know, and we can be back within twenty-four hours of receiving the message."

If we're alive after all this, Jess thought.

The agent nodded. "I'll give my people a call. They can meet your flight. Give you whatever help you need."

"Thanks," Jess said. If they were taking on Arachne, they'd need all the help they could get.

"What the hell was that about?" Jess asked after they left the station and walked back to their car.

"What do you mean?" Zach asked, neither breaking stride nor looking at her.

She hurried to catch up with him, his longer legs giving him the advantage on speed. "What do I mean? Are you kidding me? That whole boys' club thing you had going on."

He shrugged with stiff shoulders. "I did what was needed to get us out of there. Is that a problem?"

"A problem?" She stopped, grabbing his arm. He halted in his tracks.

"What?" he growled, glaring down at her.

"The problem is that we're a team. You can't just shunt me off to one side, make all the decisions and then act like what I want doesn't matter."

His eyes raked over her. "You mean, like when you decided to cut a deal with Raphael?"

Jess's cheeks flamed with heat at the accusation. "That was different," she said, realizing how weak the reason sounded as soon as it left her lips.

"How?" He edged toward her, pushing her back against the outside of the police station. "Tell me, Jess, how was it different? Because you're secret-agent girl, and I'm just some dumb geek?"

He was right, and she knew it. "That's not it at all," she said, searching for a way to save face and not finding it.

"Look at me and say that," Zach said, his body pressed against hers.

"Or you'll do what?" Jess asked, the stucco digging into

her back. She might have made a mistake but she'd be damned if she'd take Zach's heavy-handedness. "Squash me?"

Zach twitched, as if just realizing what he was doing. He backed away a few inches. "You know what I mean. Through this whole enterprise, you've made decisions for me. For my crew. Without any regard to anything but the mission."

He shook his head in what she thought was a combination of disgust and frustration. "There are people involved here. Lives at stake."

"This is *my* job," Jess replied. "And it has been from the day you took the money."

"I'll give you that." Zach lowered his eyes. "But when we decided to do this *together,* when *we* came to Rio, it became my job, too."

Together. We. It all meant one thing—a *team.* He was her team and had been since the day they'd met. There was no use denying that any longer. Jess leaned against the building with a heavy sigh. "I'm an ass," she said.

Zach took a step back. "What?"

"I said that I'm an ass."

He raised a brow as if doubting her sincerity.

"I'm not a guy," she said with a small smile. "I can admit when I'm wrong."

His brow rose higher. "Is that supposed to be an apology?"

She nodded. "As good as I can offer."

The corners of his mouth turned up, his anger fading a notch, though she still saw a hardness in his eyes that troubled her. "I was, too," he said. "I noticed that Agent Valdez was pissing you off, and I didn't discourage it."

"You wanted to make me mad?"

He nodded. "A part of me did, yes."

"You still angry?" she asked, wishing there was something

she could say to put an end to their animosity. She didn't want to fight with Zach. Hated it, in fact.

"A bit," he admitted.

Her heart fell a little, but she forced herself to smile. "At least you're honest."

He touched her cheek. "I'm not angry at you. Just at the situation." His touch traveled across her cheek and into her hair. He pulled her close. "I want to catch Mercado and put an end to this."

Jess took a deep breath, inhaling him—he smelled of sun and sweat. "As long as we're making confessions, I need to talk to you about that."

"I can handle this," he said, his head next to hers. "You won't have to worry about me freezing or hesitating."

"That's not it," she said, looking up at him. Delphi was going to be pissed with her decision, but it was her decision. She was not going to keep lying to Zach. "Mercado is a means to an end, a stepping stone. If possible, we want to catch his boss, and that's why the laptop is so important. It contains information on Arachne."

"Arachne? Like a spider?"

Before she had time to explain, noise from inside the police station, barely audible through the thick window glass above their heads, caught her attention. Someone was pleading. Begging.

She recognized the voice.

Raphael. A tiny, dark part of her hoped that Valdez was taking a pound of flesh out of the pirate.

The pleading went higher in pitch.

Dammit. She'd promised to keep the scum safe. "We should stop Valdez before he does something stupid," she said. "I promised."

"Do we have to?" Zach asked.

She nodded, and they walked back to the door. She opened it a crack and heard two distinct popping noises.

The pleading stopped.

Jess froze. She knew that noise.

A silencer. And her gut told her a single, cold truth—both Raphael and the hit man were dead.

Carefully, she shut the door, putting up a hand to signal Zach to be silent. Standing to the side, she waited, heart racing.

Valdez didn't emerge.

The wooden door was thick but warped. Staying to the side, she lowered herself until she was flat on the ground. Putting her ear next to the space between door and jamb, she strained to hear inside the police station.

"Tell Mercado it's taken care of," Valdez said.

Sudden fury raced through Jess. He worked for Mercado. She'd kill him.

Zach placed a hand on her shoulder and shook his head as if reading her thoughts.

She took a deep breath, reined in her temper and listened.

"I don't know," Valdez said. "I'll have Anderson and Smith meet them. Find out what they know then dump the bodies."

He hesitated as the person at the other end of the phone spoke.

"Just him then," Valdez said. "I'll have them bring the girl to you. No. No witnesses."

He wished, Jess thought.

Valdez laughed then there was silence.

She motioned for Zach to move. It was time to leave.

Hunched over, they hurried down the sidewalk then turned the corner as the front door to the police station opened behind them.

Ducking behind an oversize garbage container, they

pressed themselves flat against the wall. Valdez walked past them, confident in his success.

Jess motioned for Zach to remain hidden. She counted to thirty in her head. "Let's get out of here," she whispered.

Zach gave a deliberate, thoughtful nod that chilled her almost as much as hearing Valdez murder two men. "This is bad."

"Understatement," Jess replied.

Sitting in the airport terminal, Jess sipped coffee and watched Zach work on his laptop. His unfocused look was familiar. She glanced at the screen.

It was a blur of computer code.

No wonder his look was blank. She'd be brain-dead if she had to decipher the jumble of numbers, letters and symbols.

She returned her attention to the people walking past them. Families. Singles. All tanned because, hell, it was Rio and that's what people did in Rio. They tanned. Partied. Vacationed.

And occasionally were killed by DEA agents gone wrong.

She rested her head in her hands. Rafael was scum, she reminded herself. A mercenary. Killer for hire.

But she'd promised to keep him safe, and while that meant nothing to a man like Rafael, it meant everything to her.

Promises. Promises.

Just like Charles. Slowly, she exhaled, not wanting to think about Charles and the merc but unable to stop herself.

She closed her eyes, willing her mind to go blank. Thier plane was departing in an hour, and she hoped he was close to getting something, *anything,* that would give them an advantage.

"Jess." Her eyes popped open.

On the laptop's screen, what looked like schematics took the place of the earlier gibberish. "What's that?"

"Blueprints to Mercado's compound," Zach replied.

Her jaw dropped. Taking his face in her hands, she kissed his mouth. "I'm not even going to ask how," she said, "because I'm sure I wouldn't understand the answer."

Zach smiled. His first genuine one since seeing Al at the hospital. A tension she hadn't even been aware of loosened inside Jess's chest.

"What am I looking at?" she asked, scooting closer and keeping her voice low.

"A couple of things," Zach said. "An alarm system that includes cameras, motion detectors. These—" he pointed to another area "—are the perimeter defenses."

"Which are what?"

"Besides the twenty-foot wall, there's an electric fence. Cameras. Basically, the works." He leaned back. "This man believes in home security."

"Okay," Jess said, processing the information. The security would be a lot easier to deal with if they knew where to go. "How about the laptop? Any indication of where he might have it on the compound?"

"Not yet, but there are a lot of files to access, and some of the encryption is damned good."

"You can't break it?"

"I didn't say that. I just said it was good." He smiled. "I'm better, but it'll still take time."

"How much time?"

He shrugged. "No idea."

"Hours? Days? A week or more?"

"Yes."

Jess groaned. She was out of patience and time and didn't want to take her irritation out on Zach.

But she had to retrieve the laptop before Arachne picked it up. "Can you even tell if the laptop is still there?" she asked.

Zach hit a few buttons and the screen changed. "It doesn't look like anyone has visited the compound in a few days so I think it's safe to say it's still on the premises."

"Anyone coming to visit?"

He shrugged. "That, I can't tell you. Too many variables."

Jess took a deep breath. "Then we need to get inside. Question Mercado. Get the laptop if it's still there and get out."

Zach frowned. "Getting inside is going to be problematic. I wasn't kidding when I said Mercado believed in home defense. There's the fence. Floodlights. High towers at each corner, which, I'm guessing, are manned by big men with big guns."

Jess crossed her arms. "Can you work the defenses? Not just look at them?"

Zach hesitated then changed the screen again back to the previous one. "I'm not sure. He runs both a wireless system and a hard-line. The wireless runs the cameras, alarms, things like that. Anything that's hardwired, including the lights and fence, will be more difficult."

Why did drug lords have to live in freaking fortresses? Jess's mind whirled. Searched for options. Anything. And found one. The idea didn't thrill her but it would also be unexpected.

Not unexpected, a voice inside her head whispered. *Suicidal.*

She told the voice to shut the hell up. "If you had help from the inside, could you turn off the defenses?" she asked.

Zach hesitated. "Yes," he replied, dragging the word out as he considered what she was asking. "But what are you going to do? Pay off one of his people? I'm thinking that will get us caught and killed."

Jess shook her head. "No. I'm going to let Anderson and Smith take me."

Zach's eyes widened. "Are you out of your mind?"

Yes, was her first thought. "Nope," she replied.

"How do you expect to get out?"

"That's why I need you to be able to turn off the perimeter defenses. If I let them take me, getting in will be easy. It'll be the getting out that's hard—especially after I steal the laptop."

"That is the most insane plan I have ever heard." Zach's mouth thinned. "I am not letting you do this."

"Letting me?" Jess asked, bristling.

Zach continued. "I almost lost my dad. I will not lose my girlfriend."

"Girlfriend?" The bristles died down.

Zach's face flushed then he smiled at her. "Yeah. Girlfriend."

Jess scratched her arm, not sure what to say. But the thought…*girlfriend,* she liked it. She smiled back, feeling like a teenager. "We have the worst timing in the world."

"No arguments here," Zach said, putting his arm around her. "But that doesn't change the fact that getting captured is still about the worst idea I've ever heard."

"I'm running out of time."

"I?"

"*We're* running out of time," she corrected. "If we don't put a stop to this, do something over-the-top and unexpected, Arachne will outwit us and have both me and the laptop." She rested her head in her hands, wishing she could think of another option. Something less dangerous.

"That's the second time you've mentioned that name," Zach said. "Who is this Arachne person?"

Jess rubbed her eyes with the heels of her hands. "She is a blackmailer, a thief, a killer, and she wants me and anyone who is like me."

Zach's eyes widened. "There are others who can breathe underwater?"

Jess shook her head. "Not as far as I know, but there are other girls who are different. Gifted. And she will do anything to capture them. Me."

"Why?"

Jess shook her head again. "We don't know, but that's why I need that laptop. We have to find her first, and I'm running out of options, Zach."

His hand squeezed her shoulder then worked its way to her neck, massaging her tense muscles. "I know. But this is suicide."

She sighed at his touch. "It isn't," she said, her voice muffled. "I'm trained for this kind of operation."

Zach hesitated. "I don't like it."

"Neither do I." She sat up, and his hand slid down her back, giving her goose bumps. "I need you to trust me," she said. "Trust me to do my job, and I'll trust you to do yours."

He frowned, but she saw his resolution falter. "Please," she said. "Trust me."

Finally, he nodded. "You'll have to get out of wherever they put you," he said. "Get to a computer to signal me." His voice sounded calm but in his eyes, she saw the worry. The fear. For her. "What if you can't?"

"I can," she said with more assurance than she felt. "Just tell me what I'll have to do once I get in there."

For a moment, she thought he might not agree. Instead, he scrubbed at his face, and when he looked up, he was all business. "Once you're inside, I'll turn off the cameras and the alarm system. That way you'll be able to move around, get the computer and signal me. Get to a phone, steal a cell phone or whatever, and I can walk you through what we'll have to do to turn off the electricity."

"How will I know when you've turned off the alarms?"

He hesitated. "I'll sound the system for a second then turn it off."

She frowned. "Won't they suspect something?"

He shook his head. "I can make it look like a glitch. Besides, I don't leave footprints," he said with a grim smile. The smile faded as quickly as it had arrived and his eyes bored into hers. "Just be careful. I don't want to lose you."

Girlfriend.

She managed a weak smile. "I don't plan on getting lost."

Chapter 16

The flight to Colombia was one of the most nerve-racking of Jess's life. It wasn't the turbulence or the crowded, narrow seats.

It was the anticipation of what waited for her at the end.

She followed the crowd through the air-conditioned airport to customs, wishing for the millionth time that Zach was with her, but they'd both agreed that it was best if she convinced Anderson and Smith she'd ditched Zach in Rio. Thanks to Valdez, she was sure the men knew her background and would believe that a Marine would not want a civilian around.

If they bothered to check, they'd see that Zach was on a flight to Puerto Isla. Tomorrow, he'd fly to Colombia.

With luck, once they saw he was going to Puerto Isla, he'd fall off Mercado's and Arachne's radars.

If their luck went south—she shivered at the thought—her plan was going to be whole lot harder. Not impossible, she told herself as she cleared customs.

Harder.

Shouldering her small carry-on bag, she scanned the crowd as she headed toward the exit but she didn't notice anyone who appeared DEA.

Dammit, where were they?

She cleared the exit. The heat made her catch her breath. Blinking in the sun, she slipped her sunglasses on, then coughed as exhaust from the waiting taxis overwhelmed her.

The place was a madhouse, she realized. Cars were parked askew as people waited for friends and loved ones. Other cars honked, wanting a coveted curb location. And still others circled like vultures.

And amongst it all were people and luggage.

She hoped the rogue agents were able to find her or this elaborate scheme was going to be an elaborate failure.

"Ms. Whitaker?"

She looked up to see two men walking down the sidewalk toward her. One dark-haired. One blond. Broad-shouldered and tall, they sported matching sunglasses, and despite the tropical heat, both wore dark suits. They had to be Anderson and Smith.

Finally.

She stopped, taking a few seconds to observe them as they grew closer. From their carriage and movement, she knew they were trained, which was neither good nor bad, just something to deal with.

"May I help you?" she asked, playing coy and wary.

The dark-haired man held out his hand. "Agent Anderson and this is Agent Smith." He nodded toward the blonde, who looked out of place in the tropics. "Agent Valdez asked us to meet you."

No doubt he asked you to do more than that, Jess thought, but she held out her hand and flashed them a relaxed, and fabricated, smile. "Please, call me Jess. I'm glad to see he remembered."

"Of course. Mercado is a dangerous man." Anderson looked around then frowned. "Where's Mr. Holiday?"

Jess adjusted her bag, switching it to her other shoulder. "I sent him back to Puerto Isla."

Anderson's frown deepened.

"I know. I know." Jess held up her hand before he could respond. "You probably wanted to speak to him about Mercado, but frankly, he's an untrained civilian. You know how it is. Everyone wants to be Dirty Harry, but mostly they just get in the way and get agents killed."

Argue with that, she thought, as she watched his reaction through her dark lenses.

Though clearly irritated, Anderson sighed in resignation. "We can always send someone for him if needed, I suppose."

"That was my thought," Jess said, praying he didn't follow through. "But I should be able to tell you anything you need to know."

He looked at her, his eyes unreadable through his sunglasses. She could only imagine what he was thinking, but she was sure it wasn't pleasant.

"I guess it'll have to do," Anderson replied. Taking her elbow, he guided Jess to a parking garage with Smith trailing them.

"Does he talk?" Jess said, looking back at Smith.

"Very little," Anderson said, as he hurried her along. "He's what one would call stoic."

And from the way his muscles bunched and tensed, angry. At everything. She matched her steps with Anderson. "So, where are we going?" Jess asked as the entered the shade of the cement parking garage.

"To our office," he said, without hesitation.

She glanced at the agent out of the corner of her eye. He looked unconcerned. Comfortable.

Damn, he was good.

Which was *not* good.

They continued walking past rows of cars, deep into the parking structure and farther away from the crowds. "Where did you guys park? Peru?" Jess joked, although she knew exactly what was going on.

If things went wrong they did not want witnesses.

"We're here." Anderson pulled a key chain from his pocket, hit a button and a black Lincoln Continental beeped and flashed its lights.

He opened the back door for her. She glanced inside before she entered. Comfortable. Clean. Dark, tinted windows.

And no handle on the inside. She hesitated. This was it. Once she got in this car, she'd be Mercado's prisoner. The thought of intentionally putting herself in harm's way went against her nature.

"Anything wrong?" Anderson asked.

"No. Nothing," she said.

"Then get in." Anderson chuckled, keeping up the illusion of being a "good guy."

But even as he laughed, Smith cracked. "Get in. Now," he barked. And worse, there was the distinct sound of a gun hammer being cocked.

"Smith," hissed Anderson, obviously pissed.

Jess dropped her bag and slammed her fist into Anderson's sternum. He doubled over. She bolted between cars.

Not that she planned, or wanted, to escape, but with Smith's over-the-top reaction, she had to try. Had to put on a good show of panic. If she didn't, they'd know she was up to something. After all, she was a pro.

Feet pounded on the cement behind her, but no bullets followed. No doubt, they'd been ordered to take her alive.

Thank God for small favors, she thought, crouching low.

"Ms. Whitaker, there are two of us. You're not going to get away," Smith shouted.

Jess didn't respond but kept low, staying behind the larger vehicles and making her way to another row.

She glanced through the windows. Anderson was no longer next to the Continental. Good. Maybe this wouldn't take too long. She shut her eyes, listening for the second set of footsteps. *Nothing.*

"We're armed, Ms. Whitaker," Smith shouted, distracting her. He yammered on but she didn't listen.

Let them think the ploy worked. Cautiously, she glanced around the bumper of an SUV. A squeak of a shoe signaled the flight was over.

It wouldn't be long now, she realized.

Then there was a shooting pain in her head. She fell over onto the cement, and the last thing she saw was Anderson over her, a gun in his hand.

Stinging cold woke Jess, and she sputtered in surprise.

Someone pounded on her back, and she gasped as she caught her breath.

"I apologize for the abrupt awakening, Ms. Whitaker," a smooth, accented voice said. "But I have little patience, and you didn't seem inclined to wake up."

Jess finished her coughing fit, shook herself and tried to push the water from her eyes only to find her hands tied behind her back. She blinked, trying to clear her vision. Her mind.

She was at Mercado's, she realized as the fog cleared. Which meant the plan was in motion.

She was tied to a chair. A prisoner. Her throat choked at the thought.

Stay calm, she reminded herself. All you have to do is stay calm, stay focused, until Zach signals that it's safe to move about.

She shook her head and someone wiped her eyes with a soft cloth. Silk?

"Better?" the voice asked.

She looked up to see a man sitting across from her. He folded a handkerchief and slid it into his pocket.

He was handsome, she thought at first glance. Black hair. Smooth hands. Polite. Dressed in black linen pants and a pearl-gray, silk shirt, he was the perfect middle-aged, Latin lover.

Then he looked at her. His eyes were so dark they were almost black, and there was nothing behind them. They were soulless. Hard.

A chill ran through her, and though she'd never seen his picture, she knew who it was.

Mercado.

She gave a slow nod. "Much better, thank you," she said, sensing that the drug lord might value politeness. She tugged at her bonds. "If I wasn't trussed, I would be more comfortable."

Mercado smiled, but it didn't reach his eyes. "I regret your distress, but knowing your background, it seemed the safest course."

"Of course," she agreed, letting sarcasm tinge her voice. If politeness wouldn't work, why bother?

She pointedly looked away from Mercado and assessed her surroundings. Far from a cell, she was being held in a sparsely furnished bedroom. The few items she could see—a double bed, dresser and side table—were antiques. Spanish from design.

Also expensive. Originals, without a doubt.

Men like Mercado didn't do anything half-assed—she tested the ropes again—including tying up their captives.

There was no table between them, and Mercado slid his chair across the tiled floor until they were knee to knee. "We need to talk, Ms. Whitaker."

"About what?" Jess asked, wishing she could back up.

"I have put forth considerable effort to capture you. Expenses. Men. Time. I would like to know why you are such a valuable asset."

He didn't know? She wanted to smile at that small amount of good fortune, but kept her face blank. "I have no idea," she lied. If she told the truth, that Arachne wanted her because of her mutation, he'd either call her a liar or worse—he might believe her. Then who knew what he might do to her.

He leaned in until he was inches from her face. His breath, smelling of strong coffee, was hot against her skin. "I do not like to be toyed with, Ms. Whitaker, and when I ask a question, I expect an answer."

"I don't know what you mean," Jess insisted, keeping herself controlled. If she showed fear, he would use it and she was not giving him any advantage. "Why don't you ask your boss?"

"I have no boss," Mercado growled.

"Oh, sorry, your owner. *Arachne.* What's she going to do when she finds out you're questioning me instead of turning me over to her?"

Mercado's dark eyes turned black, and Jess realized she should have stuck with politeness. In that split second of back talk, she'd pushed the drug lord too far.

The first backhand slap rocked her head. She tasted blood in her mouth, and she glared at the drug lord.

The second slap knocked her sideways, sending both her and the chair to the floor.

She hit the tiles hard, but held her voice, refusing to cry out. Despite the pain, she was almost giddy. She'd been right in her assumption that the man was working with Arachne, though not as a partner.

Lackey was more like it.

"What's wrong?" Jess asked. From the tingling in her lower lip, she was sure it was split. She swiped it with her tongue and tasted blood. "Doesn't she know I'm here?"

"Arachne knows what I want her to know," Mercado replied.

Hands grabbed her, pulling both her and the chair upright. With a bodyguard flanking him on each side—she realized they must have been behind her—Mercado tilted her head up, forcing her to meet his black-eyed gaze.

There was something behind the anger and the pride. Fear. Did Arachne have something over Mercado? What would scare a drug lord? Mercado continued to glare at her.

"I will not tolerate impudence, Ms. Whitaker. What is it you know that is so important? Why does she want you?"

"I don't know," Jess said, refusing to back down.

Mercado raised his hand again, but hesitated. Held it. Taking a deep breath, he looked at Jess as if she were nothing.

Less than nothing.

Another chill washed over her, but she refused to turn away. If he wanted to hurt her, she'd show him that it would take more than a beating to make her talk.

Rising, he turned on his heel and headed to the door. "Cut her loose," he called over his shoulder. "She cannot go anywhere."

One of the bodyguards circled her. There was the *snick* of a blade and the ropes fell away from her wrists.

They walked out, locking the heavy door.

Jess rose, rubbing her hands to encourage blood flow. Now

that she could see the rest of the room, she realized there were cameras in two corners, covering the entire room.

Figured, she thought.

She walked over to the window. Though barred on the outside, she cranked open the glass panes and tested the metal rods. They were solid.

Beyond them was a wide expanse of green lawn then ocean. *Home.* She stared at the water made pink by sunset.

Finally, with a shake of her head and a sigh, she turned away. She had better things to do than watch the sunset. She needed to formulate an escape plan. One that would be easy to implement once Zach killed the alarms and cameras.

She walked over to the door, and pulled on the heavy handle. An alarm sounded—no doubt caused by her touching the door. Ignoring it, she pulled harder.

The door didn't give an inch.

But the alarm increased in pitch. Backing away, she put her hands over her ears until the noise died as suddenly as it had started.

Relieved, she uncovered her ears, but in the silence, another sound caught her attention. Something metallic. She looked up.

The camera. It swiveled to watch her

She held up her middle finger. "What did you expect?" she asked.

There was no answer and no one came.

She turned away, smiling. Their dependence on technology to watch her would be their downfall.

She had a technological genius on her side.

She glanced at the heavy, wooden door. Even after Zach killed the alarms, she would have to get out of the room. Perhaps picking the lock? Surveying the room, she frowned.

Other than the bedsprings, there wasn't much to work with, and items like bedsprings only worked in movies.

Her mind flipped through scenarios. This was going to be a bitch. Not impossible. But still, a pain.

She paced over to the window then stopped. The sun was still above the horizon.

In fact, she realized, it was higher. And the sky wasn't darkening.

It grew lighter with each passing second.

A feeling of dread crept over her.

This wasn't sunset. It was sunrise. Over the ocean.

Which meant she wasn't on the west coast. She was on the east. Her stomach rolled over as she processed the rest of the information.

She wasn't in Mercado's compound. She was somewhere else entirely.

Zach wasn't coming.

Jess stood at the window, staring at the ocean as the sun finally began its path downward. She was screwed.

She knew it. Mercado knew it.

Behind her, the door squeaked open. Whoever came in didn't speak, and she didn't turn.

There was a rustling, and the door closed.

She turned to see a tray sitting on the floor.

She walked over. Tuna salad sandwich. Cut fruit. Bottled water. Not fancy, but food.

Ignoring the sandwich—who knew what he might have laced it with and why make it easier for her keeper—she took a chance and broke the seal on the water, gestured toward the cameras in a mock toast and gulped it down, hoping that they'd provide a bathroom break in case she needed one.

Tossing the bottle to the floor, she went back to the window to watch the sunset. It wouldn't be long now. She was surprised they hadn't come back already.

Perhaps there was a problem. Maybe Zach had arrived. Brought help.

A halfhearted chuckle escaped her lips at the flight of fancy. She was on her own. She knew that. No one to save her. No backup.

Certainly no Knight in Shining Armor.

Just her. Not that she was incapable of saving herself, but she'd just accepted that she and Zach were a team.

A team of two.

"Zach," she whispered his name. Would she see him again? Was he at Mercado's Colombia compound looking for her or had he figured out she wasn't there?

He was smart, she reminded herself. A genius.

Who was she kidding? Neither of them had considered this flaw in their plan.

She leaned against the window ledge. The sky was just starting to purple, and she willed the sun to hurry into the ocean. Once she had darkness on her side, she'd try to get away. All she had to do was make it to the water, she told herself. Once she was in the ocean, she'd be safe.

But first, she had to get there. There was no way she was escaping out a barred window.

It had to be the door, but first things first. And now was the time.

She eyed the hated cameras. Grabbing a chair, she walked over to the first camera, the one that covered the door.

Standing on the chair, she glared at the camera then using both hands, ripped it from the ceiling.

Wires trailing, she tossed it to the floor then crushed it with her foot.

The large wooden door flung open, banging into the wall. Anderson barged through. "Cease and desist, Ms. Whitaker."

Jess glared at him. "Hello again, *Agent* Anderson. Taking a little vacation from catching the bad guys to become one of them?"

Storming over, he grabbed her arm and dragged her to the bed. "You will behave, or I will tie you up."

"Just you? Are you sure you're capable of acting on your own? Or did Mercado say that was okay?"

Anderson took a step toward her, stopped and shook his head. "You're not worth it," he sneered. "Touch that other camera and you'll be sorry."

She rolled her eyes in contempt, and he slammed the door as he left.

Silently, Jess sat on the bed, and stared at the door as the room darkened around her. She left the lights off. Not that the remaining camera needed it. No doubt, it was equipped with infra of some kind or perhaps a motion detector.

There was nothing in the room to pick the locks.

The hinges.

She tried not to smile at the idea. The door opened inward. The hinges were on the inside. Which meant she could get to them.

If she could find something to pop them upward. Even oiled, it would take more than fingertips to pull the pins out. She glanced around the darkening room. There wasn't much to work with.

Correction—there wasn't *anything* to work with. Frustration rose and she pushed it to the back of her mind. Focus, she reminded herself. You're a Marine. You're trained.

Use it.

There was only one thing she could think of. One way to bring them into the room under her terms instead of theirs.

She turned to the remaining camera, arms crossed over her chest. "I want to talk," she said. "Take me to Mercado."

Chapter 17

The heavy door swung open.

"Ms. Whitaker." Anderson stood aside to let Jess walk in front of him.

She stepped into the hall and the barrel of a gun pressed into her lower back. "This way, if you please," he said, herding her to the left.

Jess walked down the hallway, her feet silent on the long Persian rug. Despite Anderson crowding behind her, she kept her pace slow, allowing her mind to race as she tried to think of what she'd tell Mercado.

She could always tell him she had gills, she mused as she took in the details of the art-filled hallway. The only problem would be if he believed her.

No, she realized. The lie needed to be pertinent to Mercado. Something that he wanted to believe.

"How much farther?" she asked when they'd gone down

the length of the hallway, turned right down another hall and didn't show any signs of slowing.

"You do not ask the questions, Ms. Whitaker. We do," Anderson replied, his tone low and carefully modulated.

The passage ended at a large, carved wooden door that was as formidable as the one they'd used to hold her.

She wasn't surprised. According to the blueprints Zach had shown her, Mercado was obsessed with security and keeping people where he wanted them, whether that be inside his complex or outside the walls.

Zach. Her insides twisted at the thought of him. Where was he? Was he safe?

Had they gone after him?

The need to know almost overwhelmed her with its sudden intensity, but she held back her questions, knowing that any attention she brought to Zach would only hurt him.

"Open it," Anderson said, interrupting her thoughts. She turned the knob, stepped through and found herself in an overgrown, tropical garden. Hanging lamps dotted the edges and kept the night at bay while highlighting the bougainvillea that crept up the large, enclosing wall.

Mercado sat at a wrought iron table next to a white fountain that gave the illusion of serenity with its burbling water. "Sit," he said, gesturing at the chair across from him.

Jess sat and noticed there was a bottle of champagne in a bucket next to the drug lord.

He poured a glass and set it in front of her.

"I'd prefer water," she said, not touching the crystal flute.

The one bottle earlier wasn't enough to keep her body saturated. Since she spent the day in a cool room, she hadn't felt the effects of dehydration. *Yet.* But she needed to be at her best if she planned to escape, and alcohol would only dehydrate her.

Mercado snapped his fingers, and Jess heard the door behind her open. Less than a minute later, Anderson returned with a pitcher and glass. Setting them in front of her, he poured, sloshing the clear liquid over the ledge.

Jess drained it and held the glass out. "Do you mind?" she asked, knowing he hated serving her and perfectly happy to heap insult on him.

"Pour it yourself."

"You do not speak to my guests in such a manner," Mercado snapped.

Anderson poured.

Jess didn't bother to thank him.

"So, what is it you wish to tell me?" Mercado asked, his eyes black and dilated in the dim light of the lanterns.

So much for niceties, Jess thought, taking a quick moment to glance over Mercado's head at the wall behind him. Fifteen feet high? At the most, she decided. But what trailed along the top? Barbed wire? Electric fence? The poor man's security of broken bottles imbedded in cement?

She smiled to herself, doubting the latter. Mercado was not poor, and a man like himself wanted to make sure everyone knew his worth.

The bigger question was could she get over before they shot her?

She returned her attention to Mercado. *Please, let this work.* "Arachne wants me because I have detailed information on how the United States plans to work with the South American government to get rid of the drug lords."

Simple. Pertinent. And believable.

She hoped.

Glass in hand, she watched Mercado's expression, wondering if he bought the story.

The drug lord stared at her, tapping his chin as he considered her story. "How do you know these plans? Why are you privy to them?"

He wasn't a total fool, she thought, but neither was she. "I'm a spy. Knowing things is what I do."

Mercado snapped his fingers, and Anderson handed him a file. "This says you are a Marine. Not a spy."

"I can't be both?"

"Possibly."

She didn't miss the doubt in his voice, but she drank her water, waiting. Letting him lead.

"Who do you spy for?" Mercado pressed.

There was no way she was telling him about Oracle—not even to save herself. "Does it matter?"

He took a sip of champagne. "It does."

She shook her head. "I beg to differ."

Mercado sighed and his hand stilled. "Ms. Whitaker, you are not the first person I have *detained*. My experience is that people will say, or do, anything to save themselves."

Okay. He was smarter than he looked.

Then again, he was a drug lord, she reminded herself. A very successful drug lord. She kept her face blank but wanted to kick herself for assuming that because the man sold cocaine he was inept.

Mercado continued, "On the off chance that you are lying to me as a ruse to escape, let me assure you that escape is impossible."

"The thought never—"

Alarms sounded, cutting her off.

Across from her, Mercado's eyes widened. Moving faster than she thought possible, he reached across the table and grabbed her shirt, pulling her to him. "Who did you contact?" he screamed over the noise, his face red with fury and surprise.

"No one! How could I?" She tried to pull away but he twisted his hands in the black, cotton cloth, holding her tight.

"It is Lorenzo?"

Lorenzo? Her confusion must have shown because he pulled her closer. "Is it?" he screamed.

"Who?" she finally replied.

He pushed her away, and Anderson caught her. "What's going on?" she shouted as he grabbed her arm and hustled her back through the wooden door. "Who's Lorenzo?"

Anderson didn't answer but walked faster, almost running as he hurried her down the hall, the gun in her back again.

Lorenzo? It sounded familiar. *Lorenzo.*

She let the name cycle through her thoughts, and in seconds, found her answer.

Lorenzo Perez.

Another drug baron. Mercado's rival.

And with his timing—possibly her salvation.

Or death.

They reached her room. "Open it," Anderson barked over the sirens. She opened it and stepped inside. The agent reached over to shut the door.

Jess saw her opportunity. Perhaps her only one.

She grabbed the handle and pulled with all her strength, yanking Anderson into the room and off balance. He didn't fall, didn't drop the gun, but he stumbled forward two steps. Before he had time to recover, Jess jammed her right fist forward then her left in a lightning-fast double punch, hitting the rogue agent in his already-bruised solar plexus.

Anderson stopped in his tracks, unable to breathe, but retained his grip on the gun.

Stupid man.

"Drop it," Jess shouted, but he didn't hear her over the wailing of the sirens.

Training taking over thought, Jess grabbed the weapon and twisted until Anderson screamed. He released the weapon, and she watched it fall to her feet.

In that moment of inattention, distraction in watching the gun, she sensed her mistake. Anderson's fist connected with her jaw, knocking her off her feet and confirming the blunder.

She was not going to let him hear her scream, Jess thought, gritting her teeth. Instead, she dropped to her knees, grabbed the gun and squeezed her fingers around the butt.

Before she had time to fire, Anderson kicked her in the side. Her breath caught as he knocked the wind out of her, but when his foot came at her again, size tens in a heavy shoe, she rolled without thinking.

One. Two. Three turns.

Until she was on her side, facing her opponent.

He stalked toward her.

Without hesitation, she shot him on his second step. A double tap, just as she was trained. He stumbled backward as blood soaked the front of his white shirt.

He grabbed the wound, fell to his knees and then over onto the floor, his final expression one of surprise.

"Bastard," Jess muttered as she embraced her bruised ribs and touched her aching jaw. Slowly, she rose, not one ounce of regret in killing the agent but definite regret that she wasn't faster in avoiding his blows.

Her knees shook. "Shake it off, Jess," she said, shunting the pain to a part of her brain that was trained to ignore it. "Shake it off and get to work."

After all, this was the perfect opportunity, and she knew what she had to do. Find Mercado. Get the laptop.

Leave while the leaving was good.

There is no pain, she told herself. Just the mission. Taking a deep breath, she counted to ten. The shaking stopped at seven.

She checked the hallway, wishing the sirens would stop since she couldn't hear herself think, much less hear approaching thugs, over their blaring.

Visual would have to do. The hall was empty. For now.

She could only hope it would remain that way.

Carefully, she hurried back to the garden, hoping Mercado was there. If not, she'd go room by room until she found him.

She reached the end of the hallway. Keeping low, she looked around the corner.

Empty.

Her back to the wall, she reached the garden's door. Taking a deep breath, she turned the knob and flung it open.

"Don't move!" she screamed.

Mercado was gone.

But a man dressed in black was coming over the wall. One of Lorenzo's men? She caught him in her sights as he dropped to the ground.

He turned, a 9 mm in his hand pointed straight at her head. He didn't fire. His hand dropped.

She hesitated, her hand still on the hammer then he stepped into the light. She knew the face. Had kissed that mouth.

Zach.

It couldn't be.

Yet, there he was. Coming to save her. Walking toward her.

She didn't believe it. Couldn't believe it. Not until he was at her side and wrapping his arms around her, his warmth and strength confirming his presence.

Cupping her face in his hands, he kissed her. Quick. Hard. Fast. As if he hadn't seen her for weeks and might never see her again. "Are you okay?" he finally asked, his question barely audible over the noise.

She pulled him close, taking the time to wrap her arms around his neck. "I'm fine," she said, her lips touching his ears.

He looked at her, his green eyes black in the dim light and said something she couldn't understand.

"What?" she shouted.

He said it again.

She shrugged in reply.

Zach let her go, held up a finger to indicate "one minute." Pulling what looked like a small, handheld computer from his jeans pocket, he pushed a few buttons.

The sirens stopped. The silence sudden and welcome.

"Who hit you?" he asked, his gaze directed at her jaw.

"Anderson," she said. "He's dead."

"Good." He pulled her toward the wall where he'd come down. "Let's go."

"I can't," she said, holding her ground. "The objective stays the same. I need to get that laptop."

He hesitated. For a moment, she thought he might argue. Instead, he gave a tight nod. "Let's go."

Jess breathed a sigh a relief. She could do this without Zach, but she preferred to have him. He wasn't a Marine, but he was her partner and that meant everything. "Any idea where to go?"

"For the laptop? No." Zach looked at the handheld and typed something in. "But I have Mercado. He's in a room on the far side of the building."

"You sure?"

He raised a brow. "You have to ask?"

He'd found her when she thought she was off the edges of the map—both paper and electronic. "No. I don't."

She checked the clip on the gun she'd taken from Anderson. Full. She shoved it back in, the familiar click satisfying and the weight of the Sig as comfortable to her as a computer was to Zach. "Just show me the way."

He pointed at the door.

"His men should all be at the perimeter," Zach said in a hushed voice. "I set off charges, as well as the alarms."

She peeked into the hall. He was right. Empty. "Should I ask how you did that?" She felt absurdly pleased at what he'd done. He might be a desk jockey to most of the world, but it was stunning to see what a man with his intelligence could accomplish when motivated.

And all without killing anyone. So far.

"Later. When we have time," he said.

She nodded. "Of course. Now, let's go get Mercado."

Though most of Mercado's men were outside, as Zach said, Jess knew there would still be a few protecting the drug lord. With Jess taking point, they worked their way to Mercado, ducking into other rooms when the few men in the hacienda came too close.

Jess cracked open a closet door—their latest hiding space, to verify the hall was empty. *All clear,* she mouthed.

Zach tapped the handheld in response, pointing to a spot on a small map. Then at himself and her.

She nodded in understanding. They were here.

He pointed to another spot on the map that was just around the corner. *Mercado.* He said the name without a sound.

Almost there. How many bodyguards? she wondered. Two? Three? She hoped for two. She could handle two. Her blood raced, and her heart pounded as she prepared herself for the confrontation. She took a deep breath.

Ready?

Yes. He returned the handheld to his pants pocket, replacing it with a 9 mm.

Dammit. He wasn't trained to shoot in a firefight. She opened her mouth to tell him to put the gun away, but the look in his eyes told her he would argue. There wasn't time for banter.

On three, she said.

This time, it was Zach who nodded.

She counted off with her fingers. *One.* She raised her index. *Two.* Her middle finger. *Three.*

Making sure that Zach didn't go first, she ran into the hall and round the corner with her weapon raised and ready. The hall was as empty as the one behind them. No bodyguards. No protection.

Just a big, metal door with a keypad. "You have got to be kidding me," she muttered. She didn't have time for this. Unless Zach could pull off a miracle. "Any thoughts on getting inside?"

"Of course," Zach said, pushing her aside. Handing her his gun, he pulled the cover off the keypad, exposing the wires. Using a small penknife from his pocket, he stripped the red wire.

Next, he pulled out a thin cable.

"What are you?" Jess whispered. "Felix the Cat with a Bag of Tricks?"

"Ex Boy Scout," he said, finally retrieving the handheld. Carefully, he inserted one end of the cable into the little machine and attached the other end to the exposed wire with an alligator clip. "Now, watch and learn."

The handheld whirred to life.

At the same time, numbers started filling the screen on the alarm system. "When this is done, the lock will disengage,"

Zach said. "We won't have much time to get through and surprise them."

"I don't need much time," Jess replied, mentally preparing herself. Three numbers left.

"I should go first," Zach whispered.

"No. I'm a better shot," Jess countered. Besides, she had no intention of returning his gun.

Two numbers.

"Jess—"

One number.

The door clicked, audible in the silence.

They didn't have time to argue. Jess pushed the handle, and shoved the door open with her shoulder. Following it, she rolled to the ground, a gun in each hand.

Ignoring the sounds of gunfire and the sensation of bullets whizzing by her head, she focused on the target.

Two men. Both armed. One shot at her.

The other aimed higher and farther. Behind her.

At Zach.

Oh, hell no.

Without hesitation, she aimed for him and fired. Two shots. He fell. Three more and the bodyguard aiming at her met the same fate.

That left Mercado. Where was he?

There was a click behind her, and the hairs on the back of her neck rose. "Ms. Whitaker. So nice of you to join me."

Another click. "I'm the boyfriend."

Zach. Slowly, Jess rolled onto her back. Mercado had her at the end of his gun. Zach aimed his weapon at Mercado. He had another one?

Sneaky.

"Looks like we have a standoff," she said, slowly rising,

leaving her guns on the floor as there was no sense in making Mercado nervous.

Mercado chuckled. "Not for long. My men will return soon."

She nodded. "Good point." And in the time it took her to agree, she grabbed the muzzle of his gun and yanked it downward.

It went off, the bullet digging into the floor.

She twisted his wrist and before Mercado could make a sound of surprise, she had his weapon. He tried to grab it back, but Zach's fist was faster, and in seconds, Mercado was on the floor.

The drug lord glared up at her. "What I said still stands. My men will be back here soon. You'll never escape."

Jess cocked the hammer of the gun and pointed it at the side of Mercado's skull. "Guess I should just kill you if you have no use."

The drug lord paled. "You would not dare."

"I would," Jess said, willing him to understand that her words weren't mere bravado. The man in front of her was less than human. He'd hurt her friends. Threatened her life. And worked for Arachne.

He deserved death.

"Jess." Zach rested a hand on her shoulder, bringing her back to reality. "We need the laptop. We need him alive."

As annoying as it was, Zach was right. "For now," she said. "But we can't have him wandering around. Got any cuffs in that bag of tricks?"

Zach smiled. "No, but consider it taken care of." In less than a minute, Mercado was bound with the curtain cords and on his knees in front of Jess.

She stared down at him. It would be so easy, she mused. So easy to put a bullet in his brain and rid the world of one more bad guy.

But, there was business to be had. Important business. She propped her foot on a chair, leaning on her knee and looking down at Mercado. "Where is the laptop?"

Mercado looked up at her and shrugged. "Not here. It's at my main compound."

There was no way he would let the laptop out of his sight, but if that was the way he wanted to play it. Jess aimed at Mercado's head. "No use for you then."

Mercado looked to Zach as if for help. Zach shrugged. "Don't look at me. I want you dead."

"Wait," Mercado pleaded, flinching. "I might be wrong."

"You lied?" Jess asked, her eyes wide. "Gee. A lying drug lord. What a surprise."

Removing her foot from the chair, she pushed Mercado over with her toe. He landed at Zach's feet. "I know you're lying. Now, tell me where the laptop is."

"Or what?" Mercado asked. "You'll kill me? You do that and you'll never find it."

Jess smiled but knew the grin didn't come close to reaching her eyes. "No. I won't kill you. I will let you live and make sure that Arachne finds out what you did. That you kidnapped me and tried to pry information from me and all without her knowledge."

"She'll never believe you," Mercado said, but the blood drained from his face.

"I think she will," Jess said. "And if not, it'll set the doubt in her brain. Call me crazy, but I think that might be enough reason, *for her,* to have you killed."

Mercado glared at Jess, and she understood the meaning of the phrase, *if looks could kill.* "It's in the safe," he said.

"Here?" she asked, gesturing around the room and annoyed that he was making her ask for details.

"No. My yacht."

"Which is where?" Jess asked, becoming impatient.

"At the end of the complex," he said. "You'll never make it."

"You keep saying never, yet I keep going," she said. "Yes, we will make it. Especially if we take you hostage."

"My people might hold fire, but Lorenzo won't," Mercado said, his black eyes triumphant.

Jess realized that Mercado hadn't figured out the truth. "You want to tell him?" she asked Zach, smiling.

"There is no Lorenzo," Zach said. "Just a lot of 'shock and awe.'"

"Shock and awe?" Mercado asked.

"Well-placed pyrotechnics and explosives that this—" he waved the handheld "—operates."

"There is no attack?" Mercado asked. His eyes narrowed in disbelief.

"No," Zach said. He looked down at Mercado. "Just me. You took my girlfriend. What kind of man would I be if I didn't try to save her?"

"Save me?" Jess interrupted, brow arched.

Zach refocused his attention on Jess and shrugged. "I said *try,* but since you were already free does it really matter who saved who this time?"

Jess shook her head. Zach was crazy to try such a stunt, but it was her kind of crazy. "Would it be bad timing to tell you that I think I'm falling for you?"

"Not at all," Zach said, his eyes telling her that under other circumstances, they'd be naked and he'd be kissing her.

She could hardly wait.

Chapter 18

"What's the best way to get to the dock?" Jess grabbed Mercado's bound wrists, both helping and hoisting him to his feet at the same time.

Zach studied the handheld. "There's supposed to be a door here. Somewhere along that outside wall."

Devoid of art and with a couch pressed against it, the wall looked solid. She knew that if this was Mercado's fail-safe room, it had to have a way out.

A hidden exit wasn't a surprise. The fact that he hadn't used it when she entered was a shock.

Damn, he must either hate her or was truly scared of Arachne. She shoved Mercado forward. "Show me."

Grudgingly, the drug lord went to the keypad just inside the door. "No tricks," Jess warned. "If I hear feet or an alarm, I'll shoot you."

He glared at her then punched in a code. A narrow door opened, throwing a sliver of light on the lawn outside.

"Watch him," Jess said, pressing against the wall while she checked for "all clear."

It appeared to be safe, but voices were close. Too close. "Have any more of that 'shock and awe' left?" she asked Zach, keeping her attention focused outside.

"A few explosives. And they're big."

"Good." That was what she wanted. Something Mercado's men couldn't ignore. "How about setting off one of those charges to give us a little distraction?"

"You got it."

She turned her gun on Mercado while Zach worked his technical magic on the handheld.

"Get ready," Zach said. "Three. Two. One."

An explosion rippled through the air, lighting up the night sky. Mercado's eyes widened. "Geez," Jess said, realizing that whatever Zach set off was large enough to do damage.

Serious damage.

"Do I even want to know where you found that kind of explosive?" she asked.

"Not really," Zach said.

She put Mercado in front of them, keeping one hand on his bound wrists. "Let's go," she said. Pushing the reluctant drug lord through the door. Once outside, the sounds that had been somewhat muffled by the thick adobe of the hacienda became sharpened in the night air.

Shouting. The occasional crash.

On the far side of the house, the trees burned.

She guided Mercado to a stand of jacaranda trees that traversed the lawn and ended at the beach. "Where to?" she whispered, standing in the shadows.

"That way." He gestured to the left.

"I don't see anything," she said, squinting in the dim light of the quarter-moon.

"It's on the other side of the grove," Mercado said. "Fifty feet on the far side."

"Zach?" she asked, not trusting Mercado. "Anything you can tell me?"

"From what I saw on the blueprints, that sounds about right," he said.

Jess took in the landscape. Right now, they were in shadow but once they cleared the trees, starlight would be enough to spot three figures sneaking across the sand. They needed to get to the pier before Mercado's men got the fire under control and discovered their boss was missing.

"Let's do this." They started making their way along the edge of the grove.

Jess stumbled on a root, almost dragging Mercado down with her. For a moment, she thought the man might try to escape, but she increased her grip. He stilled. "Clumsy bitch," he muttered.

Jess chuckled at the insult. The man was a fool if he thought mere words would make her falter in her determination or lose her temper.

A shout sounded from the direction of the house. Jess couldn't make out much but it came from the safe room.

They'd been discovered.

Now it was Mercado who chuckled.

"Damn it," Jess swore, "They know. Move." She shoved him, hard, and the three moved faster, almost running.

"You will never escape now," Mercado panted. *"Aqui! Aqui!"* He shouted the words before Jess dragged him to the ground and clamped her hand over this mouth.

He tried to bite her. She rapped his head with gun. "One more word, and I swear, I will kill you," she said through clenched teeth.

Beyond the trees, she heard shouting. Calls. All growing closer with each second. "Dammit," Zach muttered. "Are you sure you don't want to just shoot him? He's not making a convincing case for keeping himself alive."

Against the skin of her palm, she felt the drug lord smile, but she refused to give in to the negative thoughts that passed through her mind. She focused on the positive.

She was free. Zach had found her. Mercado might be smart but they were smarter.

"It is tempting," she whispered. "But not right now."

Zach chuckled. "Let me know when you change your mind."

"You got it," she said. She squeezed Mercado's face with her hand. "I'm going to uncover your mouth. If you make a noise, if you so much as breathe hard, I will make sure the only thing your men recover will be a body. Do you understand?"

He hesitated then nodded. She removed her hand. He remained silent.

She sighed in relief. "Got one more explosive?" she asked Zach.

"One more," he whispered.

"Now would be the time."

He opened the handheld, and the soft glow illuminated the dark. He pushed the button.

Nothing happened. No explosion. No fire. Nothing.

He pushed it again. And again.

"Dammit," Zach whispered.

"Problema?" Mercado asked.

Jess bristled at the pleasure in his voice, and in the dim light, Zach frowned. "Something came loose. A wire. Something." He pocketed the handheld. "I can go back. Fix it. It'll distract them enough to give you a chance to get away."

"Go back?" The thought made her stomach tumble and she swallowed hard. "No."

"We need a distraction," Zach insisted. "They'll be all over us in a minute."

"We have him as hostage." She pushed Mercado forward, trying to ignore the voices that grew closer with each breath. "That's enough to keep us safe for now," she said, praying that neither man heard the doubt in her voice.

Kneeling at the end of the grove, Jess yanked Mercado to the ground as the beam of a flashlight swung over them. With her pushing Mercado, it hadn't taken long to reach the pier. But even seconds were too long, Jess realized as she hunkered down behind a tree, her gun pressed into Mercado's forehead.

Another light swung toward them, hesitated and moved on. She exhaled in relief and raised her head.

Fifty feet away—just as Mercado said—was the dock. Using Mercado as hostage was risky. Damned risky. There was always some trigger-happy idiot looking to get in good by saving the big man.

That's all it would take to stop her, because no matter her bravado, she wouldn't shoot Mercado. Not like this.

She wasn't an executioner.

All she could do was minimize the risk.

"Any ideas?" Zach whispered.

"A few. None perfect."

"We're not going to get perfect," Zach said. "So settle for imperfect. The longer the wait the harder it's going to be due to sheer numbers."

"I know," she snapped. She ran her fingers through her hair. "Sorry. I just don't want this to go bad."

"Me, neither." He squeezed her shoulder.

"Thanks." Mercado, she knew, was going to be nothing but a hindrance. She imagined that when they ran for the yacht, he'd do whatever he could to screw her up.

There wasn't much alternative but to leave him behind.

In which case, they'd be shot in seconds.

Voices grew close. She stilled. They passed, and she breathed easier.

"What are they waiting for, and why is *he* behaving?" Zach asked, his voice going no farther than Jess's ear.

"If I had to guess, daybreak," Jess replied. It wasn't a bad tactic. Time-consuming but sensible. "They still don't know how many people they're looking for. Who. Anything. They won't take a chance on shooting Mercado."

"Well, they aren't dumb," Zach said. "That's unfortunate."

They didn't know there were only two people to seek.

The phrase resonated through Jess's head. All his men knew was what they assumed. Suppositions based on how they would have run a similar operation.

She glanced at Mercado. The drug lord lay on the ground but he was smug. He knew that when the sun rose, his men would discover the deception.

They didn't know.

She had an idea.

She smiled at Mercado, knowing he couldn't see it but not caring. "Strip," she said to him. She turned to Zach. "You, too."

"Excuse me?" Zach said.

"We need Mercado as hostage but we don't want some idiot taking a wild chance and shooting us. So, we make it more difficult for them."

"And being naked helps how?"

"You two switch clothes. I'm going to hide your faces and take you both hostage. They won't know which is which and, with luck, won't take stupid chances."

She heard Zach unzip his jeans. "With luck?" he asked.

"It's dark," she said, "You're both tall. Fit. Tan. It'll have to be enough."

"I am not stripping," Mercado said, his voice loud.

Jess clamped her hand over his mouth. "Give me your socks," she said to Zach. "I am tired of listening to this man."

Zach held his gun to Mercado's head while Jess stuffed the sweat socks in the drug lord's mouth and took off his pants, ignoring his muffled protests. She untied his hands for the seconds needed to switch clothes, with the whispered promise to shoot out his knees if he put up a fuss.

In minutes, Zach was dressed in Mercado's clothes, and the drug lord's hands were tied in front. Grabbing the back hem of Mercado's shirt, she pulled it upward and over the drug lord's head and down to below his chin, creating a hood. She pushed him to the ground to wait.

"Hands," she said to Zach. He held them out and she used Mercado's socks to tie them in front of him, as well. Though it was too dark to see his eyes, she felt them on her.

"Jess, if this goes wrong—"

She put her finger over his lips. "Don't say it." Standing on her toes, she replaced her finger with her mouth. "Don't even think it," she whispered, a superstitious part of her scared that giving the worst-case scenario words would make it real.

And the thought was unbearable.

He placed his weapon in her hand in answer. She tucked it in her pocket, and pulled his shirt over his head in the same manner she'd used with Mercado.

Now, only she knew who was who.

"Let's do this," Zach said, his voice muffled.

"Just stay quiet," Jess whispered. "No matter what."

She yanked Mercado to his feet. "You behave and you will live. You give me any trouble," she promised, whispering in his ear, "and I will kill you and take my chances. If you think I won't, then you remember what you did to my friends. To Zach's father. I swear." She ground the words out. "I swear, if you fuck this up you will die screaming. Do you understand?"

He gave a slow nod. She believed it.

"Straight ahead," she said, prodding both men with her gun. They stumbled onto the grass. Seconds after they were in the open, Jess heard a shout and saw men running toward her in the dark. "Stop!" Jess shouted, pointing the gun at first one man then the other. "Stop or I'll kill him."

The men slowed. She heard more coming but the others waved them back. "Are you unharmed, Mr. Mercado?" one of them shouted, addressing Zach.

"Keep walking," she murmured to her two hostages. To Mercado's men she said, "He's fine." The men came closer. Despite the cool night air, a bead of sweat slid down her spine. "Blindfolded and gagged, but fine, and I said *stop*."

She emphasized the word by cocking her gun. Zach and Mercado stiffened but kept moving, with Mercado's men following the other men's lead and stopping to let her pass.

"I am going to tell you how this goes," Jess shouted as she walked. "I am getting on that yacht. You will not stop me. And for those who want to be heroic, please be aware that these triggers are cocked. If you shoot me, my last action will be my muscles contracting which will make me pull the trigger and shoot your boss."

The pier was only thirty feet away. We might make it, she told herself. Just stay calm. One step at a time.

"I will board," she continued. "Then I will pick up the rest of my men, and they will board. When we are safely away from this crappy place, we will release your boss in a dinghy with a signal buoy. You can come get him."

"Why should we trust you?" someone asked.

"Because you don't have a choice," Jess said. The yacht was in sight now. Against the silhouette of the sky, the boat looked small—perhaps forty-two feet in length but no more. A Tierra, from the lines.

It was also the only boat in sight. She said a small prayer of thanks. They reached the short pier. Zach's and Mercado's weight made the wood squeak and groan.

Almost there.

Then they were on the deck. "You—" she gestured to one of the men as she turned Zach and Mercado so they could go up the gangplank "—get the ropes then leave."

He did as she asked.

Jess breathed a sigh of relief and pushed the men into the cabin. Finding safety in the dark, she shoved Mercado to his knees and pulled the shirt back over Zach's head to untie him. "We're clear," she said.

He cupped her face and kissed her. "You were amazing."

"So were you." She smiled, absurdly pleased. "Can you drive this thing?"

"Of course," Zach said. "They're built for people with minimum skills." Closing the curtain, he flicked on the lights and went to the helm.

"How fast can you get us out of here?" Jess asked.

"Fast enough," he said. "How long do you think we'll have before they come after us?"

Jess peeked out between the curtains. Though there were no other boats at the pier, she didn't doubt they were somewhere close. "It'll be a while. Let's go."

Zach punched a button, and the engines roared to life. Not caring if he caused a wake, he threw the yacht into Reverse.

Jess looked out through the curtain and saw Mercado's men running down the pier, finally fed up with waiting. Fiberglass flew as they shot at the yacht. "Move it!" she shouted.

There was splashing as Mercado's men jumped for the moving yacht and missed. She nodded in satisfaction and headed back to the bow of the ship where Zach piloted the yacht. "How fast can you get us to safety?"

"A few hours," he said. "Everything taken care of?"

"For now," she said. She cocked her head. "A few hours? Where the hell are we?"

His brows arched. "You don't know?"

She shook her head. "They knocked me out at the airport. I woke up in this complex."

"We're in Colombia, but on the northern tip," Zach said, keeping his eyes on the instruments. He adjusted course.

"How?"

"Some of it by car so I wasn't sure where you were, but then they flew you to Cartagena. That's where I picked up your trail and found out about this complex."

Cartagena and the northern tip of Colombia? That was more a day's jaunt. "How long have I been gone?" she asked, not sure if she wanted to hear the answer.

"Three days," Zach said.

Three days? It seemed like three hours. Had they questioned her? She chilled at the thought then realized that if they had, they hadn't learned much. Otherwise, Mercado wouldn't be so insistent on finding out what she knew. She sighed in relief and turned her thoughts back to Zach. "And you still found me?" she said, amazed.

He nodded. "It wasn't easy, but when I realized you weren't at the main compound as planned, I knew…" He hesitated then put the yacht on autopilot. For a moment, he stared at the floor and when he looked up, she saw his eyes were wet. "I thought you were dead."

"And you still came?"

"Of course I came." He glared at Mercado still gagged, tied and blindfolded on the floor. "To kill him."

For a minute, Jess stared at Zach in wonderment as myriad emotions raced through her. There was so much to say,
but there were no words. None big enough to say what she needed. Sliding her arms around his waist, she rested her head against his chest.

"When I saw you in that garden. Alive." He kissed her forehead. "You can't imagine my relief."

She flashed back to his accident underwater. To the bomb. So many close calls. In each one, he might have died. And to think of losing him broke her heart. "Yeah, I can," she replied, kissing him.

He wrapped his arms around her and held her tight, burying his face in her long, dark hair. "Would now be a bad time to tell you that I'm falling for you?" he whispered.

"Not at all," she whispered back. "In fact, it's the perfect time."

Jess gazed down at the trussed drug lord, drumming her nails with one hand and keeping her gun trained on him with the other. Still on the floor, he hadn't said a word since she'd taken off the blindfold and gag.

"Where is the safe?" She stopped drumming her fingers. "Tell me or I will make you tell me."

Part of her hoped Mercado would defy her. He deserved punishment and, given reason, she'd like to mete out a little bit in his direction.

He paled and she realized she was smiling, unpleasantly.

"It is in my bedroom," he said.

She rose. "Show me."

He rose.

"Just a minute," she said. "Zach? Any sign of pursuit?"

"Nothing on radar," he replied.

Jess turned back to Mercado. "If you lie. If you try to get away. If you do anything that annoys me, I will toss your ass overboard."

He nodded and walked toward the back of the yacht.

The yacht wasn't as big as *One For The Money*, but Jess didn't doubt that with the teak walls, gilding and original works of art, it cost as much as the research vessel, if not more.

He pushed open a carved door, turned on the light and Jess's breath caught in her throat. Mercado might be a killer and the scum of the earth, but he had excellent taste.

Silk the color of warm gold covered the walls. The furniture was shades of blue and gold with accents of other colors.

Stunning. That was the word for it.

And purchased with cocaine.

"Show me the safe."

Mercado crossed the room and pulled a picture off the wall. "She will come after you," he said as he turned the combination.

"What did I tell you about annoying me?" Jess said, keeping her gun on him.

He shrugged. "She will come after you, and she will kill you. And if not you, she will kill everyone you love."

There was something in his voice that caught Jess's attention. Something personal. Was that why he defied Arachne and questioned her? "She threatened you, didn't she?" Jess asked.

"The greedy bitch threatened my daughter," Mercado snarled. "My Anna is only five."

Jess shook her head in disgust and amazement. Although she knew it wasn't her place, and he didn't deserve it, Jess pitied the drug lord and the daughter who was caught up in his illegal life. He had everything, or thought he did, and saw himself as strong. Beyond emotion. Exempt from the law or repercussions of his actions.

And he was. Except when it came to his child.

A drug lord who specialized in ruining lives brought to his knees by love.

That, she thought, would be amusing if it wasn't so sad. "Is she okay?" Jess asked.

"I sent her away. She is safe for now."

There was a click, and the door to the safe swung open. Mercado stepped away and held up his tied hands. "I'd give it to you, but as you can see, it would be difficult."

Her gun still trained on him, Jess grabbed the laptop and the logs. She opened the first log, keeping an eye on her prisoner. *Paradise Lost,* was written on the first page.

Relief rushed through her. This was almost over. Her life returned. It had been so long since she'd felt free that the thought was heady.

Plus, the information wouldn't just help her. It would help the women of Athena Academy, Jess and even Mercado's daughter. She shut the safe. "If this is the right laptop, it might save your daughter."

"Then let me have it," Mercado said. "I can do more with it. I'm not bound by your laws."

"Or morality," Jess said. "And I can't trust you not to use it against me and mine."

She motioned him to walk. "When Zach confirms this is the laptop we need, I'll let you go, and your men can pick you up."

"You are making a mistake," Mercado said.

Jess didn't miss the underlying threat, but it didn't sway her. "Possibly. But it's mine to make."

Chapter 19

Zach had been able to confirm that the laptop was from *Paradise Lost,* and with that, she'd set Mercado adrift. The life raft shrank into the distance as the yacht motored away.

Jess watched him until the rising sun made her eyes water then she returned to Zach, satisfied Mercado would survive. They'd left him with food, water and a beacon. His men were undoubtedly in pursuit by now and would be looking for him.

Which meant that when they found him, they'd be coming after her and Zach.

"How are we doing?" she asked, finding Zach at the helm.

"Making good time," he said. "It'll still take us a while, but we have a decent head start so I don't think they'll be catching us." He flipped a switch, turning on the autopilot. "You did it."

Jess leaned against a console, the smooth metal cool against her back. "We did it. Not me."

"We then," Zach said. "We should celebrate."

"A little early, don't you think"?" Jess teased. "You've been driving all night. Wouldn't coffee be better?"

"Nope. I'm a big believer in champagne with my girl."

His girl. She smiled, liking the title. "You stay here. I'll find something," she said, giving him a brief kiss.

The galley was as beautiful as the rest of the boat. Teak. Marble. No expense spared. She opened the small fridge and found two bottles of Cristal Rose inside.

Opening one, she poured the sparkling beverage into two crystal flutes, spilling a little on the floor.

"Do you know how much that costs?" Zach asked.

Jess jumped. "Geez. Warn a girl, would you?" she said, her smile belying any snappishness as she handed him a flute. "And shouldn't you be watching the road, as it were?"

He shook his head. "It'll warn us. This ship has all the amenities."

He took the offered glass and held it up. "To us." His smiled softened. "And to lost friends."

"To us." Jess raised her glass. "To Chuck." She downed the glass and let the flute drop to the chair, the goose-down cushions softening the fall. Her eyes watered, and she wiped them with the back of her hand. She was a Marine.

Marines didn't cry.

"Hey, it's okay," Zach said.

Jess sniffed and wiped her cheeks again, shocked and annoyed by the sudden tears. "Sorry. I don't usually get all weepy."

Yet she didn't seem to be able to stop.

"You lost a friend, and you haven't been able to grieve. I'd be more shocked if you didn't cry." He pulled her against him, wrapping his arms around her. "Cry all you want. I'll be right here."

With that, the floodgates opened, and when she finally stopped, her cheeks felt raw.

"You okay?" Zach whispered.

"I'm fine," she said. "Just goofy looking."

He tilted her chin up. "Not at all. Your eyes don't even get puffy."

She stared into his eyes and they were, once again, the emerald green she remembered from when they first met. Sexy. Mesmerizing. "Kiss me," she whispered.

He answered her by kissing her forehead, tasting her tears as he worked his way to her mouth. His hands glided under her shirt and up her back then he hesitated. "Sorry," he said. "I know that now is not the time."

"Make love to me," she whispered in his ear. "Here." She wrapped her arms around his neck and he picked her up by the waist, sitting her on the galley table.

"We could go find a bed," Zach teased. "That would be new for us."

"Later," she said.

He chuckled, and pulled her T-shirt over her head, tossing it to the floor. She tugged at his shirt, and he stopped her. "You asked me to make love to you, so for once we're taking our time." He pushed a bra strap off her shoulder, kissing the now-exposed skin. "Or at least I am." He followed the strap with kisses. "I'm a scientist, Jess. That makes me thorough."

She shuddered at his implication. "Okay," she said, her voice cracking. "I can live with that."

He chuckled again.

"Smart-ass," she whispered, wrapping her legs around his hips and pulling him closer. Perhaps this would go at his pace—and she wasn't going to argue with thoroughness—but she wanted to touch him. Needed to feel his heat. The weight of him.

"Bad girl," he teased, tickling the bottom of her foot and making her giggle. She retaliated by tightening her legs. He wrapped his arms around her waist and picked her up.

She squealed, sure he was going to drop her on her ass, but without missing a beat or stumbling, he took her out to the deck.

"Where are we going?" she asked, burying her head in the crook of his shoulder, not wanting to watch.

"Here," he said, setting her on the outside table. "The galley is too small, and I like to see you in the morning sun." He set her down on the teak table, unhooking her arms and guiding her backward until she was lying down.

He stared at her, and she felt her skin warm with the combination of the sun, embarrassment at the appreciation in his stare and sheer desire. "If you don't take your shirt off," she said, running a hand over her waist and down her hip, his eyes following her movements, "I shall have to find my gun and shoot you."

He grinned, the breeze ruffling his dark brown hair. "You're the boss." He pulled the shirt over his head and tossed it to the deck.

Her breath caught. "You look nothing like a geek."

"And you don't look like a mermaid," he said, leaning over to kiss the hollow between her breasts. "But you are."

"Mermaid?"

He unsnapped her bra, "*My* mermaid. Now, be quiet so I can concentrate."

Jess shut up, and an hour later she understood what Zach meant by thoroughness. She was pleased, satiated twice over, and he was still clothed.

Leaning on his elbows, he laid a pale blue, cotton towel over her. "I don't know about you," he said, "but it's getting hot out here. Want some water?"

"Hot is an understatement." She leaned up to kiss him. "How about sweltering?"

"Back in a minute."

Jess sighed and stared up at the few clouds marring an otherwise perfectly blue sky. The day was perfect. Zach was perfect.

Life was perfect.

An alarm blared out over the speakers. "Son of a bitch!" Jess shouted, putting her hands over her ears.

The sound was decidedly imperfect in her perfect moment, and the Marine in her roared to life. Wrapping the towel around her body, she ran to the helm, vowing not to let her guard down again until the damned laptop and logbooks were in Allison Gracelyn's hands.

When she reached the helm, Zach was already there. "We have company," he said, killing the siren. "Three vessels. Varying sizes."

"I didn't think Mercado would be so dumb as to try and capture us." Jess swore at the drug lord's stupidity. "But I guess some people need the beat-down put on them before they learn."

Zach nodded at the radar. "Whoever they are, they're coming from the opposite direction. I don't think it's Mercado."

They might be fishing boats, but they could also be the authorities, and either way, she didn't want to answer questions. The adrenaline rush slowed. "Then speed up and let's get out of their way."

"You got it." Zach punched in coordinates for the new heading, then frowned.

"What's wrong?"

He held up a hand, asking for silence. He punched in the numbers again. Gunned the engine. "The boat isn't responding. We're not changing course and can't go over five knots. In fact—" he checked the compass and the radar "—I have no idea where we're heading. From the looks of it, we veered off course around twenty minutes ago. It's as if the boat is driving itself, and it's taking us right toward our unexpected company."

Unexpected? Perhaps. She shivered despite the heat that still turned her pink. But not unknown. She turned on the radio. "You out there, Arachne?" she asked, even though she knew the answer.

"Hello." Arachne's voice was smug, and Jess's hand tightened on the knob.

Arachne continued. "I was wondering how long it would take you to figure out you couldn't escape—"

Jess turned the radio off and whirled away, her hands clenched into tight fists and her eyes squeezed tight as she searched for a solution. She found nothing but frustration in her jumbled thoughts.

Zach lay his hand on her shoulder. It was warm and firm and promising. She opened her eyes. She may not have a solution but she had Zach. Her brilliant, wonderful geek, and with him at her side, they were bound to figure something out. "How much time before we intersect?" she asked.

"Thirty minutes."

"How the hell can they be doing this?" Jess growled. They'd spent ten minutes, searching for something, anything, that might be controlling the ship and were back at the helm, watching the boats grow closer with each passing second.

"It's not in the engine room," Zach said, dripping with sweat. "If it is, I can't find it."

"Maybe we should check the console again," she said. The panel was off and the wires intact but jumbled.

"It's not there," Zach said. "If it was, I'd know it."

"Okay," Jess said, trusting Zach's judgment. But trust didn't alleviate the frustration or the fear. They were on a collision course with Arachne, and when that happened, she'd be taken prisoner and Zach would be killed. She paced the small area, aggravation growing. "Where would they put it?"

"Someplace they wouldn't think we could get to. Or Mercado. Or whoever they think might be on this boat," Zach said.

Jess stopped pacing. "She probably set the hardware up a while ago, knowing she'd need it, but not necessarily for us."

"So, where is it?" Zach asked. "It's not on this boat."

She knew that look. He was calculating. Thinking.

Figuring out what she couldn't see.

"It's outside the boat. On the hull." He pounded his fist on the console. "Of course! If it's radio-controlled, being outside the boat would provide the best, clearest signal and be easy to place without being caught." He shook his head again. "Brilliant. Even if someone figured it out, they couldn't get to it without gearing up."

"No one but me," Jess said. "With your help."

Zach paled as he understood what she was suggesting. "Go under the boat while it's moving?"

"Do you have a better idea?"

He hesitated.

"You don't," she said. "And we're running out of time."

He took a deep breath. "I can put on a tank and do this."

Jess took his hand in hers. As much as she appreciated the thought—his desire to be the protector—he didn't have the skills for this. She did. Plain and simple. "We've had this conversation before Zach. This is what I do."

He squeezed her fingers. "I know, but it's so…"

"Dangerous?" She shrugged. "I'm a jarhead. I eat danger for breakfast."

He didn't smile.

She couldn't blame him.

"What can I do?" he asked. "We're going to need to keep you attached to the ship, somehow, so you can disable the device."

She gave a slow nod. "I have an idea about that."

Jess hung on to the rope with both hands as Zach lowered her over the side. Looped around her waist and tied in a make-shift climber's rigging, it dug into her flesh but there wasn't time to make it better.

She glanced at her watch. Ten minutes before intercept.

The waves tugged at her feet and she put one hand on her mask.

Seconds later, she was in the water and being dragged next to the boat. She inhaled, breathing in the cool, salty water.

This was insane, she realized as she fought to keep from being beaten against the hull. Even with the yacht at only a low cruising speed, it was going to be difficult to see what the hell was going on. She yanked on the rope as hard as possible, and Zach gave her a few more feet.

With gloved hands and using the barnacles as shallow hand-holds, she pulled herself along and under the moving craft.

Slow, she told herself. Careful.

You can do this.

As soon as she cleared the edge, the rough water dimin-ished, and she found herself gliding in the current created by the yacht. Out of the corner of her eye, she spotted a red pulse of light.

The transmitter. Damned if Zach wasn't right. Again.

She smiled, knowing she should be used to his brilliance by now.

Using her feet as rudders, she worked her way over to it. In the flickering shadows, it didn't look too complicated. A metal box that she only need yank off, snip a few wires and watch it drift away in their wake.

They'd be on their way. Safe. Simple.

She also knew that Arachne was not so uncomplicated. The criminal mastermind made tasks look easy, but there was always a hidden trap. And so far, when it came to boats, she seemed to be leaning toward explosives.

Why would this be any different?

Clearing her mask, Jess guided herself closer while taking care not to dislodge the tiny machine. It looked simple enough from the outside. A metal plate bolted to the fiberglass with a transmitter attached to the plate. It looked as if it would detach if she twisted it clockwise.

Carefully, she let go of the rope with her right hand, taking a deep, relieved breath when she didn't spin out of control.

Slowly, she reached into the small dive bag attached to the rope, groping until she found a pair of wire nippers.

Putting the nippers between her teeth, she grabbed the transmitter housing, taking care not to twist it until she was ready.

Deep breath.

Slowly, she turned the housing.

The yacht veered to the left, sending Jess into a spin but not before she ripped the housing away, leaving it hanging in the moving water.

Dammit! She fought to stop the out-of-control spin, and slammed into the hull of the boat. She shrieked at the pain, but at least she'd stopped moving.

She looked at her watch. Seven minutes. She hadn't realized how long she'd been underwater. The others had to be visible by now. Very visible.

Now on a new course, the yacht slowed.

That was not a good sign. She had to get the control off the boat before Arachne boarded. She hurried to the metal box, which flopped in the slowing current.

Four wires. Red. Blue. Yellow. Black.

No timer.

That meant it would blow if she cut anything besides the defuser. Not a comforting thought, but if she didn't take the chance, then she would be captured and Zach would die.

A twenty-five percent chance wasn't good, but it was all she had.

Red wire. Blue wire. Red wire. Blue wire.

Her chant of good luck.

Grimacing, she snipped the black wire before she could hesitate. Opening one eye, she realized she was still alive.

They were also still moving in the direction of the oncoming boat.

Great. Maybe the right wire. Maybe not.

What she knew for certain was that it wasn't the wire that connected the control box to their helm.

Five minutes. Time was almost up. Arachne was almost on them. And all she could think about was Charles. How he had died. Drowned. She didn't want that to happen to Zach. No matter what happened to her, she wanted him to live.

She took a deep breath, filling her gills with water and held it. She reached out. Her hands shook. Not good.

Another breath. She squeezed her trembling hands into fists. She couldn't do it. Couldn't take the chance.

Do it.

A banging on the hull vibrated through the water. Zach, telling her that there was no more time. She had to either take the chance and cut a wire or return topside and prepare for a gun battle they were certain to lose.

Make the decision, she told herself. Make the decision. She held her breath and snipped the yellow wire.

The mine didn't explode, and she screamed with success. A few nerve-racking seconds later, the props increased in speed and the yacht circled to the right, turning away from their pursuers.

Relief washed over her, so intense she wanted to cry. She'd done it. She'd beaten Arachne.

Saved Zach.

A tugging on the rope caught her attention, and she felt herself moving upward as Zach reeled her in. She cleared the waterline, and seconds later, found herself sitting on the deck with the breeze blowing across her skin as the yacht barreled through the water.

Zach helped her to her feet. "Are you okay? Were you hurt?"

She shook her head. "I'm fine. Fine. How about you?"

"I had the easy job. I just had to wait."

She looked over him. The other boats were following, and though they'd faded into the distance, they were close enough for her to see the men on deck. All in black. All armed. All pissed, she was sure.

No one liked to lose what they considered an easy prize. "Not so easy," she said, her arms around Zach's neck and not caring that she got him wet. "Nerves of steel for such a geek."

"Now, let's get the hell out of here." Back at the helm, they turned the radio on. "I win," Jess said, knowing her nemesis would be listening.

"This time." Arachne's voice crackled over the airwaves.

Jess's mouth thinned in a tight smile, not wanting to discuss or spar. There was only one thing she needed to say. Only one thing a person like Arachne understood. "If you come within ten feet of anyone I care about, I will hunt you down and put a bullet in you."

Arachne chuckled, but Jess didn't miss the edge of anger in the low sound. "Say what you will. You and I both know—"

Jess flicked off the radio, cutting her off in midsentence. "Screw that."

"Hunt her down? Normally I'd say that was a little extreme," Zach said, keeping an eye on the radar. "But I feel the same way."

"It's over," Jess said. She held her hands out. They shook, but she no longer cared.

One hand on the helm, Zach reached out with his other hand, his fingers wrapped around hers, giving her strength. "Ready to go home?"

She didn't know what waited for her, court martial or acquittal, but she was ready to face whatever the navy threw at her.

As long as Zach stood next to her.

"Yeah," she said. "Let's get the hell out of here."

Epilogue

"Jess. Zach. Thank you for coming," Allison said, as the pair entered her office.

"Our pleasure," Jess replied. She'd heard about the enigmatic Allison Gracelyn and even seen her a few times, but until now, she hadn't formally met the woman behind the name.

Jess glanced around the room as she and Zach took seats opposite Allison. The walls were covered with nautical charts and satellite images. One in particular caught her attention— a series of pushpins and dark thread connected Puerto Isla, Brazil and Colombia. "That's me?"

"It was," Allison said.

Jess frowned. "I'm sorry I wasn't more help."

"Jess, you and Zach—" she smiled at him "—put your-selves in danger and regained valuable information. I couldn't have asked for more."

"But Arachne." Jess frowned in disappointment. "She's out there."

"I know. And we'll catch her. Even now, Nikki Bustillo is tracking a hot lead."

"Nikki?" Zach asked.

"A good friend of mine," Jess said, soaking in the information that Nikki was an Oracle agent. "We're trying to use all the information we have to determine Arachne's location."

Allison turned her attention to Zach. "Have you been able to get into the laptop?"

Zach nodded. "Yes, but the information I've recovered so far is limited. Arachne was tapping into bank funds."

"Any in Florida?" Allison asked.

Zach raised a brow. "No. Why?"

Allison shook her head. "We were tracking a bank account in Puerto Isla when the money disappeared. We traced the signal back to the Florida coast, but there was nothing in that location." She sighed. "I don't think it's Arachne, but nothing else makes sense."

"Unless there's another player," Jess said.

"Yes," Allison replied, her lips tight for a split second then relaxing again. "We're looking at that option, but not to worry, we'll get it figured out." She closed the file in front of her. "But we have more important things to discuss in regards to Jess's career."

The inquest. Jess reached over to take Zach's hand. He squeezed hers in return.

Allison smiled. "I could go into details, but to keep it brief, you've been cleared."

Jess's jaw dropped. "How? I wasn't even here."

"Information was provided. Inquiries were made. Evidence was regained." Allison's smile broadened. "You're free."

"And my rank? My job?"

"All intact."

"Thank God," Zach said. "But what about Arachne? She's tried to kill Jess three times already. Who's to say she won't go for a fourth?"

Allison tapped a pencil against her thigh. "We don't think she was trying to kill Jess."

"Excuse me?" Zach said, almost rising. Jess touched his arm, signaling him to stay seated.

Zach glared at her but sat back down.

"Continue," Jess said.

"The first explosive, the one that killed Chuck, was designed to ruin your career and make you vulnerable."

"It did that," Jess said. "But she took quite a chance. I could have been killed."

"Doubtful," Allison said. "It was more pyrotechnics than lethal. Charles's death was an unfortunate by-product."

Unfortunate. That was an understatement.

"And the others?" Zach asked.

"The one in the engine room was to scare away Zach and the crew. To make Jess work alone."

"How did she know we'd find it?" Jess asked. Arachne was either a sociopath who truly didn't care if she killed her target or she was smarter than anyone realized.

"Arachne is no fool. She researched Zach as thoroughly as she researched you. She knew he'd find it. However, I don't think she'd thought you'd stay to disarm it, not after what happened with Charles." A smile played on Allison's lips. "But then one never knows what an Athena might do."

Allison's smile died. "The pirates set the third on their own and were killed for the presumption."

"And the fourth?" Jess prompted.

"Bad luck. She didn't expect you to steal the boat, and I'm sure she thought to overtake you before you found the device."

"So we got lucky," Zach said.

"A little good and a little bad, but yes," Allison confirmed. "And while Arachne is smart and thorough, she tends to overestimate herself and underestimate the women of Athena."

"Let's hope she continues that trend," Jess said. "Luck can't last forever."

"You don't need luck. You have brains and skill," Zach said. Pulling Jess to her feet, Zach cupped her cheek in his hand. "And you have me."

"I do? After all that's happened?"

He wrapped his arms around her in response.

Relief flowed through her, and a tension she hadn't been aware of dissolved, leaving her almost limp in Zach's embrace.

"I'll, uh, give you two a minute," Allison said, her cheeks pink. "I need to run this file down the hall."

She slipped past them and closed the door.

"How can you think anything else?" Zach said. "I thought you were smart." Then his mouth was on hers. His tongue tasting her and his hands in her hair, messing up her tight braid.

Jess pressed her hands against his chest and kissed him back, until he broke contact and traced a path down her jaw to her throat. "There were so many times I almost lost you," he murmured.

"Never," she whispered.

He leaned back, his green eyes dark and staring into hers. "You don't understand." He stroked her hair, his gaze intense. "If I lost you I'd never get over it. Never recover."

She brushed his cheek with her fingertips. Call her crazy, but she felt the same way. Now that Zach was in her life she couldn't imagine a day without him. She wasn't just falling for Zach.

She was over the edge. A smitten kitten.

Head over heels.

"You going to say it?" she said.

"Do I need to?" Zach asked, a small smile turning his lips upward.

"It would be nice." She mouthed his mouth, tracing his lips.

"I love you, Jessica Whitaker." He leaned in. "Gills and all."

She smiled, trying not to whoop with joy.

"Well?" he asked, "Are you going to stand there grinning or are you going to say it back?"

The grin broke and she laughed aloud. He stared at her, arms crossed, waiting. Still laughing, she grabbed his shirt and pulled at him until their lips met.

"You sound like a crazy person," he said as his mouth traced hers, featherlight and warm.

"Well, this crazy person loves you back," she said.

His mouth pressed harder, and she sank into him, knowing that she could take anything—accusations, guilt and the acceptance that she was a mutant—if she had Zach by her side and his arms around her.

* * * * *

Don't miss the next
ATHENA FORCE *adventure*
WITHOUT A TRACE
Available March 2008

Turn the page for a sneak preview....

Lieutenant Nikki Bustillo knew the shrimp boat her Coast Guard crew had just boarded for inspection was hiding something. It was as plain, she thought wryly, as the nose on her face.

"Problem?" Ensign Rich Mansfield, the boarding team's rookie member, joined her in the trawler's pilothouse.

"The *Montoya* is carrying more than dinner."

Mansfield gave her a measured look. "How do you know?"

Nikki nodded at the fidgeting shrimper crew. "They look nervous to you?"

"Yeah. Sort of."

The truth was, these men didn't look any more nervous than any other crew Nikki's command had stopped in the past three weeks along Florida's coastline. But to put it mildly, they reeked of fear. The vessel was definitely carrying something besides shrimp. Cocaine was a good guess.

Mansfield hovered at her elbow as she thumbed through the vessel's shoddily kept logs. She would've had the fresh-out-of-cadet-training ensign pegged merely as a nuisance, except back in February she'd received an encrypted e-mail message from someone called Delphi warning her to watch her back: Somebody called Arachne was getting her jollies kidnapping Athena Academy students and alumni, and Nikki's name was on the wish list.

This Delphi had never contacted her before but had known too many students—too many facts about too many of Nikki's friends—for Nikki to doubt she knew what she was talking about. Along with that e-mail had come a visit from a former classmate, Dana Velasco, confirming Delphi's assertion. Nikki had gotten the impression she—Nikki could only think of Delphi as *she*—was never wrong.

And Mansfield had a habit of pestering Nikki with a lot of questions she preferred not to answer.

He'd been particularly intrigued by her schooling. The Athena Academy for the Advancement of Women was unusual and he'd wanted to hear all about it. Fair enough. She'd given him the *Cliff Notes* version and moved on to her rapid-fire years at Florida State University studying literature, then to her decision to join the Coast Guard.

The truth was, the Athena Academy was the first place she'd felt she belonged. After an early childhood with seven raucous older brothers, she'd felt as though an all-girls school was somehow coming home. Her orientation group, the Hecates, had consisted of four other girls, each talented, gutsy and strong. How could she possibly explain her sense of sistership with these women? Especially to someone she didn't know. It didn't seem…right…to share that with a stranger.

With Mansfield still at her elbow, she radioed her captain

aboard the cutter *Undaunted* and let him know what was going down.

"Another hunch?" Captain Pickens's voice growled in response.

"Yes, sir."

"Go with it."

"Yes, sir." She turned to Mansfield. "Let's see what they've got in the hold."

She set two members of her boarding team to stand guard over the trawler's captain and crew while the rest fanned out and started a routine search for drugs.

When Mansfield yanked open the main hatch, fear musk—a cross between burnt coffee and battery acid—surged from the general vicinity of the shrimper captain.

"Got a problem?" Nikki asked the captain in Spanish.

He shrugged, looking sullen, though his gaze kept darting to the guardsmen disappearing into the hold.

"How long have you been piloting this vessel?"

Nikki asked the usual questions while her squad members poked through the compartments where the shrimp were stored. The captain muttered his answers, which she jotted down in a small notebook. The *Montoya* rolled gently as fat waves slid beneath her, and the sun glared off the water and steel.

After a few minutes, Mansfield was back, wiping sweat from his face and looking queasy.

"Nothing," he said.

"You've been thorough." She made it a statement, so he'd understand thoroughness was expected, no matter how bad the job stank.

"Yes, ma'am."

Nikki narrowed her eyes at the shrimp-boat captain. Burnt

coffee assaulted her nostrils. The man was scared, and not just because he had more than his allowed catch aboard.

"Look again," she told Mansfield.

"But—" He caught himself before protesting a direct order.

She leveled a measuring gaze at him. Maybe that was why she didn't trust him. Because he couldn't stomach the job. Hell, she knew what that was like, but it didn't mean she'd cut him any more slack than her CO had ever cut her. "You'll get used to it. Come on."

Nikki gripped the edges of the storage hatch, took a deep breath, held it and leaned into the hold. Something hard touched her shoulder; Ensign Artie Jackson held out a heavy-duty flashlight, which she took. Light splashed over the dead shrimp and rusting steel hull. The plastic liner that held the shrimp was cracked and stained from years of use. Stifling heat pressed in on her, bringing a quick burst of sweat to her face and neck. From the looks of it, this shrimp wasn't a fresh catch.

She let go the breath she was holding and sniffed.

The musk of coffee bored past the acrid, salty smell of dead sea creatures and washed over her in a hot wave. Nikki gritted her teeth against nausea. Terror. Terror like nothing she'd ever smelled before. Terror and…grief?

She leaned away from the hatch and squinted into the afternoon sun. "Get me a rake or shovel or something!" The wind lifting over the trawler's rail cooled her face.

Jackson handed her a shrimp rake. Nikki coughed hard a few times, then shook herself mentally. *Get a grip. It's just rotting critters.*

The days-old dead sea life she could handle. It was what lay beneath that that had her reeling.

She reached the rake down and scraped a bare spot inside the storage unit, then dropped through the deck hatch. A few minutes of hard work had cleared a broad swath, revealing another hinged hatch immediately beneath her feet. It was roughly two feet by two feet, with a pull handle. She would have smiled at her success, but the bitter scent of fear ratcheted her nerves another notch tighter.

Nikki stepped aside, pulled her sidearm, grabbed the handle and yanked the hatch open.

People in ragged, stained clothing lay piled on each other, huddled, clutching pillowcases or battered backpacks. One, a boy no more than thirteen, stirred and opened his eyes, squinting against the flashlight's beam but too weak to hold up a hand for shade. The rest were still.

Nikki raised her head. "We've got refugees!"

ATHENA FORCE

Heart-pounding romance and thrilling adventure.

When Coast Guard lieutenant Nikki Bustillo's inside contact is brutally murdered on the streets of Hong Kong, Nikki's manhunt is compromised. Her only hope: the help of a maverick, martial arts-wielding police detective. Nikki and her new partner set out to follow the enemy's shadowy trail— but will they fall right into his trap?

Look for

WITHOUT A TRACE
by *Sandra K. Moore.*

Available in March wherever you buy books.

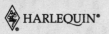

REQUEST YOUR FREE BOOKS!

2 FREE NOVELS PLUS 2 FREE GIFTS!

Silhouette® Romantic

SUSPENSE

Sparked by Danger, Fueled by Passion!

YES! Please send me 2 FREE Silhouette® Romantic Suspense novels and my 2 FREE gifts. After receiving them, if I don't wish to receive any more books, I can return the shipping statement marked "cancel." If I don't cancel, I will receive 4 brand-new novels every month and be billed just $4.24 per book in the U.S., or $4.99 per book in Canada, plus 25¢ shipping and handling per book plus applicable taxes, if any*. That's a savings of at least 15% off the cover price! I understand that accepting the 2 free books and gifts places me under no obligation to buy anything. I can always return a shipment and cancel at any time. Even if I never buy another book from Silhouette, the two free books and gifts are mine to keep forever.

240 SDN EEX6   340 SDN EEYJ

Name	(PLEASE PRINT)
Address	Apt. #
City	State/Prov. Zip/Postal Code

Signature (if under 18, a parent or guardian must sign)

Mail to the **Silhouette Reader Service™**:
IN U.S.A.: P.O. Box 1867, Buffalo, NY 14240-1867
IN CANADA: P.O. Box 609, Fort Erie, Ontario L2A 5X3

Not valid to current Silhouette Intimate Moments subscribers.

Want to try two free books from another line?
Call 1-800-873-8635 or visit www.morefreebooks.com.

* Terms and prices subject to change without notice. NY residents add applicable sales tax. Canadian residents will be charged applicable provincial taxes and GST. This offer is limited to one order per household. All orders subject to approval. Credit or debit balances in a customer's account(s) may be offset by any other outstanding balance owed by or to the customer. Please allow 4 to 6 weeks for delivery.

Your Privacy: Silhouette is committed to protecting your privacy. Our Privacy Policy is available online at www.eHarlequin.com or upon request from the Reader Service. From time to time we make our lists of customers available to reputable firms who may have a product or service of interest to you. If you would prefer we not share your name and address, please check here. ☐

SRS07

nocturne™

Dark, sensual and fierce.
Welcome to the world of the
Bloodrunners, a band of hunters
and protectors, half human,
half Lycan. Caught between two
worlds—yet belonging to neither.

Look for the new miniseries by

RHYANNON
BYRD

LAST WOLF STANDING
(March 2008)

LAST WOLF HUNTING
(April 2008)

LAST WOLF WATCHING
(May 2008)

Available wherever books are sold.

™ *Silhouette*®

Desire

NEW YORK TIMES BESTSELLING AUTHOR

DIANA PALMER

A brand-new Long, Tall Texans novel

IRON COWBOY

*Available March 2008
wherever you buy books.*